25TH FEB

The
BOUNDLESS

KENNETH OPPEL

David Fickling Books
31 Beaumont Street
Oxford OX1 2NP, UK

www.davidficklingbooks.com

The Boundless
is a
DAVID FICKLING BOOK

First published in Great Britain in 2014 by
David Fickling Books,
31 Beaumont Street,
Oxford, OX1 2NP

Text © Firewing Productions Inc., 2014
Illustrations © Jim Tierney, 2014

978-1-910200-10-0

1 3 5 7 9 10 8 6 4 2

David Fickling Books supports the Forest Stewardship Council (FSC), the
leading international forest certification organisation. All our titles that are
printed on Greenpeace-approved FSC-certified paper carry the FSC logo.

Mixed Sources
Product group from well-managed
forests and other controlled sources
www.fsc.org Cert no. TT-COC-2139
© 1996 Forest Stewardship Council

DAVID FICKLING BOOKS Reg. No. 8340307

A CIP catalogue record for this book is available from the British Library

Printed and bound in Great Britain by Clays Ltd, St Ives plc

For Julia, Nathaniel, and Sophia

THE LAST SPIKE

Three hours before the avalanche hits, William Everett is sitting on an upturned crate, waiting for his father.

The town doesn't even have a name yet. Nailed to a crooked post at the side of the train track is a messy hand-painted sign that says only: *Mile 2553*. Paint has dribbled down from the bottom of each number and letter. Yesterday when Will and his mother stepped off the train, the conductor shouted, "End of the line! Farewell Station!" But Will wasn't sure if Farewell was the town's name or if the fellow was just in a hurry to say "Good riddance."

The station is an uncovered wooden platform. There is a water tower and coal shed to fuel the trains. A telegraph pole slings a wire to a shack, where the station master dozes on his stool, his crooked door shut against the November chill.

The town feels like it's just been carved from the forest. Behind Will is a halfhearted jumble of wooden houses set back from a street of churned mud and snow. There is a general store, a church, and a large rooming house, where his mother waits. She's tired out after their five-day journey from Winnipeg, and so is Will. But he's had his fill of small spaces, and people everywhere, and he wants to be alone and breathe fresh air.

He's grubby. His hair needs a wash. He's not sure, but he might have lice again; it's itchy back behind his ears. In their rooming house the single bath was in high demand last night, and Will didn't get a turn.

On the wooden planks beneath his boots someone has carved the initials of two lovers inside a clumsy heart. He wonders if he'll ever put his initials inside a heart. He pulls his collar closer about his neck. The cold seeps through the worn patch under his right armpit. He's too thin, his mother says. But right now his body doesn't want to be any other way.

At least his feet are warm. The boots are the newest things he owns. The laces keep coming undone, though, even when he double knots them.

He looks at the track, gleaming as though it has just been set down. Will imagines his father helping lay those long measures of steel. He follows the track west, where it's quickly swallowed up by dense, snow-cloaked forest. His eyes lift to the towering mountains—like the very world has raised its gnarled fists to keep you out. How could you cut a road through such wilds? Clouds graze the icy peaks, painting restless shadows across the furrowed slopes of rock and snow.

That's the direction his father will come from. Maybe today, maybe tomorrow. And Will's going to be here to greet him.

From his coat pocket he takes his sketchbook and pencil. The sketchbook is homemade from the pieces of packing paper his mother brings home from the textile factory. Will has learned to fold the pieces in a special way and slit the edges to make a booklet of sixteen pages. A few quick stitches bind them together. He peels off his threadbare glove so he can get a good grip on the pencil stub.

Across the tracks two big tents and several smaller ones are set up in an otherwise vacant lot. Amongst the tents are carts, some still loaded with luggage and crates. Horses nose the scraggly earth. Across the biggest tent is written: KLACK BROS. CIRCUS. Several shabby men set up booths. The sound of their hammers echoes, lonely off the hills.

Will chews at his pencil for a few moments, then tentatively roughs in the scene. Next he begins to capture the texture and folds of the canvas tents, the fitful light on the foothills.

"What are you drawing?"

He looks up to see a girl about his age standing before him. Why didn't he see her coming? She wears a drab gray dress, her straight, fair hair parted in the middle and pulled back into two braids.

"Nothing much." He closes his sketchbook.

With dismay he watches as she steps closer. Talking to people isn't something he's very good at, especially strangers. Especially girls.

Beneath thick eyebrows her eyes are grayish blue and lively. When she smiles, he sees a slight gap between her front teeth. She isn't all perfect and pretty like Theresa O'Malley, but there's something striking about her that makes him want to keep looking. Maybe if he drew her, he could figure out what it is. But he's better at things than people. People are very tricky.

"Can I see?" she asks.

He doesn't like showing people his drawings. It's something he mostly keeps hidden, especially from other boys, because they think it's girly. This particular girl just waits patiently. Her face is awfully bright.

He shows her.

Her eyes widen. "Dang! I wish I could draw so well! Who taught you?"

"No one. Just me, I guess."

A couple years ago he was ill, and bedridden for weeks. As a trick to distract himself, he invented a drawing game. It didn't matter what he drew: a chair, a shirt on a peg, a shoe. He pretended his eyes were the point of his pencil against the paper. And as he moved his eyes very slowly over the outline of the object, he moved his pencil, too—without ever looking at the paper. He got so lost in it that he forgot about his burning ember eyes and aching limbs. Time disappeared. And he was often surprised at how accurate these blind contour drawings were—better than anything he could have done while looking at the paper. And when he recovered, he kept drawing, so that now he took a hand-stitched sketchbook everywhere.

Without asking, the girl takes the book from his hands and starts turning pages.

"Hey!" Will says.

"And these, too! Where's this?" She points to a picture of a trestle bridge under construction across a deep gorge.

"The Rockies." She seems so friendly and interested, he can't really be angry with her.

"Do you work on the railroad?" she asks.

He laughs at the idea, though he's pleased she thinks he's old and strong enough. "My father does. He's building the Canadian Pacific Railway." He feels proud when he says it. "I draw the things he describes in his letters."

"They're so good, it's like you've really been there."

"No, I ain't been anywhere really."

He doesn't tell her that this particular sketchbook is a present for his father. He hopes Pa will like it, as a keepsake of all his adventures on the railroad.

The girl turns a page and pauses. "Is that a sasquatch?"

He nods.

"Your father's seen one?"

"Look at this." From his pocket Will pulls his most prized

possession: a tooth, yellow and curving to a sharp point, that his father sent back months ago. "This one's from a big male they had to shoot."

She examines it with great attention. "A lot of people think they're not real. This could be a bear tooth."

Will's indignant. "It's no bear tooth! They're real. They're awful trouble up in the mountains."

"How long's he been away, your pa?"

"Three years. But he's done now. We're here to meet him. We're moving west."

She follows his gaze up into the mountains and is silent for a moment.

"You live here?" he asks.

"Just visiting."

"You waiting for someone too?" He's heard from their landlady that the town will soon be flooded with men coming down from the work camps.

The girl shakes her head mysteriously, then turns and steps off the platform. The workers have left a long plank across two rickety sawhorses. The girl hops up onto it. Arms out, she steps across, one foot in front of the other, chin high. Midway she does a handstand.

Will blushes at the sight of her pantaloons. He knows he should look away, but he's so amazed, he can't stop watching. She walks the rest of the way across the plank on her hands, then flips herself upright and curtsies.

"You're in that circus!" he exclaims. "An acrobat?"

"A wire walker." She hops down and returns to the platform.

"On a tightrope, you mean?"

Will has only ever been to the circus once, on a birthday, and he was enthralled by the people crossing the high hempen rope.

"They call me the Little Wonder." She wrinkles her nose. "It's a silly name. It's just because I started when I was six. One day I'm going to cross the Niagara Falls. That's eleven hundred feet! But what I really want to be is a great escape artist. There'll be no chains that can hold me, or locks bind me."

Will is speechless at her aspirations.

"Try to hold me. I can escape any grip."

"I believe you," he says shyly.

"Grab my arm. Both hands!" She takes his hands and places them on her upper arm.

Awkwardly Will clenches his fingers.

"Harder than that!"

He squeezes tighter.

Then she does something, very simple and fast, and is free of his grip before he knows what's happened.

"That's something," he says. He nods at the tents across the tracks. "Who're the Klack brothers?"

"Uriah and Crawford. Crawford's dead. He was the smart one. It's a pretty rotten mud show. But it's work for the time being."

Will feels suddenly childish. Unlike his father, the only adventures he's ever had have been in his head, or drawn in his sketchbook. This girl seems from another world. Looking at her is like catching a glimpse of unknown track: and immediately he wants to travel it to the horizon, to know what's at the end.

"You could be an artist," she says, pointing at his sketchbook. "Is that your dream?"

"Don't know." He is shy again. He wishes he were full of plans and dreams. "Just somethin' I do."

"It's silly not to use the talents you have."

"I ain't so good."

"I think you are."

Heat comes to his cheeks. Why does he blush so easily? It's a curse. To change the subject he asks, "You know all sorts of tricks, then?"

"Like what?"

"Can you do a disappearing trick?"

"Of course," she says after just a moment's hesitation.

"Go on, then."

"I don't feel like disappearing just yet."

When Will grins, one of his eyes closes more than the other. "Can't do it, can you?"

Her eyebrows lift haughtily. "It's rude to call someone a liar."

"I didn't call you—" he begins.

A distant locomotive gives a blast, and Will stands eagerly. He sees the train, still far away, but it's coming from the wrong direction.

"That's not your father?" the girl asks.

Will shakes his head.

"Come see the circus tonight," she says to him.

"How much is it?" He knows Mother is worried about money. She's been worried about money all their lives.

"Nothing for you," she says. "Bring your parents, too. Just tell the man at the tent flap, '*Jeg inviterte*.'"

"That some secret circus code?" Will asks excitedly.

"It just means 'I'm invited' in Norwegian."

"You're Norwegian?"

"Half-Norwegian, half-French," she tells him with a shrug.

It seems incredibly exotic to Will. "I'd like to come," he says.

With another blast of its whistle, the train makes its slow approach. The station master stirs from his stool and steps out from the shack.

"Will you do the disappearing act?" Will asks the girl.

She grins. "Promise you'll come?"

"Yes, all right. Promise."

He looks over at the train and sees it's not a freight. It's carrying only two cars, and they look fancy.

"Wonder who's on this one?" he says, and when he turns, the girl's gone. He looks all around and sees no trace of her. The locomotive pulls past him, alongside the platform. Surely she didn't bound in front of it! He smiles to himself. Maybe she really could do the disappearing trick. He realizes he doesn't even know her name—

And that she still has his sasquatch tooth! Frantically he pats his pocket to double-check. Empty. The train comes to a halt. The engineer and the brawny fireman drop down from the locomotive and holler instructions to the yard workers.

"She needs to be watered and fed, lads!"

Will runs along the platform to get around the train. Maybe he can catch up with her. From the passenger carriage a man suddenly steps down, and Will barrels right into him and goes sprawling. Before Will scrambles up, he catches a glimpse of gleaming shoes, still firmly planted on the platform.

"Sorry, sir!" he pants to the gentleman.

He's a stocky fellow—no wonder he didn't go over. He has a neatly trimmed mustache and beard. His hair doesn't start till halfway back on his square head. A solid stomach swells his expensive vest and coat. Will is surprised to see that his eyes don't flash with anger but with amusement.

"You're in quite a hurry, lad."

"I'm sorry, sir, but . . . there's a girl. . . . She . . . took something. . . ."

"Ah. Stole your heart, did she?"

Will's face blazes. "No . . ." he mumbles, mortified. "My sasquatch tooth."

"Really?" says the gentleman, intrigued. He bends and picks up Will's askew sketchbook. His eyebrows lift as he takes in the drawings.

Will just wants to disappear—with or without a puff of

smoke; he's not picky. But he can't leave without his sketchbook. And he can't very well demand it back.

"Fine pictures," the gentleman says. "I'm guessing someone in your family works the rails."

Will forces himself to meet the gentleman's eye. "My father, sir. I'm waiting for him."

The gentleman is starting to look familiar, though Will doesn't know why.

"Up in the mountains, is he? What's his name?"

"James Everett."

The gentleman gives a gruff nod. "A fine man."

Will thinks he must be joking. "You know him?"

"Of course. I make it a point to know my best workers. I'm the manager of the CPR. My name's Cornelius Van Horne."

Van Horne thrusts his hand toward him. For a moment Will's paralyzed. Of course this man is familiar! Will's seen his portrait in the papers. His name has appeared in his father's letters. For the past five years Van Horne has overseen every detail of the railway's construction. He is general manager, engineer, visionary—slave driver, some call him, according to Will's dad. But Will's father has also told stories about how Van Horne has cut through virgin forest with a forty-pound pack on his back and forded a raging river. Will shakes his hand. The rail baron's grip is swift and powerful.

"What's your name?" Van Horne asks him.

"William Everett. Sir."

"Been a while since you've seen your pa, eh?"

"Yes."

"Tell you what, William Everett, why don't you come up with us. We're headed into the mountains ourselves." His eyebrows rise, and his high forehead creases with sudden mischief. "You can surprise your father and come back with him before nightfall. And maybe find yourself another sasquatch tooth."

Something shifts inside Will, like a door opening. Maybe it was meeting the circus girl, maybe it was the view of all these new mountains like a gateway to a new and dangerous world—but he feels like his whole life is about to be upended. His father's had so many adventures—maybe he'd be impressed if Will did something daring. Anyway, he hasn't seen his father in ages, and how could he pass up the chance to see him all the sooner?

"Is there time to go tell my mother?" Will asks.

As if in answer, a uniformed conductor leans out from the carriage and calls, "All aboard, sir!"

"Are you coming, William Everett?" says Van Horne. "It would make a good story, don't you think? And it's always good to have a story of your own."

The rail baron turns and starts back to his carriage.

Will looks toward the boardinghouse, where his mother waits, then up at the mountains. The train whistle blows. He grits his teeth and inhales sharply. He looks over at the station master, who's watching him with curiosity.

"Will you please tell Lucy Everett I've gone to the camp to

KENNETH OPPEL

meet my father? She's at Mrs. Chester's rooming house!"

And it's done. He bounds toward the train and up the steps.

Inside the carriage he comes to an abrupt halt. Instantly he feels shabby and out of place. He's never been in a fancy parlor like this, or amongst such finely dressed gentlemen. They are all muttonchop whiskers and top hats and vests. They trail their own atmosphere of cigar smoke and brandy. And they are all looking at him.

"I see you've brought an urchin with you, Van Horne," one of them says.

"Bite your tongue, Beddows," says Van Horne sharply. "This is William Everett, the steel layer's son. He's coming up to meet his pa."

Will notices one of the gentlemen open a window. He can't imagine he smells worse than all the cigar smoke. Still, he wishes he could fade into the velvet wallpaper.

But Van Horne puts a large hand on his shoulder and begins introductions with a satirical grin. "William, this bearded fellow here is Mr. Donald Smith, the president of the CPR. And *this* bearded fellow is Walter Withers; and this *excessively* bearded gentleman is Sandford Fleming, another of our surveyors and engineers. . . ." And so it goes, Will taking in none of this, just nodding and trying to meet the eyes of these famous, wealthy gentlemen. His insides twist. "And this beard*less* man here is Mr. Dorian," Mr. Van Horne finishes, indicating a tall man with curly black hair.

"How do you do, Will?" Unlike the other gentlemen, he approaches Will and shakes his hand. He has strikingly high cheekbones, a warm hue to his skin, and a dark, penetrating gaze.

"Good, thanks," murmurs Will.

"Mr. Dorian here," says the rail baron, "has taken a great liking to a painting of mine."

Mr. Van Horne walks over to the parlor wall where an oil painting hangs, and he smiles at Will. "I saw your drawings, lad. What do you think? Is it a good piece?"

Will studies it. There's a house in winter, with several sleighs outside. A blacksmith tends to one of the horse's hooves.

"I like it," he says.

Mr. Dorian tilts his head. "I'm offering a fine price."

"The price is irrelevant," Van Horne says, laughing. "I won't be parted from it. She's my pride and joy. Don't you have enough pretty baubles in that circus of yours?"

"Some baubles are prettier than others," says Mr. Dorian. His voice is deep and carries the faintest hint of an accent. *Is it French?* Will wonders.

"Do you work for that circus near the station?" Will asks impulsively. Maybe he knows the girl and can tell him her name.

"Alas, no."

"I heard they have a good wire walker," Will says, wanting to sound knowledgeable.

"Is that so? Well, I'm always looking for new talent."

To Will's relief the gentlemen all resume their conversations with one another. He retreats to the very back of the car and sits quietly. He watches and listens. He dares not even take out his sketchbook, in case that might be rude.

The man called Withers seems to be a photographer, because he and his assistant keep checking through several large cases holding a camera and all sorts of equipment.

The train shudders and surges higher into the mountains. Will hasn't seen a single sign of human habitation since Farewell. Often all he can see are the vast pines that grow along the track, but sometimes they thin and he catches a sunlit glimpse of a high bony crag, or a cataract of black water spilling over a cliff. Will jolts when the train steams across a wooden trestle and he peers down to the jagged, churning gorge, hundreds of feet below.

An attendant comes through and serves a luncheon of cold chicken cutlets, steamed vegetables, and boiled baby potatoes. Van Horne, after taking his meal, points the attendant back to Will, and the fellow grudgingly hands him a plate and napkin. Will sits for a while staring at the food, wondering how he's supposed to eat it, then realizes his cutlery is wrapped up in the thick napkin.

Copying how the gentlemen hold their forks and knives, Will tries to eat neatly. The food's very good—certainly better than the boiled something-or-other last night at Mrs. Chester's. Some sauce plops onto his vest. He tries to dab it off with his napkin but seems only to spread it, so he rubs it in as hard as he can until it disappears.

"I like to keep a sketchbook myself," says Van Horne, sitting down near him. "What do you think of this, eh?"

In his hands he holds a beautifully bound volume. The paper is so thick and creamy, Will can't help stroking it. Across two pages are drawings of a machine so extraordinary that it takes him several seconds to figure out what he is looking at.

"Is it a locomotive?"

"Indeed."

"It can't be so big, can it?"

"Mark my words, once she's built, she'll ride these tracks. Maybe you'll ride upon her."

"Van Horne," says Sandford Fleming, "you are hopeless at keeping secrets."

"There's no need to keep this secret," he replies, winking at Will. "I'm the only one who can build this train, and build it I will. And who knows, maybe one day someone like William here will drive it."

"What will you call her, sir?"

"The Boundless."

Laughter rumbles from a gentleman with an enormous white beard. "Building the track nearly bankrupted us ten times over—and the nation with it. I marvel at your appetite for risk."

"It's a keen appetite I have, Smith," Van Horne replies, "and without it we wouldn't have finished the railway."

"Not to mention blind luck," says Smith. "Now, who's up for a game of poker?"

The carriage suddenly darkens, and Will thinks they've entered a tunnel. But when he looks out the windows, he sees dense trees on both sides, so close that their branches scrape and snap against the carriage.

"Why haven't these blasted trees been cut back?" Van Horne demands angrily. "I told them last time I was up. It's not—"

There's a loud thump, and Will turns in time to see a dark shape climb swiftly past a window onto the roof. Heavy footsteps sound overhead.

"Gentlemen, we have an uninvited guest," says Van Horne, drawing a pistol from his jacket.

"What is it?" Will asks, his throat tight. "Is it a—"

"Yes. Head down, keep away from the windows," Van Horne tells him.

Will can only stare, petrified, as the other men draw guns. Sandford Fleming takes a rifle from a rack on the wall and loads it. The railway men walk smartly to the windows, slide the glass down, and lean far out. Squinting, they take aim and begin firing.

The reports are deafening, but Will can still hear the frantic pounding of footfalls overhead. The ceiling beams shudder under the thing's massive weight.

Withers the photographer is crouched on the floor, his terrified gaze ricocheting about. His assistant whimpers softly. Mr. Dorian is the only other man without a gun, and he stands calmly in the center of the room with an air of faint amusement on his face.

"Quickly, gentlemen!" cries Van Horne. "If he gets to the locomotive, he'll kill our engineer."

They reload and redouble their efforts. Gun smoke stings Will's eyes. Still the footfalls pound against the roof, making their way steadily forward—then pause.

"Can't see him anywhere!" hollers one of the gentlemen.

Mr. Dorian takes the remaining rifle from the rack and walks calmly to the front of the carriage. He stands listening, the color high in his cheeks, and then fires a single shot through the ceiling.

There's a massive thump against the roof, then a scratching sound. Will whirls as a brown shape drops past the window. He hurries over and catches just a glimpse of a massive, furred creature crumpled alongside the tracks. He feels hot all through, and his heart's suddenly hammering. He sits down.

"Steadies the nerves," Van Horne says, offering Will a small glass of brandy.

Will accepts it with a shaking hand and downs it in one fiery gulp.

"Nearly there," Van Horne tells him, clapping him on the shoulder. The rail baron looks over at Mr. Dorian. "Well done, sir. You're a useful fellow."

Windows are closed, guns disappear, cigars are relit, and brandy is poured all around. As the train climbs higher, the ride gets rougher. The train jounces over uneven sections of track, screeches around corners. Despite the two stoves in the carriage, it becomes chilly. Staring out at the landscape of granite and forest and snow, Will wonders if he should have stayed back in Farewell.

After thirty more minutes the locomotive gives a whistle blast and begins to slow.

"Well, gentlemen," says Van Horne, rising, "are you ready to make history?"

When the train stops, Will waits for the gentlemen to get off first. He hopes Van Horne will tell him where to find his father, but the rail baron seems to have forgotten about him. Will is left alone.

"Off with you, then," says the attendant with a grimace.

Will steps off. There is no platform, just gravel. Despite the sun, it's very cold up here, and the snow is deep on either side of the rail bed. The smell of pine is keen in his nostrils. He fills his chest and starts walking.

To the left of the tracks, the land slopes down into sparse forest that ends at an abrupt precipice. From below rises the sound of a swollen river. Up ahead, to the right of the tracks, some of the trees have been cleared for the work camp.

Wood smoke rises from the chimneys of rickety bunkhouses. Men mill about outside. Will is too shy to call out his father's name. He supposes he should go over and ask someone but dreads the prospect.

The company dignitaries are walking up the tracks toward a gathering crowd. Withers the photographer brings up the rear, he and his assistant lurching under the weight of their equipment.

"William?"

Will looks over and sees someone walking toward him, not a gentleman but a tall working man in a cap. His face is tanned by wind and sun, and he is leaner than the person Will has drawn and redrawn from memory over the past three years. But when James Everett grins his familiar lopsided grin, he is suddenly and powerfully Will's father.

"Will!" he says, and pulls him into a tight hug. Beneath the musty clothing, his father's arms and chest feel as hard as the granite he's blasted from the mountains. Will feels completely safe.

"Mr. Van Horne said you came up in the company car!"

"He invited me!"

James Everett shakes his head. "Well, that's something."

"There was a sasquatch on the roof!"

"I'm not surprised. Where's your mother?"

"Waiting back in Farewell."

"Good. She knows you came, though?"

"I sent a message."

His father holds him at arm's length. "You're a good height. You'll be taller than me soon. A fine fellow through and through."

Will grins, trying to find himself in his father's face—and sees it in the lopsided grin. Will is built like him, though he has yet to fill out. His red hair is his mother's, but he has his father's large hands. His father reminds him of those trees he saw on the train trip from Winnipeg, the ones that thrive on hardship and get stronger and more stubborn.

"I brought you something," Will says tentatively, for he's worried his father might not like the gift, might think it childish. He reaches inside his pocket for the sketchbook, but there's the sound of a bell being rung.

"Will you show me after the ceremony?" says his father. "They're starting in a minute. You'll want to see this. They're going to hammer the last spike."

The last spike. It's a phrase Will has read many times in the papers, and his father's letters—and it has such power that it hangs in the air like the echo of a thunderclap.

Will leaves the sketchbook inside his pocket. His father leads him toward the growing crowd. Will smiles, enjoying the weight of his father's hand on his shoulder. Set off a ways from the main work camp is a second. There are no wooden bunkhouses there, only tents and miserable lean-tos, where Chinese men are drinking tea and packing up their tattered bags.

"Aren't they coming to the ceremony?" Will asks.

"Not them," his father answers quietly. "They've got no love for the railway, and I don't blame them. They had the most dangerous jobs and lost a lot of their countrymen."

Then Will sees something that makes him stop and stare. Spiked to the top of a tall pole is a head. Flies churn about the rotted flesh, and for a moment Will thinks it's human, until he sees the mangy, sun-bleached patches of fur.

"Sasquatch?" he asks his father.

James Everett nods. "That one came in the night, killed one of the Chinese blasters, and tried to drag him off."

"Why did they do that to its head?"

"Some of the men think it scares them off. It doesn't, though. Not since we started shooting them."

Will has read all of his father's letters so many times, he has them nearly memorized. Last year, when the first crews entered the mountains, the Native Canadians warned them of the *sasq'ets*, the "stick men." Plenty of the workers thought it was superstitious nonsense. It wasn't. The young ones came first and were merely a nuisance, filching food from the mess tents, playing with the workers' tools like comical monkeys. But there was nothing comical about the adults.

"Come on," his father says.

They near the fringes of the crowd. Will's father jostles him closer to the front. Nobody seems to mind as James Everett passes, for he has a friendly word for everyone, and people say, "Is that your lad?" and "He's the spitting image!" and "Let him get a good view!" Before long Will finds himself standing not far behind the dignitaries he rode up with. With his top hat Mr. Smith is the tallest, and Will can make out Van Horne, talking to the man with the ferocious beard. Their woolen coats are buttoned snugly against their ample bellies.

Spread out on either side of the tracks are the workers, like Will's dad, humbly dressed, some smoking, all looking like they could use a hot bath and a square meal.

"Gentlemen, are we ready?" asks Withers, bent over his camera.

Will watches as Van Horne steps forward.

"This mighty road," the rail baron cries out, "will connect our new dominion from sea to sea. Men, you've all toiled long and hard for this moment, and there's not one of you who doesn't have a share in the glory. Be proud of that, for there will never be another job like this in our lifetimes—and you will forever be a part of history!"

Will finds himself cheering along with the rest.

"And to complete this great enterprise," says Van Horne, "Mr. Donald Smith, the president of the CPR, will drive the last spike!"

Another cheer as Mr. Smith steps forward, holding a silver sledgehammer.

A weedy-looking railway official approaches with a long, ornate velvet case.

It seems to Will that every man in the crowd takes a small step toward it. Like a sigh of mountain wind, a collective gasp rises. Will stands tall on his toes as Smith lifts from the case a six-inch rail spike. The dull luster of gold is unmistakable, as is the sparkle of diamonds, set deeply into the side of the spike, spelling out a name he can't see.

"Heard it cost more than two hundred thousand dollars," Will hears a man whisper bitterly behind him. "I could work ten lifetimes, wouldn't make half that."

Will glances back and sees a man about his father's age, sandy haired, a bit of gray coming into his beard. He has chilly blue eyes. His nose looks like it's been broken more than once.

"You ask me, it's criminal, spending that much on a spike, after we slaved two months without the pay car coming. Bet Van Horne didn't go without his pay."

The man raises his eyebrows challengingly at Will, and Will turns away.

Quietly Will's father says, "Van Horne came through for us in the end, Brogan. He kept his bargain."

"Let's just say he got the better end," Brogan says, and sniffs.

"Ready when you are, Mr. Smith," says Withers behind the big camera.

Donald Smith positions the spike atop the final steel plate and grips the sledgehammer.

"Everyone still now!" cries out the photographer. "And, Mr. Smith, I'll need you to hold your pose once you hit the spike."

Smith strikes and freezes.

"And . . . wonderful!" cries the photographer.

But Smith's aim was off, and Will sees he has only bent the top of the spike without driving it in properly.

Van Horne gives a hearty laugh. "Smith, you've spent too long behind a desk."

"Let me straighten that out for you, sir," says the assistant, try-ing in vain to yank out the spike with his hands.

Van Horne steps forward and pulls it out with one swift tug. He takes the hammer from Smith and with a sharp blow straightens the priceless gold spike against the rail.

"Do the honors, Van Horne," says Smith good-naturedly. "No one has given more of his life to build this road."

"Perhaps." Van Horne looks about the crowd, and his eyes settle on Will. "But this road is for a new generation that'll use it long after we're gone. Lad, would you like to try your hand?"

Will is aware of every set of eyes in the crowd fixed on him, more intense than the sun's glare.

"Go on," he hears his father whisper, and Will feels his hand upon his back. "You can do it."

"Yes, sir!" Will says, so nervous that his voice comes out much louder than expected.

He steps forward, his legs feeling strangely disconnected from his body.

He takes the silver sledgehammer Van Horne holds out to him.

"One hand close to the top," the rail baron tells him quietly. "Tight grip. Now you'll want to raise it to your shoulder. Look at the spike the whole time."

Will can now see the diamonds set into the spike's side and the name they spell. He murmurs the word: "Craigellachie."

"That's the name I'm giving this place," says Van Horne. "Now strike!"

Will tenses his muscles and strikes.

He doesn't even know if he's been successful until he hears the cheer rise up from the crowd.

"Well done, lad!" Van Horne cries. "The last spike!"

"You finished the railway, Will!" his father says, slapping him on the back.

"All aboard for the Pacific!" shouts Donald Smith.

From down the tracks the company locomotive blasts its whistle. Men take out their pistols and begin firing in the air. The shots echo between the snow-laden slopes, one great firework crackle.

When the shooting subsides, the rumble is so low that it is barely audible, but Will can hear it, and he looks at his father in alarm. James Everett is shielding his eyes and staring at the summit. Will sees a patch of perfect snow pucker and slip raggedly away from the pack. A dreamy white haze rises like sea spume as it plows a growing crest before it.

"Avalanche!" James Everett bellows, pointing. "Avalanche!"

All is chaos as men run for cover, looking up at the plunging snow, trying to guess where it will hit. There are cries of "Not that way!" and "Climb a tree!" and "Stick close to the rock face!" Withers seizes his camera and tripod and pelts after the dignitaries toward the locomotive.

"Move the train! Back it up!" shouts Van Horne. "Men, take cover! The snow sheds are your best bet!"

"This way!" Will's father says, sprinting. Will knows the sheds are supposed to keep the snow off the track as the railroad skirts the mountain face, but are the sheds strong enough to withstand an avalanche?

The sound of thunder builds. He runs after his father and trips, sprawling hard on the tracks. His wretched bootlaces! He tries to stand, but the toe of his boot is jammed beneath one of the ties. Fire jolts up his ankle.

"Pa!"

His father turns and rushes back to him. "Is it broken?" he pants.

"Jammed." He's trying to pull it free, but each tug only gives him more pain.

The ground begins to tremble.

"Never mind, never mind! Just undo the laces and slip out." Will sees his father glance up at the snow and then back to the boot, fingers clutching at the laces. "Almost there. . . . Ease your foot out now."

With a grunt of pain Will pulls his foot from his boot, and his father hauls him up.

"Lean on me."

Not far away Will glimpses a man bent over the track, trying to lever up a spike with a crowbar. Then Will looks up at the snow and knows they're too late. His eyes meet his father's.

"I'm sorry," Will says as the ice-streaked wind hits them.

"Stay on top of it!" his father yells above the din. "Swim!"

His father disappears in the blizzard, and Will is running, the pain in his foot forgotten. He runs blindly. The ground is a white rug being pulled out from beneath him. He staggers, and knows that to fall is certain death. He throws his body forward and thrashes wildly, trying to stay atop the churning sea of snow. It pushes and pummels him with a terrifying weight. There is no time for fear, only a wild animal scrabbling as he tries to keep on top. He goes under, claws his way back up, gulping air, hurtled along by the avalanche's mighty muscle.

Something long and narrow whips past, nearly taking off his head—and he realizes it's a twisted measure of steel rail. Off to his right he catches the dim shadow of his father, swimming alongside him, before he vanishes once more. Some high branches of a buried tree jut out of the blizzard, and he makes a grab, but is swept past. He knows he is being washed down through the sparse woods that grow right to the edge of the gorge.

Another set of boughs looms up, directly in front of him, and he clutches at them and this time holds fast. His body is lashed about by the driving force of the snow, but he won't release his grip, even as his head is covered and snow rammed up his nostrils. He gags, choking for breath.

Stillness then, and silence. He releases one hand from the branches and burrows it back to his body to clear space around his face. Then he thrusts his arm high, scooping wildly and breaking free. Packed snow melts inside his collar, slithering down his back and chest. He sees a flash of sky and fills his lungs hungrily. Slowly he hauls himself from the snow and into the arms of the tree.

Shivering, he beholds a landscape transformed. The snow must be piled twenty feet high amongst the trees, some of which have keeled over. Debris is scattered everywhere, branches, steel rails jutting up, wooden ties. He can't see beyond the woods to the track or the snow sheds. Overhead the sun shines. Birds resume a cheery chorus. Will thinks of the sketchbook in his snow-sodden jacket, the pencil lines smearing on the wet paper.

From the trees comes a sound Will has never heard before, a series of gruff animal hoots that taper off into a kind of mournful sigh.

"Will, are you all right?"

Twenty yards to his left his father clings to a tree.

"I'm fine!"

"I'll come to you!" his father calls.

At the same moment they see it. A little higher up the slope, jutting from the snow, is the gold spike.

A rustling draws Will's attention. A snow-caked man clings to another nearby tree, a scarf tied around his face, revealing only his eyes.

"All right?" Will's dad calls up to him.

The man says nothing, just lifts a hand. His eyes, Will can tell, are on the gold spike.

"Help!"

This cry is muffled and comes from down the slope, where, not forty feet from Will's perch, the ground drops into the gorge and the rioting river. Will squints. On the very edge, clutching the branch of a spindly bent pine, his legs dangling over the edge, is Cornelius Van Horne.

"Hold tight, sir!" Will's father calls out. "I'm coming!" He looks at the man with the scarf. "Help me!"

The other man makes no reply and stays put.

From the trees comes another series of gruff hoots.

"What is that?" Will asks, but instinctively he knows.

"The branch won't hold long!" Van Horne calls out with amazing calm.

"Pa?" Will says, a terrible fear spreading through him like cold.

"Stay there, Will. It'll be fine."

Will watches as his father carefully paddles down over the snow toward the rail baron, digging in with his hands and feet to slow himself. Off to the right a heaping drift mutters and creaks and spills itself into the gorge. Will feels the vibration through his body. Everything piled up along the edge could give at any moment.

"You'll be all right, sir," Will's father says as he reaches the spindly pine and wraps his legs around the trunk.

He reaches out toward Van Horne. "I'm going to take your wrist, sir, and you take mine."

The rail baron is a large man, and Will hears his father grunt as he takes his weight. Bracing himself against the trunk, James Everett pulls.

Will's heart is a small panicking animal against his ribs as he watches his father struggle on the precipice. Van Horne's other hand stretches out and seizes a sturdy branch, and he pulls now too. After a minute, with both men straining, the rail baron reaches the trunk and holds tight. They lean their heads against the bark, catching their breath.

Will exhales and hears a rustling behind him. He turns to see the man easing himself down the slope toward the gold spike. He looks at Will and holds a swollen finger to his mouth.

"Shhhhh."

He plucks the golden spike from the snow.

"You and me," he whispers to Will, "got an understanding, ain't we? You call out, I'll find you and your pa and slit your throats. Got that?"

Terrified, Will just stares at the man's obscured face, at the narrow band of skin around his chilly blue eyes.

I know you, Will thinks, but he says nothing.

The man called Brogan turns and begins churning his way back up the slope. He brushes a broken branch, and the end twitches and then clutches his ankle.

With a grunt Brogan tries to kick himself free, but the branch flexes and grows longer. Like some mutant tree unfolding itself from the earth, a long arm stretches out and sprouts a bony shoulder and narrow head, matted with snow. Brogan gives a cry of horror as he's dragged back.

A skunky stench wafts across to Will as the sasquatch thrashes itself up from the snow. Will knows now why the Natives call them stick men, for their limbs are so thin yet powerful that they look like they're made from the indestructible ingredients of mountain forest.

Will can see that it's a young one, quite a bit smaller than him. Though its mouth is wide, teeth bared, Will isn't sure if the beast is attacking or merely clambering atop Brogan like someone trying not to drown. Brogan beats at the sasquatch. From a pocket he pulls a long knife and stabs the creature in the shoulder. It crumples, sending up a terrible shriek.

For a moment Will thinks a treetop has snapped and fallen, for something thin and very tall hits the snow beside Brogan. But it's no tree. It is seven feet of fury, jumping down from above to protect its child. Will's insides feel liquid with fear. The creature's arms are vast knotted branches, its clawed feet gnarled roots. The adult sasquatch reaches down and grabs Brogan by an arm and a leg and in one movement hurls him. The golden spike flies clear of his clothing and lands in the snow, not far from Will. Brogan himself sails through the air, skids across the snow with a squawk of terror, and disappears over the edge into the gorge.

Chest heaving, the sasquatch checks on its young, and then turns and looks straight at Will.

"Pa!" Will hollers.

"Stay still!" his father shouts. "Don't turn your back! I'm coming!"

Gripping the tree, Will stares at the sasquatch as it shakes the snow from its furred body.

"She just wants her child, Will," his father is calling. "Show her you're no threat. Don't look in her eyes."

Will feels a tremor and sees the snow sliding slowly past his tree like a river toward the precipice. Great rafts of it pour over into the abyss. An ominous creak emanates from his father's pine. It begins to tilt toward the gorge.

"It's giving way!" Will cries, seeing the snow's surface pucker all around.

"Swim!" Will's father cries out to Van Horne, and the two begin thrashing their way uphill toward Will. The snow slips and shoves against them. To Will it looks like they're scarcely moving, but they fight on against the tide.

When he turns back to the two sasquatch, they're skidding straight toward him on the current of snow. Will clambers round to the far side of the trunk. Sliding with the snow comes the gold spike, and as it passes, Will seizes it.

"We're coming, Will!" his father shouts behind him.

But the sasquatch are coming faster. He can't help it—he looks into the creature's face and sees eyes as old as the mountains and as merciless.

"Move back, Will!" he hears his father cry, and then there's a sharp crack.

Will looks over his shoulder and sees Van Horne with a smoking pistol in his hand.

The mother sasquatch has collapsed in the snow, and her limp body is being carried by the current. The young one sets up a frenzied shrieking, its sharp mouth wide. It's coming right for Will.

A huge net unfurls from the air and drops over the small sasquatch. The creature knocks against the tree, struggling and yelping. Will leans far out of its reach.

"Don't shoot it!" calls a voice from the trees.

Mr. Dorian emerges on snowshoes, along with three other large men carrying thick measures of rope over their shoulders. The snow has finally stopped moving.

"We've got him, gentlemen. It's quite all right," calls Mr. Dorian. "Take our ropes!"

Ropes are thrown out for all of them, and Will grabs hold. Mr. Van Horne and Will's father are pulled up alongside him.

"Will," his father says. "You're all right?"

Will nods, unable to speak.

"Well, Dorian," puffs Van Horne, "you didn't come just for my painting, did you?"

"I came for many reasons," says Mr. Dorian. "To see the greatest railway in the world finished—and to find a sasquatch for the greatest show on earth."

CHAPTER

2

THE BOUNDLESS

THREE YEARS LATER

"How long is the train exactly?"

"How many people is she carrying?"

"Will she arrive on schedule for her maiden voyage?"

The reporters' questions come in a barrage as Will and his father stand on the platform beside the massive locomotive. Despite the chill of the April day, Will can feel the heat from her mighty furnace.

"Well, gentlemen," says Will's father, smiling easily at the reporters, "quite simply the Boundless is the longest train in the world. When we're finished coupling the last of her cars, she'll be pulling nine hundred and eighty-seven."

"Is she strong enough?" cries out a reporter whose body is all angles.

Will's father looks astonished. "Is she strong enough? Gentlemen, *look* at her!"

Will stares up too. The locomotive steams, her hot breath curling from the smokestacks atop the three-story boiler. He can feel the tremor of her expectant power through the station platform, through the very air. Massive and black, she's like something forged with lightning and thunder. A steel galleon on nine sets of towering wheels. Behind the boiler jut metal scaffolds where soot-blackened men stand ready to shovel coal into the furnace and set the Boundless in motion.

"She's the most powerful engine in the world," Will's father tells the reporters. "She'd pull the moon out of orbit if we could get a tether on it. As for her length, if you care to walk from locomotive to caboose, it's more than seven miles. According to our manifest we have 6,495 souls aboard for the journey. And I think I'm all out of statistics, gentlemen!"

Applause and good-natured laughter erupt from the churning crowd. Will's never seen the station so utterly crammed. Half of Halifax has turned out for the send-off.

Will looks at his father enviously. He would've been tongue-tied, and yet his father answers with such ease, in full sentences, without faltering. Will has grown used to seeing his father in fine suits and in the company of other important gentlemen.

But even now he still feels a bit bewildered at how different his father is—and how much all their lives have changed in the last three years.

At the back of the crowd, several photographers are busy taking photos, their cameras perched high atop tripods. Will hopes the reporters are done with them—but it's not to be just yet.

"Mr. Everett, is it true that just before his death Mr. Van Horne handpicked you to expand his empire across the Pacific? Even though his board recommended someone with more experience?"

Will notices his father's nostrils narrow as he inhales.

"I'm very honored that Mr. Van Horne gave me such a position of trust," he answers. "And it's my ardent goal to make sure his steamships sail across the Pacific just as grandly as his trains steam across our nation."

"There's some talk that the Boundless is too big," another reporter says.

Will's father laughs. "How can she be too big?"

"Too long for the turns, too heavy for the bridges, too tall for the tunnels."

Will catches the flash of indignation in his father's expression. "Sir, when Cornelius Van Horne built this railway, his eye was always on the future. He was sketching designs for the Boundless long before the last spike. She is exactly the kind of train he imagined running on this track."

Will remembers how Mr. Van Horne showed him his

sketches in the company car and asked his opinion. Over the years the rail baron sat at their table often, and he always took time to talk to Will. There seemed nothing he wasn't interested in. Insects, battles, gambling, famous artists . . .

"How safe is the route?" yet another reporter demands. "We hear those muskeg bogs can eat a train whole."

"Not this train."

"The mountains, then," the reporter persists. "Avalanches. Sasquatch."

"I wouldn't recommend walking," says Will's father, "but stay inside the Boundless, and you'll be absolutely fine. Now then, gentlemen—"

"Are you superstitious about carrying his funeral car on the maiden voyage?"

Will looks at his father, wondering how he'll reply to this one. James Everett shakes his head.

"Not at all. It was Mr. Van Horne's wish that, upon his death, his body be carried across the nation on the railway he built."

"And where will his body finally rest?"

"It will not rest. Like the man himself, it will remain in motion, crossing and recrossing the country forever."

A murmur of amazement wafts through the crowd, and Will sees some people exchange nervous looks. This is the first he's heard of it too.

"If you're inclined to believe in ghosts," Will's father says, "I can assure you, we'll have the most able-bodied and benevolent ghost looking over us. Now, if you'll excuse me . . ."

"Is it true his coffin carries the gold spike?"

"Thank you, gentlemen, and good day!"

"How's your boy feel about being on the maiden voyage?"

Will feels like all the air in his lungs has been sucked out. The reporters stare at him, silent and expectant. For what feels like a long moment, his mind is blank. Then he takes a breath and tries to smile like his father.

"It's going to be an adventure," he says.

"All aboard, Ladies and Gentlemen!" his father says, guiding Will through the crowd.

His heart still racing, Will walks past the locomotive, and then the triple-decker tender, filled with the tons of coal and water.

"What's this one?" he asks his father, pointing at the small carriage coupled behind the tender.

"A bunk car," he replies. "For the engineers and firemen driving the locomotive."

Will doesn't need to ask what the next car is. There are so many people knotted around it, he can't get close enough to read the inscriptions on its black steel side. A portly guard warns the spectators not to touch.

Will was at the funeral. His father was one of the pallbearers, carrying the enormous coffin down the aisle. In the vast cathedral Will felt small and insignificant amidst all the dignitaries, politicians, and magnates. He'd liked Mr. Van Horne an awful lot. Many fine speeches were made about him, but they were all about his achievements and service to the nation, and they didn't seem to be about the person Will remembered.

"We're up ahead, just a few more," Will hears his father say as they pass several plain cars that Will guesses must be for crew and cargo.

And then suddenly the train carriages become altogether different. Gleaming shells of mahogany and brass and spotless glass, they rise gracefully two stories above the track.

"This is ours," Will's father says at the very first of the fine carriages. Will steps up the fancy iron steps to a small canopied platform. A white-gloved porter is waiting for them.

"Welcome aboard, Mr. Everett," the porter says to his father; then he nods at Will. "And Master Everett. You're in the first stateroom to your right."

"Thank you, Marchand," says Will's father.

Will steps through the thick wooden door after his father. The car smells of new carpet and wood polish. On the left a narrow, wood-paneled hallway with large windows and a brass handrail runs the length of the carriage.

This is hardly his first time on a train, but when Will walks into their stateroom, he's speechless. He's used to a comfortable cushioned seat, but before him is a luxurious parlor with armchairs and sofas and side tables and electric lamps and fresh flowers in vases.

"Mom would like this," Will says.

He can imagine her stroking the red velvet wallpaper, giving a delighted little sigh at the Persian carpet, and admiring the tasseled silk blinds, which are discreetly lowered to block their view of the rail yards.

"Oh, she was perfectly comfortable on the Columbia," his father says.

Six weeks ago Will's mother went out West with the twins and their nurse, to get settled and organize their new home in Victoria.

Will opens a door and pokes his head into a washroom gleaming with porcelain and polished brass.

"Do our beds pull down at night?" Will asks, searching the walls for handles.

"No," says his father, and he opens another small door, which Will assumed was to a closet. Instead it reveals an elegant wrought iron staircase. "Our bedrooms are upstairs."

"Upstairs!" Will hurries up to a small hallway with two doors. The first opens onto what must be the master bedroom, for there is a large bed—not a pull-down like in the usual Pullman sleepers but a proper bed. The second door leads to his own room. It has a single bed, a night table, and a wardrobe.

Will sets about opening every drawer and cupboard. Everything is marvelously designed to make the most of the small space. It's a bit like being on a ship, he supposes, a very long and narrow land ship steaming across the continent. Best of all he has his own large window, which he'll be able to see through while lying in bed.

He feels a restless surge of excitement. He wants the train to be in motion right now. He wants to be going somewhere. But weirdly, even going across the whole country from sea to sea, starting a new life in a new city doesn't seem like enough. He has moved before, to new places, to new and bigger houses. What he wants is something else.

When he goes downstairs, his father is already sitting at the rolltop desk, writing. This image of him—his back, his powerful shoulders, head bowed, and the *scritch* of the nib upon paper—is all too familiar to Will from the past three years. When his father is home, that is, and not traveling.

"Is it in his coffin?" Will asks.

Distracted, his father looks up.

"The spike," Will adds.

His father's smile is amused. "Planning a career in newspapers?"

"You must know," Will says. "You were one of the pallbearers."

His father looks at him carefully. "Well, I suppose you have a right to know. After all, you drove that spike."

"And saved it after the avalanche," he reminds his father.

He still dreams about that spike. He's always searching for it. He thinks he knows where it is. There are clues. People tell him it's just up the hill. People tell him it's just around the corner. If he hurries, he can grab it. But the dreams always end the same. He's about to turn that corner. He's about to climb that hill, but then he wakes up, unsuccessful.

"Yes," his father tells him. "He wanted it buried with him. But that information is for you alone."

"Of course," Will replies. "Why would I tell anyone if I want to steal it myself?"

Will is never sure his father appreciates attempts at humor— he is a serious man—but James Everett chuckles briefly.

"I have some work to do. Why don't you go explore the train? Once we're under way, I'll join you in the Terrace car for the bon voyage reception."

Will leaves their stateroom and turns down the hallway, pressing himself to the wall to allow the ladies and gentlemen and stewards to pass with their luggage. At the end of the corridor, he opens the door and is outside on a small platform. He walks across to the next car, where the door is opened from the inside by a waiting steward.

After ten minutes or so he loses track of how many stateroom cars he's traveled through. All of them have famous names: MacDonald, Crowfoot, Champlain, Brock, Van Horne. He wonders if someday there will be one named after his father.

Entering the Vancouver car, he finds himself in a cozy library, with long reading tables and green shaded lamps and floor-to-ceiling walnut bookshelves between the windows. A pretty librarian glances up. Will isn't saying anything, but she shushes him anyway.

Beyond the library the hallway takes him past a barbershop, where a man with excessive sideburns is tipped back in his chair, getting his nostril hairs clipped. Next door is a fancy salon, and after that a tailor's, and a shoe blacking stall, and a shop where you can buy anything from cigars to DeWort's sleeping powders.

The train seems endless, and Will knows he has hardly made a dent in first class. It's like a rolling city. In the next car he emerges into the billiards room. Two gentlemen are already strutting around the table with their cues, muttering about the despicable state of the stock market.

Down another corridor Will opens a door to a gymnasium tiled in blue and gold and resembling a Turkish bath. He goes in and sits atop a complicated exercise machine, pulling levers. He gets off before it can stretch him or break his legs.

The next car is an enormous lounge with leather armchairs, side tables, and thick rugs. Light slants through angled shades. Large ceiling fans silently circulate the air. Waiters in black vests lean over discreetly to take orders. In the corner a man plays the grand piano. There are a great many people here already, sitting in small groups, talking, drinking tea or coffee.

Will looks about hopefully for anyone his age, and is disappointed. He passes between cars and enters another lounge, this one with stairs.

So this is the famous Terrace car! The walls on either side are built entirely of reinforced glass, veiled right now by muslin curtains to hide the view of the rail yards. Behind an enormous semicircular zinc bar stands a uniformed bartender with smoke coming out of his neck. Will hurries closer. His father has told him about this bartender, for he is entirely mechanical and powered by the same steam that drives the Boundless's pistons.

The automaton is pouring a drink for a gentleman. He picks up the tumbler with mechanical fingers, tight enough for a good grip, not so tight as to break the glass. With a gasp of steam he lifts and extends his arm toward the gentleman.

"Whiskey, please," Will says before the mechanical bartender.

The machine stands, motionless. It's disconcerting, for its head is plaster and is painted with a pleasant but immovable expression.

"Whiskey," Will repeats.

"Maybe a ginger beer," the machine says, and Will starts. Then he sees a human bartender farther down, wiping the counter. "Nice try, though, kid."

Will waits for the machine to pour him a ginger beer, and then takes it upstairs. The second level of the Terrace car has a vaulted glass ceiling, giving a panoramic view. There are only a few people here, maybe because it's a bit chilly. A man writes a letter on an elegant table that folds down from the wall. At the back of the car, a door leads to the sizable terrace. Will steps out and leans against the brass railing.

The train, he's surprised to see, has actually pulled ahead

without his even noticing. All the first-class cars are now out of the station, to give the second-class passengers a chance to board from the platform.

He supposes the Boundless will have to pull ahead again for the third-class passengers too. And then there's the colonists, who don't even get to use the station platform. From his vantage point he can see beyond the station building, where the gravel sidings are thronged with humbly dressed passengers carrying odd, tattered suitcases and sagging boxes and bundled crying babies. Will's used to seeing them in Halifax. Every week ships bring them to Pier 21 from all over the world.

All around him in the vast railyards, more freight cars and baggage cars are being shunted about and readied to join the Boundless as it edges forward bit by bit.

Will chews on his pencil meditatively, then fishes out his sketchbook. It's a beautiful slim thing, brand-new for the trip. The pages are thick enough for watercolors—but mostly he just likes to sketch with pencil.

He spots a boy standing atop an old rusted boxcar, waving. And for a moment Will feels like he's waving at himself across time. Before he was rich, he was poor. And just three years ago he lived in a Winnipeg rooming house that backed onto the rail yards.

He doesn't miss their old apartment, with its splintered, cold floors, its mean windows, and the hallway smell of cabbage and wet sock. But he often thinks about what Van Horne said to him at Farewell Station. About how you need a good story, one of your very own.

That day, in the mountains, he was given a story, and a grand one at that. He felt then like his life was about to properly start—that he'd finally have adventures of his own, maybe with his father. But then almost right away his story got derailed and he was just watching his father's life trundle merrily along the tracks.

After the avalanche Mr. Van Horne promoted Will's father to engineer of the Maritime Line. Within the week they were moving—not out West as planned but back East, beyond Winnipeg, to Halifax. Their new apartment was clean and bright and spacious. Shiny store-bought furniture stood beside their shabby beds, tables, and chairs.

It was a big promotion, and Will's father said it was Cornelius Van Horne's way of saying thank you for saving his life. But it soon became clear that the rail baron wasn't done with James Everett. Van Horne said he showed unusual promise. Before long Will's father was promoted again, to assistant regional manager of the Maritime Line.

After that they moved into their first house, not far from Point Pleasant Park. It had a garden that belonged only to them. Will's shoes got shinier; his clothes got more buttons and fastened more tightly around his neck. He stopped going to the local public school and started at a small private academy.

Will liked that. He wasn't so embarrassed to be good at

his studies. But he never felt like he fit in properly with the sons and daughters of wealthy businessmen and politicians. He stayed on the fringes.

Nonetheless there was an art teacher there who encouraged him and gave him extra lessons once a week after school. Drawing changed from being a hobby to a passion.

At home they got a cook and a housemaid. His parents began entertaining their new friends and going out to social events around the city. His mother seemed to slip into her new life as easily as into one of her new gowns.

And for the first time in Will's life, his father slept at home more often than not. But sometimes it was as if he were still far away. Mostly he was at his office, and when he came home, there was always work waiting for him, huge ledgers and books that needed studying.

If Will pestered him enough, he'd occasionally talk about his days laying tracks, or his adventures up in the mountains. When he did, Will felt like he had his old father back—the father he'd imagined from his letters, anyway. Will never tired of those stories. But they started to seem more like stories from books—and ones his parents were keen to forget.

After his father's next promotion they moved to an even larger house, with a manicured lawn that swept down to the water of the Northwest Arm. One day a piano appeared in the parlor, and with the piano came a little old lady with mothball breath who tried to teach Will how to play it. Will hated the piano, and no matter how hard he banged the keys, how much he mangled his scales, his mother would not let him stop the lessons. One day his father threatened to drag the thing out into the backyard and take a hatchet to it. Will waited hopefully, *desperately*, wanting his father to splinter the piano to kindling, but his father changed his mind and went back upstairs to his study.

Just last month came the biggest promotion of all. His father was offered the job of general manager for the railway's new steamship line, operating out of Victoria, where the great ships left for the Orient. And so here they were moving across the entire continent again to start a new life.

Rapidly Will draws the rusty boxcars at the rail yard's edge. But instead of a boy atop it, he finds himself sketching a girl doing a handstand.

He never got his sasquatch tooth back.

It is late afternoon when the Boundless is finally ready to depart. On the Terrace deck Will feels the brisk Atlantic wind pick up. By now the locomotive has pulled the first-class cars alongside the Bedford Basin. Miles away, out of sight, he knows the last cars are being coupled back in the rail yard.

The terrace is crowded now, and when he hears the long shrill whistle from the locomotive, an excitement beats within him, in time with the train's connecting rods. A huge plume of steam bursts from the locomotive's smokestack.

Cho—

And again.

Cho-cho . . . *cho*-cho-cho . . .

And the train is moving, not the sluggish pulls from earlier but an intent straining.

Cha-cha-cha . . . *cha*chachacha . . .

Picking up speed now, the grayish plume rising high into the spring sky; smaller, alternating plumes jetting from the pistons.

Cha-ch-ch-cha-ch-ch-tchtchtchtchtchtchtch . . .

They are finally on their way!

"Some champagne, sir?" a waiter asks him, holding out a platter filled with slender glass flutes.

"Thank you," says Will, taking one. He has a sip, savors the crisp nutty flavor before letting it bubble down his throat. He smiles, pleased with himself. He couldn't fool the bartender, but he's fooled this waiter. And why not? Everyone tells him he looks older than his age, as tall as his father now, and likely to be taller still. His first champagne.

He closes his eyes. He is going somewhere. And he has a plan.

His father just doesn't know it yet.

THE EVENING'S ENTERTAINMENT

Back in the stateroom Will and his father dress for dinner. Will's father has gained weight since his years laying steel, but he still cuts a fine figure, with his closely trimmed beard and piercing eyes.

Will feels like he may as well be wearing a suit of armor; his shirt is so stiffly starched, it scarcely bends when he moves.

"Can't I ride in the locomotive with you?" Will asks.

"Not possible, William. I've already told you."

His father is going to be chief engineer on the maiden journey of the Boundless. Tomorrow, at the first stop, Will's father will board the locomotive and take shifts with the other engineer driving the train. When he is off duty, he won't even sleep in their sumptuous stateroom but in the sooty bunk car right behind the tender. It's his father who will guide the train over the Rocky Mountains—and after tomorrow Will won't see him again until Lionsgate City.

This is no surprise; he knew all this ahead of time. But it still rankles—he's getting left behind. Again.

"You'll be much more comfortable back here anyway," his father tells him. He straightens Will's bow tie. "Hungry?"

They leave the stateroom and join the procession bound for the dining car. As his father exchanges pleasantries with the gentlemen, Will once more looks about for anyone even close to his own age. He feels beardless and out of place.

He's seen some fancy restaurants in the last few years but never one quite so opulent as this one. Though long and narrow, it gives the impression of palatial grandeur, with mirrored walls and a ceiling painted like the sky, complete with little angels peeping around the edges. Spiral staircases lead to galleries running the length of the carriage. From a small balcony a woman sings opera.

The waiter leads Will and his father to their table. With a flourish he places napkins on their laps and hands them each a slim leather booklet. Will stares at the menu, trying to decide, but his thoughts are aswirl.

"The lamb, please," he finally tells the waiter. "Medium rare."

When his father has ordered and the waiter has left, Will says hesitantly:

"I've been thinking about next year."

"Me too," says his father. "When you finish your studies, I'd like you to join the company."

James Everett raises his eyebrows and grins, as though he's just given Will a present.

"What would I do?" Will asks, startled.

"You'd start as a clerk, I imagine, but once you show promise, you won't remain one for long."

He thinks of his pencil, writing numbers in ledgers instead of drawing.

"I'm not sure," he murmurs.

"Not sure of what?"

He swallows. "I'm not sure it's what I want. There's an art college in San Francisco, a good one. I was hoping to study there."

"Study to become an artist?"

Will nods.

"You're talented, Will," says his father, frowning. "No question."

Will's pretty sure his father is lying. He's never taken much interest in his drawings. Will wonders if his father has even kept that sketchbook he gave him in the mountains.

"What I'd like to see," his father says now, "is you putting that skill to use as an engineer or an architect for the company. Think of the things you could create! I saw the way you looked at the locomotive."

Will nods. "It's very impressive. . . ."

"The CPR will need men to design new fleets of ocean liners and bridges to take our tracks all the way across the world. There's even talk of spanning the Bering Strait so we can pass from Asia without need of ships."

Will adjusts his cutlery. "I'm not sure it's what I'm meant to do."

"*Meant* to do? That's nonsense. A man does what he *needs* to do, to make his way in the world, to support a family."

The lamb is placed before Will. It is one of his favorite dishes, but he suddenly has no appetite.

"There's no living to be made as an artist, William," his father says. "Your mother and I have been happy to let you draw and paint—as a hobby. But these artist fellows, they live very wretched lives."

"I don't mind being poor," Will replies, and then adds, "We were poor once."

"And there's no shame in being poor," James Everett replies, though Will notices that he glances about the dining car. "But it's foolish to seek it out when there are better opportunities."

"There's nothing I want to do more," says Will simply.

His father looks at him closely, and for a moment Will

thinks he sees sympathy in his father's eyes. But then James Everett sniffs.

"William, my boy, I see it as a fruitless course."

Will forces himself to take a mouthful of his meal; the meat is heavy and tastes of blood. He washes it down with water.

"I've done the things you thought best," he says. "I studied hard—"

"And why wouldn't you?" his father counters in exasperation. "You had an opportunity, a rare opportunity, to get a superior education. Studying hard was the least you could do."

"Yes, I know," Will says, tracing the small pattern on the tablecloth to focus his thoughts, "and I'm grateful. And I did work hard. I even played piano for a year because mother wanted me to, even though I hated it!"

"You made a terrible sound with that instrument."

"I did it on purpose. Drawing is what I love most."

His father shrugs. "And you draw every day. So keep drawing. But *after* your proper work is done."

"It's not enough. I need training, that's what Mr. Grenfell said. I'm good at *copying* things. But I'm a terrible painter still. And when I do people, they're not right. They're all missing . . . *something*."

"And you think this fancy school in San Francisco will fix that."

"I won't know unless I try."

"Ah. And you expect me to pay for this foolhardy experiment?"

"I'll pay my own way!"

"Will you?"

Will feels his cheeks redden. "Why not? You worked when you were my age."

"I never would have done the things I did if I'd had your opportunities."

"What about building the railway? You said it was a grand adventure." He takes a breath. "I want my own adventure."

His father's eyes look past him for a moment. "You saw what it was like in the mountains, William. Rough men doing back-breaking work. Frostbite in the winter, and a plague of mosquitoes in the summer. Bad food. Late pay. Every day a fair chance we'd get torn apart by a sasquatch or blasted to bits." More gently he says, "You could've died up there that day. Your mother was furious with me. She and I, we don't want a hard life for you. You're not suited to it."

Will feels another sharp sting of humiliation—though this isn't the first time his father has said such things. His father thinks he's too shy, too sensitive. Too *soft*.

"I don't know what I'm suited for," Will says quietly. "But I mean to find out."

After dinner Will and his father make their way to the Lionsgate parlor car, which has been transformed into a theater while they dined. Rows of velvet chairs face a small raised platform with Japanese folding screens on either side.

Will sits down beside his father. The rest of their dinner was quiet and tense. Nothing was decided.

More men saunter in with their cigars and glasses of port and brandy, their ladies on their arms, and take their seats. Will spots a Mountie in a scarlet uniform.

"Is that Sam Steele?" he asks his father.

"He helped keep law and order in the mountain work camps, so we invited him to be on the maiden voyage."

To Will it's like seeing a picture torn from a book. Steele really is as mountainous and powerful as the stories said.

"We'll have at least one Mountie on every voyage," his father says. "To do the rounds of the cars."

When everyone's finally seated, a short, finely attired gentleman steps onto the platform, and the audience grows quiet.

"Welcome aboard the Boundless, Ladies and Gentlemen, the world's largest and most glorious train."

There is a polite splattering of applause and a few gruff "Hear, hear"s from the audience.

"My name is Mr. Beecham, the conductor. I am delighted to have such a fine group of people aboard for our maiden journey. In this room is an unparalleled collection of our nation's best and brightest. I salute you Ladies and Gentlemen, nation builders all! And in honor of your first night aboard, we have a program to entertain, delight, and even thrill you. First some recitations from our poet laureate, Sir Allen Nunn."

When the famous writer stands and begins to proclaim, Will's attention wanders. The poet seems to be talking about pulling weeds from a garden, but Will isn't sure. The man's voice drones on, rising and falling with the monotony of an ocean swell.

From somewhere comes the unnaturally loud sound of a flushing toilet. It flushes for a very long time, water gurgling and sucking through the walls in an invisible tangle of pipes. Everyone in the room is trying to ignore the noise, and Will bites his lips together. But he can't stop a muffled explosion of laughter inside his mouth.

The historian who follows the poet is more interesting, talking about the building of the railway. Will has heard most of the stories already, but at least they're good ones.

"Some of you may have noticed that our train is a large one," Mr. Beecham says when he resumes the stage. "Our rolling city comprises first class, second class, third class, colonist class, and behind these, several miles of freight cars. But amongst these freight cars is a little town, a string of eighty carriages belonging to the world-renowned Zirkus Dante. The Boundless is conveying the circus to Lionsgate City, where it will begin its tour of the continent. And kindly joining us tonight is the ringmaster himself, here to inspire and confound us with his wizardry. Ladies and Gentlemen, I give you Mr. Dorian!"

Will sits up straighter. From behind one of the screens steps the circus man that Will first met three years ago. Dignified, he walks to the center of the platform, hands clasped behind his back.

The gaslights in the car are dimmed by attendants, leaving only Mr. Dorian brightly illuminated.

"I do not believe in magic, Ladies and Gentlemen. There is no such thing. What people call magic is just the unexplained mystery of our world. And there is no end of wonders along this road we're on. Cut from the wilderness, these tracks take us from sea to sea, through landscapes scarcely seen by civilized man. And so this steel road has revealed things to us that we might have assumed were the stuff of legends. Muskeg that devours trains, the man-eating Wendigo of the northern forest. Perhaps a lake leviathan or the mighty sasquatch."

A hush has fallen over the parlor car, so Will can feel the thumpety-clack of the track like a startled heartbeat in his chest. He knows firsthand how real the sasquatch is, and some of his father's letters mentioned these other mysterious things—stories told from other people's stories. He never knew how much to believe.

"Yes, Ladies and Gentlemen," Mr. Dorian continues, "the wonders of our world are many, and I have seen things that would startle and terrify you. But let me share with you now a marvel of a different sort."

After pausing dramatically, he walks closer to the audience.

"Mesmerism, the art of hypnosis, is one of the world's most powerful forces. Monsters and armies mean nothing compared to the power of one man's eyes, and the power of one man's voice, and the power he can muster when people listen to him of their own free will—listen to his voice, and look at his eyes, and let themselves accept an invitation to listen and then to listen once more. . . ."

Will wonders if the light in the car has dimmed further, for it's as if Mr. Dorian's face has grown brighter. And Will is aware of the man's fathomless black eyes, and his mouth, inviting him to do something, he doesn't know what because he can no longer hear what is being said, until—

He looks around the car, which seems brighter suddenly, to find himself standing along with everyone else in the theater. He has absolutely no memory of moving at all, and everyone else seems just as startled as he is. Nervous tittering and a few gasps erupt.

"Ladies and Gentlemen, forgive me," says Mr. Dorian with a smile. "Most rude of me, but I merely suggested that you all stand up, and you did so most willingly. Please sit down, sit down. . . . You've been most kind."

Everyone sits, grinning foolishly.

"It's a trick," grumbles a stolid man through his whiskers.

"Not at all, sir," says Mr. Dorian. "It is the power of mesmerism. Would you care to help me demonstrate?"

The whiskery fellow waves his hand grumpily, but others

are eager to volunteer. Will watches, amazed, as one after another, people go to the front and Mr. Dorian puts them into a kind of trance. One woman chirps like a canary, another sings a lullaby from his childhood, a third fellow thinks he's climbing a ladder, huffing and puffing with every imaginary step.

Whenever Mr. Dorian asks for another volunteer, Will wishes he were not so shy. He likes the idea of being hypnotized—what would it feel like to not be himself?—but can't imagine being watched by so many people.

"Ladies and Gentlemen," says Mr. Dorian, "as I said, I do not believe in magic but only the power of the mind. And we have, I believe, in our audience a very great mind indeed. Mr. Sandford Fleming, am I correct?"

"You are," says a gentleman.

Will cranes his neck and recognizes the "excessively bearded man" Mr. Van Horne introduced him to on the company train. If anything, Mr. Fleming's beard is even more massive, fanning out sharply over his collar so he seems to have no neck at all. Will notices that the man's wife sits a good distance from him.

"Sir, I applaud you," says Mr. Dorian. "If you did not know, Ladies and Gentlemen, this is the genius who invented the notion of standard time and time zones. In this age of lightning and steam, we move at such great speeds that it's necessary for us to adjust the time, hour by hour, as we hurtle across the continent. It's remarkable, isn't it, that within the space of a single second, it can be ten o'clock, and then the next second, nine o'clock! And if I'm not mistaken, we are about to pass through one such time zone, are we not, Mr. Fleming?"

"We are indeed," he concurs.

"Have you ever wondered, Ladies and Gentlemen, what happens when we pass *through* a time zone? Do we truly lose or gain an hour? Does it appear or disappear? How can time be altered? Surely time does not really change. And I believe, Mr. Fleming, you've also invented the term 'cosmic time,' which is the same all over the world."

"True again," says the gentleman.

"So we have standard time, constantly changing as we move, and cosmic time, which remains steady. Now, here is a curious thing. It seems that when we move with speed through time zones, there is a moment when reality catches up with cosmic time. I invite you all now to look at your timepieces."

Will, along with all the men in the room, dutifully takes out his pocket watch.

"Now observe the second hand as it makes its way around the clock. And remember that we're about to gain another hour! You will travel back in time an entire hour. Is it true? Of course not, and yet . . . behold."

Will stares at his watch face. The second hand moves smoothly.

Tick . . . tick . . .

"Watch carefully now," comes Mr. Dorian's deep voice. "Making its steady way. Watch now . . ."

Tick . . . tick . . .

"It moves and it moves; it knows its path," Dorian's voice says, as if from a great distance. "Keep your eyes on it, Ladies and Gentlemen."

And then Will's eyes widen as the second hand leans forward but doesn't move, only stutters in place—for how long, he doesn't know, for he can't take his eyes away. Will is dimly aware of gasps around the room, and a few people muttering, "Impossible!"

And then the second hand begins to move again, and Will blinks and looks back at Mr. Dorian.

"What happened, Ladies and Gentlemen? I shall tell you. Your bodies, all the matter in this room, were simply readjusting to the new reality, the new time. But what if I were to tell you that in this small stutter of time, I slipped from the front of the room and walked amongst you, and took some things, without your even knowing?"

"Outrageous!" calls someone.

"Is it?" he says. And he pulls from his pocket a wallet. "Sir, I believe this is yours, is it not, with the monogrammed initials HD?"

"How in the devil . . ."

"And a pair of jade cuff links from you, sir, there!"

"Incredible!" says the man, looking at his loose shirt cuffs.

Will laughs with his father, until Mr. Dorian points at them.

"And from the gentleman over there . . . an important-looking key on a chain."

Will's smile fades when he sees the concern on his father's face.

"Now, if I can ask you all to come and collect your things, please," says Mr. Dorian. "Oh, and please do remember to set your timepieces back an hour!"

"Go on," his father says quietly. "Take it back."

Will's heart thumps.

Impatiently his father says, "Now, Will."

Will stands, and as he walks toward the front, he feels his heart give a few panicked thumps. It doesn't help that Mr. Dorian seems even taller as he draws closer to the platform. The ringmaster smiles as he hands Will the key, and he shakes Will's hand but doesn't release his grip. Is there a hint of recognition in his eyes?

"And since you're already here, young sir, perhaps I might prevail upon you to assist me in the final act."

Will finds he cannot speak.

"Excellent," says Mr. Dorian. "And now, Ladies and Gentlemen, please welcome Zirkus Dante's unparalleled escape artist, the Miraculous Maren!"

A girl emerges from behind the screen like an exotic bird, her clothes bright and extravagant. Will has never seen anyone so vividly made up, her lips rouged, eyebrows lined with charcoal. Her legs and arms are bare. Will feels the heat in his cheeks.

"No lock can hold her! No chains can bind her!" proclaims Mr. Dorian.

She carries with her a length of rope and several heavy chains.

"Now, I know you think there will be some trick to this, my friends. Which is why I've asked this young gentleman from the audience to fasten these chains and this rope in any way he sees fit."

The girl holds out the rope and chains for Will.

"Examine them first," Mr. Dorian instructs. "Make sure they are strong."

Will tests them, but he's distracted by the girl, who smiles at him. There is a narrow gap between her teeth. Her eyes have a lively angle and a light that doesn't seem to be a mere reflection from the gas lamps.

"What shall I do now?" he asks.

"Tie me up," she replies.

Nervously he starts winding the rope around her body.

"Tighter, young sir, tighter!" cries Mr. Dorian.

"I don't want to hurt her," Will says.

Laughter rises from the audience.

"You won't hurt me," she says, just to him. "Go ahead."

"It's you, isn't it?" he whispers.

She gives a quick, almost imperceptible nod.

He knots the rope many times. "You have my sasquatch tooth," he murmurs.

"I know."

Will winds the chains around her and fastens them with heavy padlocks, then tests the locks to make sure they are secure.

"Thank you, young sir. Now if you will step to one side . . ."

Her eyes meet his once more before she turns her attention to the front.

With a flourish Mr. Dorian throws an enormous silk scarf over her, and she's transformed into a giant cocoon, wriggling about to the sound of clanking chains as she tries to free herself. Will can hear the steady sound of her breathing.

"Surely that's long enough!" exclaims Mr. Dorian after only fifteen seconds, and he impatiently grabs hold of the silk scarf and yanks it off.

The audience gasps, for the girl is no longer there. All that's left is the rope and chains in a pile on the floor.

"Ladies and Gentlemen!" cries Mr. Dorian with a tip of his hat. "The disappearing act!"

The applause is still going strong when Mr. Beecham, the conductor, takes Will's arm and says, "You can go back to your seat now, lad." Will watches as Mr. Dorian strides behind the screen and is gone.

"I want to talk to them."

"William!" his father calls. He turns to see his father looking at him expectantly.

"Where are they staying?" Will asks Mr. Beecham. In his haste he's forgotten to be nervous.

"They have rooms in second class for the night. Tomorrow they'll return to their own cars during our stop."

"Will!" his father calls again.

More than anything Will wants to run after Maren and talk to her, but he reluctantly hurries back to his father.

"The key," he says to Will.

Will fishes it out of his pocket and presses it into his father's hand. "I wanted to ask the magician something," he says.

His father looks a bit surprised but then nods. "I'll see you back in the stateroom."

Will's on the move at once, squeezing his way between people and chairs. When he reaches the Terrace car, the crowd thins, but then thickens again near the dining car. She can't be too much farther ahead. Past the kitchens a child is sprawled on the floor, having a temper tantrum as his weary mother cajoles him to stand. Will jumps over him. He spots a steward.

"The circus man and his assistant?" he asks. "Did you see them?"

"Just a few moments ago."

Will jogs through the hurtling train. He reaches the end of another carriage and opens the door to a gust of startlingly chilly night air. A brakeman in coveralls stands at the corner of the small platform, the tip of his cigarette flaring orange. He nods curtly at Will.

Through the next door—and he's suddenly in a garden, as warm as a hothouse. Tall plants rise all around him. Birds shriek from the high glass ceiling. It smells like summer. Fairy lanterns light a paved path. He rushes past a burbling fountain.

Will barrels on through the pungent fug of a cigar lounge. In the next car he slows down to cross the slippery deck of the swimming pool. The water flashes with color, and, startled, he looks down to see all manner of exotic fish darting about. Peering harder, he realizes they're contained in a shallow aquarium along the pool's bottom.

He keeps going, past a small cinema and the smell of roasted almonds and popcorn. How can Maren and Mr. Dorian have gotten so far ahead? The train is endless, juddering, shuddering, steaming along its steel road. He smells soap and bleach as he passes a laundry.

Damp with sweat, he's brought up short by a formidable door that says: TO SECOND-CLASS ACCOMMODATION. Eagerly he grasps the brass handle, but it won't turn. He tries again, looks about for a catch. A crisply dressed steward appears from a vestibule, pen in hand.

"Can I help you, sir?"

"I'd like to go through, please," Will says.

"It's second class through there, sir."

"Yes. There's someone I want to talk to."

The steward tries to smile patiently. "Do you have a second-class ticket, sir?"

"No."

As if he's trying to explain something to a small child, the steward says, "Then you can't enter the second-class carriages. The doors do stay locked. It's more comfortable for everyone that way."

Will sees the ring of keys clipped to the steward's belt. "The circus man went through, didn't he?"

"Ah yes, he did, sir. But that was by special arrangement."

"I have something I need to ask him."

The attendant nods sympathetically. "It's train policy, sir. The doors between the classes stay locked."

For a brief moment Will wants to tell him who his father is and demand the door be opened, but he can't quite do it.

"If there's a message," says the steward, "I'd be happy to send it back."

"It's all right. Thank you."

What on earth would he write anyway? He shakes his head as he imagines it.

I would like my tooth back, please.

P.S. I've wanted to talk to you for three years. You did a tight-rope walk. Then you disappeared. You are the most remarkable person I've ever met.

A complete idiot

Unsteadily he walks back toward the front, feeling the train's shake and shudder, and wondering how long it will take to get used to.

At the Terrace car he climbs the stairs and lets himself out. Though the deck is at the back of the car, and protected from the wind, he shivers in the cold night. A number of other passengers stand, taking in the view. Will tilts his head and is awed by the intensity of the stars. Constellations he's seen only in books are suddenly blazing above his head—every star in Orion's belt and cudgel! It's like a whole new world, only now visible to him.

He looks back along the Boundless, the long endless dark line of it. Green lamps illuminate its flanks. Far away he sees the lighted windows of the second-class dome car, not nearly as big and grand as theirs. A figure stands silhouetted before the bright windows and is joined by a much taller one wearing a top hat. They seem to be facing him.

The shorter figure raises a hand and waves, and Will instinctively waves back.

When Will returns to the stateroom, his father is wrapped in his robe, smoking a cigar and reading some papers in a pool of amber light.

"Did you get to ask your question?" he asks, looking up.

Will shakes his head. "They were already in second class; the steward wouldn't let me through."

Will's father nods. "Strict train policy. What did you want to ask him?"

"About the disappearing act," Will says. He doesn't want to tell him about the girl; he doesn't know how to explain his urgent desire to talk to her. It would just embarrass him.

On the desk he sees the key Mr. Dorian spirited from his father's pocket. It's unusually thick, with a great many notches. Instinctively he knows what it does.

"It's for Mr. Van Horne's funeral car, isn't it?"

His father's lips compress in a moment of hesitation, but then he answers, "Yes, and I rather wish Mr. Dorian hadn't drawn attention to it."

"Well, no one could know what it's for, could they?"

"*You* did."

"It was the way you looked when you saw him holding it. I could tell it was important. But didn't you say the funeral car had no door?"

"That's what we've told the papers. The car's made from the hull of an old battleship, steel plates half an inch thick. But even so, there's a door."

"Where?" Will asks.

His father's expression is poised between amusement and annoyance. "There are limits to what I'll tell you," he says. "But the key isn't just for the door. Before you can even *open* the door—if you can find it—there's another lock that needs attention."

"And what's that one for?"

"It turns off the high-voltage current traveling through the outer walls of the car."

"You're joking!"

He shakes his head. "Enough to knock you out cold. Van Horne designed it himself. I remember him showing me sketches years ago. He wanted his coffin and the spike safe from grave robbers."

Will frowns, thinking about it. "But doesn't the guard get electrocuted?"

"He's never inside or on top. He has his own little room at the back of the adjoining maintenance car."

Will watches his father closely. "What else is inside?"

James Everett releases a mouthful of smoke. "Plenty of things. Van Horne was quite a collector and he wanted his favorite belongings with him."

"You've been inside, then?"

Will doubts his father would be this forthcoming at home, but maybe there is something about the moving train that makes him more talkative.

"Yes, I oversaw the loading of the car. It was done in secret in the middle of the night." His gaze drifts away, as if remembering something amazing—or alarming. "Good luck to anyone who gets inside, is all I can say."

Will wishes he could have seen it, a treasure trove illuminated by lantern light.

"And you've got the only key?"

"There's one other. The guard has it."

Will remembers the guard, a portly bearded man, shooing spectators away.

"There," his father says, stubbing out his cigar. "You know things that only a handful of people know."

Will's glad his father has confided in him; he feels encouraged.

"We never finished our conversation at dinner."

His father's face closes. "Yes, we did."

"How?"

"You said you wanted to go to art school in San Francisco. I'm against it. I'll pay for proper training at a university if you mean to study something sensible. But you'll not go to study art. I forbid it."

Forbid. Standing before his father, Will feels a hot tremor move through him, and knows he cannot speak. His voice will shake with rage, and he refuses to look weak before his father.

Instead he turns and climbs the stairs to his bedroom.

Standing before the window, all he can see is his own reflection. He doesn't want to look at himself, so he turns off the electric light. He leans his head against the cool glass, tries to breathe evenly.

He thinks of Maren. Is it her real name? Don't circus people have special names? She shed her chains; she disappeared right before everyone's eyes. It was incredible. He wishes he could do something like that.

Tomorrow when the train stops, he'll step off and catch up

with her as she's heading back to the Zirkus Dante cars. He wants to know what she's done since he last saw her, all the places she's been, all the new tricks she can do.

He takes out his sketchbook and tries to conjure her stepping out onto the stage. Over the years, he has tried to draw her many times, but the results never satisfied him—and this time is no exception.

The train is surprisingly noisy clattering down the tracks, hurtling through the night. He gets ready for bed. On his night table is a small brick of waxed cotton, which the porter said you can put in your ears. But Will doesn't want to block out the sound of the train. He likes it. The endless motion.

Through the night his sleep is filled with whistles, long and short—and the image of a black horse galloping along the tracks, always just ahead of him.

His dreams bound after it.

CHAPTER 4

THE JUNCTION

It's not until after lunch that the Boundless nears the Junction. Will feels the train slow, and rushes to the Terrace car for a better view. Outside on the deck he realizes it's much colder now that they've swung farther north. Pine trees grow close against the tracks. He can see no sign of a town or station yet.

Back in the stateroom he finds his father packing himself a small valise. He's dressed simply in shirt, trousers and vest, and an engineer's cap. He seems leaner and younger somehow, more like the man Will met in Craigellachie three years ago. Will can tell he's excited.

"She's quite a train to drive," his father says.

Will is still angry with him, for his stern words last night and for leaving him alone while he has another adventure. He says nothing.

"You'll mind yourself while I'm away," says his father. "If you need anything, ask Beecham."

Will grunts. The train gives several short blasts and slows even more. Beyond the windows the trees draw back from the gravel shoulders of the tracks. He sees a few stalls and vendors, and then more stalls, and small tents, and then larger canvas buildings, and yet more stalls and people crammed amongst them, so many people, waving at the train as it slowly trundles past.

"It springs up whenever a train makes a stop," his father says. "They put it up overnight and take it down after the train leaves. It's mostly for the colonists. There's no meal service on their cars, so they have to lay in provisions for the journey."

Will feels a restless pulse of excitement as he watches all the merchants calling out and waving up at the train, grinning. It feels like a carnival—and a gigantic one at that, for it stretches on and on, all the way to the edge of the station platform.

When the Boundless finally comes to a halt, Will's father picks up his valise and they leave the stateroom together. Stairs have been lowered from the front of their car, and Will steps down onto the platform. His body feels as though it's still in motion, and he sways like a sailor just come ashore. As the gentlemen and ladies disembark, tastefully dressed merchants offer flutes of sparkling wine, oranges from a wicker basket, silk scarves.

"I'll see you in Lionsgate City, then," his father says.

Will nods, unwilling to let his father know he's hurt. "How long is the stop here? I'd like to have a look around."

"Just make sure to be back aboard by six. That's when we leave. And watch out for pickpockets."

Will glances at his watch. He has a good four hours. Plenty of time to find Maren. He hurriedly pats his jacket pocket to make sure he has his sketchbook and a few pencils.

Lots of other passengers from first class have stepped out by now. They saunter about, taking the air. A crowd is already knotted around the funeral carriage, and Will pauses to get a good look. It is night black, with ornamental metal plumes spiking high at each corner. The carriage is the size of a boxcar and gives an impression of immense thickness and strength. He can easily believe it was welded together from battleship steel. It even looks like something dredged from the ocean deeps, for its sides are festooned with intricate decorations, like barnacles.

"Have a good look, Ladies and Gents," the guard says from the other side of a velvet cordon. He has a meaty square face and looks strong enough, but his belly makes too tight a bulge against his jacket. "Keep your distance, please, or you'll get a nasty shock."

He points at the large white letters painted along the bottom half of the car: DANGER! DO NOT TOUCH! HIGH VOLTAGE!

As if for emphasis a crow lands on top of the car. There is a violent snap and a flash of light, and the crow falls, stunned, to the gravel. Several people step back with gasps.

"Discourages vandalism, is all," says the guard with a stretch and a yawn.

On the side of the carriage is a tombstone-shaped sign with the words:

Herein lie the remains of William Cornelius Van Horne.
With the building of the great railroad, he did more than any other
Man to ensure forever that:
"He shall have dominion from sea to sea." (Psalms 72:8)

"Fine tomb," says a fellow in a brakeman's overalls and cap, "for an old slave driver."

The guard's eyes widen. "You knew him?"

"Blasted rock for him in the mountains. He'd sooner send a man to his death than wait a minute. He was never a regular working man like you or me."

The guard says nothing. The brakeman offers him a cigarette, which the guard takes.

Will wouldn't mind getting a sketch of the funeral car, but he's in too much of a hurry to find Maren. Surely she'll want to look around the shantytown too. Shouts and laughter and music lilt through the air, drawing Will like a siren song. He plunges into the crowd.

Just beyond the platform eager boys are selling warm sticky

buns and cider. A toothless man thrusts a paper cone of sugared almonds into Will's hand, and Will decides it's easiest just to drop some coins into the man's cup. Someone is playing the accordion. Standing beside his cart, a farmer proclaims his apples and pears the finest in the land. A group of silent brown-robed monks arranges rounds of cheese on an overturned wooden crate.

Will doesn't mind the noisy tussle of the crowd. He walks and walks. His eyes search for Maren, and then he realizes she probably won't be wearing last night's outfit. The thought of her shapely legs makes his cheeks feel hot. How will he find her in this crush? He's alongside third-class now, and a small city is pouring off the Boundless. But maybe Maren is looking for him too.

"Sasquatch urine!" a man bellows from behind his plank counter. "You won't find it anywhere else!"

Will tries to give him a wide berth, but to his dismay the man's eyes lock on his.

"Young sir! For you, a special rate!" He holds out a vial.

Will stares at his shoes but feels rude just walking past. And he has to admit he's curious.

"What's it for?" he asks.

The fellow's face creases with surprise. "What's it for? My son, this ain't the city. I don't know where you're going—"

"Victoria," Will tells him.

"Well, there you are. That island is filled with bears and

mountain lions—and worse." He gives the vial a little shake. "This here's your surefire protection. This urine is guaranteed from a male sasquatch. Obtained at great personal risk! Put a bit of this on you, and all the other animals stay away. You're untouchable!"

"How do they collect the urine?" Will can't help asking.

"Well, my son, these people are brave souls. Fearless. You've never seen one of these animals up close."

Will says nothing.

"But maybe you don't plan to leave the city," says the merchant, taking in Will's clothes and shoes, "in which case, you'll have no need of it."

"I have seen one, actually," Will says.

The vendor's eyes narrow, taking a second look at him. "Then you'll want some."

"I'll take a vial."

"My special price of just one dollar."

It seems a lot for a little bit of urine, but Will supposes it was quite difficult to collect—unless it's just well water. He finds the coins in his pocket and hands them over.

"And there you are," says the fellow, smiling. "Use it wisely."

As Will walks away, he can't resist wiggling out the cork and taking a sniff. His nostrils flinch. It certainly smells bad, with an unmistakable skunky whiff which makes his skin prickle for a moment. He recorks the vial and puts it carefully into his breast pocket, padded by his handkerchief.

Looking at his watch, he sees he's been walking for a good hour. His feet are beginning to get sore. He's alongside the colonist cars now, and there are all kinds of stalls selling food and clothing. People noisily compete for the potatoes, a pair of boots, a jar of spirits, a side of bacon. A woman in a spattered apron twists the neck of a chicken and begins to pluck it. Sausages spit on braziers; soup pots bubble. Smells billow past him like steam from a locomotive.

Near one stall he sees a boy and a girl his age talking. Their bodies are angled expectantly toward each other, and when he looks back after a moment, he sees them kissing and then laughing shyly. The boy's fingers touch hers.

Will hurries on. Where is Maren? It's such a different world from the perfumed hush of the first-class carriages. A dozen different languages graze his ears. He realizes he loves this. He passes a stall with a modest scattering of items: a rusty bottle opener, a compass with a cracked face, a few Native arrowheads—and a pair of spectacles with cloth for lenses.

"What are these for?" he can't help asking. Will only now notices that the man's eyes are milky with cataracts. His gaze goes right through him. And yet the man seems to know exactly what Will is talking about.

"Those are for the muskeg," is all he says.

Will feels the same chill he did last night when Mr. Dorian uttered the mysterious word. What he knows about the muskeg is this: It was nearly impossible to build tracks across it. Gravel and steel sank into the bog. An entire train disappeared once. His father told him stories of workers throwing themselves into the bog in despair, never to resurface.

"But what do they do?" Will asks, picking up the spectacles.

"Put them on."

Will lifts them to his face. The cloth is very fine. He can still see, but only the outlines of things. The man before him is a pale shadow.

"Can you see my eyes?" the man asks.

"No."

"That's right. You don't want to see the hag's eyes."

Startled, Will removes the glasses. "The hag?"

"She lives along the northern shores of Lake Superior. The tracks will take you right through. If her eyes meet yours, then it's too late."

"What happens?" Will asks.

"Oh, she'll just give a nod. And then it don't matter none if you look away, 'cause next time you look back, she'll be a little closer."

"I'll be on a moving train, though," Will says with a nervous laugh. "Can she chase after me on a broomstick?"

"She doesn't need no broomstick. She travels with you." The man grins, revealing stained stumps of teeth. "When you first see her, she'll be standing just beside the tracks. But next time you see her, she'll be sitting right beside you on the train."

Gooseflesh erupts across Will's neck.

"She'll sit beside you, nice and calm, and you won't be able to move or call out. Wouldn't do you no good anyhow, because no one else can see her but you. And you're helpless because you can't move, and you can't stop her when she leans in nice and slow and whispers in your ear."

"What does she whisper?" Will asks, unaware that he is whispering himself.

"They say it's different for everyone. But some people, after they've listened awhile, they get up and go between cars and throw themselves off. Sometimes they get run over by the wheels; sometimes they roll and land in the bog and get pulled down."

"That's quite a story," says Will.

The man shrugs. Will buys the spectacles.

He walks on. The sun is out and it's suddenly warm. He looks everywhere for Maren, even though he knows it's probably hopeless. There are just too many people. He buys a fizzy apple drink from a vendor. It's so refreshing, he has another.

Beside the tracks a man in brakeman's overalls calls out:

"Five cents to run the deck of the Boundless, the best and longest train in the world!"

Atop two boxcars a pair of brakemen sprints back and forth along the running boards, jumping effortlessly over the gap.

Will wonders if the conductor knows this is going on, but it seems a different world down here, far beyond first class, where the colonist cars give way to freight.

"Who wants a try!" brays the man.

"I do," Will hears himself say. He's had no luck finding Maren so far, but maybe with a better view . . .

"Ah, the young fella wants to try. I'll take that nickel, and up you go!"

Will grabs the ladder's thin metal rungs and hauls himself up as swiftly and confidently as possible. A short, wiry brakeman with pouchy eyes helps him onto the roof.

Will likes being up high. He can see along the rooftop of the train in both directions. He figures he's about four miles from the station by now, though he can't even see it, nor any sign of the town. Forest embraces the track. His gaze sweeps the crowded shantytown, looking for Maren, without luck.

Wind moves his hair, and for a moment he imagines the train is moving, carrying him with it to the horizon.

"Ever walked a boxcar?" the brakeman asks with a pouchy-eyed smirk.

"Nope. But my father used to be a brakeman."

"Was he now?" The fellow looks at Will's clothes. "He done well for himself, ain't he? Let's see how you do! Do a walk."

The running boards are no more than a foot wide, laid along the center of the roof. With the train at a standstill, it's not hard to step smartly along them. There's a bit of a crowd watching him now, but he tries not to look.

"Not bad," says the brakeman. "Try running it now, in them fancy shoes of yours."

This doesn't go nearly as well. He loses his balance a couple of times and steps off the running boards onto the roof.

"Lad!" the brakeman calls from behind.

He turns sharply.

The fellow laughs. "Look ahead. Never turn your back to the track! First rule. A sudden curve can send you flying!"

Will nods sheepishly. He remembers his father telling him that. He can see a line of other people now, waiting their turns.

"You want to try a jump?" the brakeman asks.

Will looks at the gap. If his father could do it, he can do it.

He backs up, sucks air through his nose, and runs. Looking straight ahead, he jumps, sails across, and clatters down on the other side. The second brakeman is there to steady him.

Applause rises from the ground.

"You've got a knack, lad," says the second brakeman. "The union's always looking for new men!"

The crowd below laughs. Will blushes, but he's proud, not embarrassed. He didn't feel scared when he jumped. He wishes Maren could have seen him—not that it would be anything special to her. But still. He has one more look around for her before he climbs down.

Outside a canvas building men and women are lined up. Through the doorway Will glimpses a crowd perched on sawhorses, balancing tin plates of greasy food on their knees.

Will's suddenly aware of people looking at him, and he supposes it's his fancy clothes. He removes his jacket and slings it over one shoulder—tries to slouch a little as he walks.

Around a crude pen, cheering men are crouched, intently watching two roosters lash out at each other. Their claws are tipped with blades. The men trade paper money and coins, betting, urging the birds on. It makes Will feel a little sick, and he hurries away.

From a makeshift saloon come squalls of laughter and shouting. Two men emerge, squinting and swaying unsteadily. With surprise Will recognizes the portly guard from the funeral car and a brakeman in overalls. They seem the best of friends, slapping each other on the shoulders, rocking with laughter.

Will is nearing the far edges of the shantytown now, and still the Boundless's freight cars go back and back along the track—several miles, Mr. Beecham said. He can't even see the circus cars. He looks at his watch and is surprised at the time. He should be starting back soon.

Why didn't she come to see the shantytown? To see *him*?

With a sigh he starts back, but he has to go to the bathroom. Looking around, he can't see anywhere obvious, and he doesn't want to go into the saloon. He'll go in the woods.

Stepping amongst the trees, he looks back over his shoulder to check if he can be seen—still lots of people milling about in plain view. He goes deeper, twigs crackling underfoot. The sounds of the shantytown begin to fade, and then suddenly disappear altogether, replaced by birdsong. Will makes sure to walk in a straight line so he doesn't get lost.

The forest is amazingly noisy, all sorts of things snuffling in the undergrowth. Some sound quite large. From his pocket he takes the vial of sasquatch urine and pops off the cork. He puts a drop on his index finger and dabs himself behind his ears, as he's seen his mother do with perfume. The smell is pungent. Better safe than sorry. He can wash it off before dinner.

Behind him he hears a grunt and turns in alarm. Half-hidden in the bushes is a man with his back turned, peeing against a tree. He's muttering to himself, leaning against the trunk—more like clutching on to it for dear life. Then he steps back, drunkenly tries to hoist his trousers. He staggers, falls down chuckling, and takes two tries to get back on his feet. It's the guard from the funeral car.

Will walks on a bit more and finds his own tree. He quickly relieves himself and then starts back to the tracks.

Amidst the greenery the silver keychain is easy to spot. Will bends to pick it up. It holds only a single key, unusually thick, with plenty of notches. At once he recognizes it as the key to the funeral car—same as his father's. The guard must have dropped it. Will pockets it.

He is hurrying back toward the shantytown to catch up with the guard, when he hears a grumble off to his right. Likely the fellow has fallen down again. Will wonders if he should tell his father. The guard's clearly unfit for his post. Will walks through the trees in the direction of the noise. Through the thick foliage he catches a glimpse of the guard's jacket.

"You dropped your key!" Will calls, drawing it from his pocket as he steps into view.

The guard is pushed back against a tree, his eyes wide with surprise. A second man has an elbow against the guard's throat and is pulling a knife from between his ribs. Will can't tear his eyes from the knife, darkly wet. He feels like he's been touched with something searingly cold.

The man with the knife turns. Will recognizes the busted-up nose—and the blue eyes that lock onto the key in Will's outstretched hand.

Brogan runs at him. Will's terror breaks free inside him, and he bolts into the forest. Blood pounds in his ears. He ducks beneath branches, his face whipped with twigs, his ankles crackling through shoots and shrubs. He runs and runs, deeper into the forest. When he finally dares look back, there's no sign of Brogan.

Pain spiderwebs across his side, and he can't run anymore. He slows down, looking all about, listening for footfalls over the noise of his own wheezing. Up ahead is a tree with branches low enough to grab. He drags himself up as high as he can. Hidden behind thick boughs, his breathing slows. His view is not good, but he can see around the tree for several yards.

He hears nothing. He waits. Shivering, he realizes it has

become much colder, the sun almost sunk below the horizon. He checks his watch. The second hand keeps ticking, but his heart skips a beat.

It's almost six o'clock.

He turns his head, straining for the noises of the shantytown, but he can't make them out. He has no idea where he is. The wind has picked up and shushes through the branches, making one of the loneliest sounds he's ever heard.

And then, a single long blast of a train's whistle.

The Boundless is getting ready to leave the station.

He clambers down the tree, heedless of the noise he makes. He can't be left alone here, night coming on—*that knife coming out, slick*. He hits the ground running, hoping he's headed in the right direction. A second blast of the train's whistle tells him he's on course. He doesn't care if Brogan hears him now. He needs to get back on that train.

But he didn't realize how deeply he'd wandered into the woods. With mounting desperation he hurls himself through the thickets and undergrowth, waiting for the trees to thin, waiting for the sight of the Boundless on its tracks.

Above his heart's roar he hears the slow, rhythmic thumping of cars moving along the rails. It's leaving without him! He pushes himself hard, gasping. Some roots trip him up, and he hits the earth, one of his shoes flying off. No time to get it. Scarcely able to breathe, he runs on.

A growing brightness between the trees. His legs surge with

strength. Beyond the trees, boxcars shuttle slowly past.

He breaks from the woods. There's no sign of the platform, or the shantytown, for that matter. With increasing swiftness the freight cars trundle past, and behind them comes the caboose—the last car on the Boundless.

He pelts toward the tracks, toward the red caboose. Alongside now, he struggles to keep up. He sees the metal steps and the handrail of the platform and knows he has just one chance, for the train is gaining speed, and his is failing. Grabbing the handrail, he feels its cold hard pull. He loses his grip, takes it back. With all their strength his fingers clench.

Just before he's dragged off his feet, he gives a leap and lands on the lowest step. His knees nearly buckle. Every one of the four steps is a hardship, and then he is on the metal platform and falling back against the railing, breathless and numb.

CHAPTER 5

T H E   C A B O O S E

Will has hardly taken three wheezing breaths when the red door of the caboose bursts open. All he registers is a pair of worn denim trousers, and then there's a hand clenching his collar and hauling him to his feet. Will looks into the furious face of a young man in overalls.

"Not on my train!" the guard shouts, and with both hands he drags Will toward the platform's edge.

Terrified, Will looks down at the ties flashing past. "No!" he gasps. "Wait!"

"You hopped on. You can hop off!"

"What's this?" asks another fellow, appearing in the doorway. This one is an older Chinese man with silver hair and an unlined face. His left pant leg flaps loosely and ends with a peg.

"Stowaway," says the younger fellow, and William feels the guard's fists clench. His eyes are slightly too close together. This and his sharp-tipped mustache make his demeanor even angrier. "Giving him the heave-ho."

"Wait a moment, Mackie," says the other fellow. "He's just a lad."

Will can scarcely choke out the words: "Not a stowaway. Passenger." And then after a few more gasps, "First class."

Mackie scoffs, and Will glances down at his own clothing. His jacket is shredded, and his trousers are grimy and torn at one knee. He lost one of his shoes. He doesn't look like a first-class passenger. He doesn't look like *any* kind of passenger. Even the people from the colonist cars are better turned-out than he is.

"Where's your ticket, then?" demands Mackie.

Will swallows. He didn't even think to bring it with him—just assumed they'd know him when he reboarded.

"My name's Everett!" he gulps. "William Everett! My father's James Everett!"

"The general manager of the railway?" says the Chinese guard, raising an eyebrow.

"He's just a hobo, Sticks!" Mackie retorts in exasperation.

"Those aren't hobo clothes," Sticks says, looking Will carefully up and down. "Just ripped and dirty."

"He's only got one shoe!" exclaims Mackie.

"But it's a fine one," replies Sticks with a trace of a smile.

"I lost the other in the woods," Will murmurs.

"Stinks, too," says Mackie. "He's lived in them clothes a good long time."

"It's just sasquatch urine," Will says.

Mackie frowns. "What?"

"To keep the animals away. I bought some at a stall."

"The boy's an idiot on top of everything," says Mackie. "Everyone knows that stuff don't work."

All the frantic energy that fueled Will through the woods and to the train leaves him in an instant. He feels sick and cold. His limbs begin to shake.

"He's gone pale," says Sticks. "Bring him inside."

Mackie lets out a bad-tempered breath but turns Will toward the door and gives him a shove.

"You're likely chilled," Sticks says, ushering Will into the caboose and toward the potbellied stove. "Sit there."

Will jerkily lowers himself into a chair and watches as the guard scoops in a few lumps of coal. It's hard to tell how old he is. He has kind eyes. A welcome warmth seeps from the stove, and William shivers. He didn't realize how cold he'd gotten in the woods. He puts his feet as close to the cast iron as he dares, leaning forward with his hands.

There are several covered pots on the stove top, one of them simmering slightly. A delicious smell fills the caboose.

Sticks pours a mug of something and offers it to Will. "Hold this without spilling?"

Nodding, Will gratefully takes the mug in both hands. For a moment he just wants to feel its warmth against his fingers. When he lifts it to his mouth, he discovers it isn't tea but some kind of wonderful broth. He drinks greedily.

Sticks takes a neatly folded blanket from a cot and drapes it over Will's shoulders.

"Thank you," Will says.

After a few minutes, as the soup's warmth spreads through his belly, the shivering stops.

"You're the caboose guard?" Will asks.

"I am. My name is Paul Chan."

Will shakes his hand. "I'm pleased to meet you, Mr. Chan." He glances over at the younger fellow, who's slouched in a chair with his arms crossed suspiciously.

"And that's hotheaded Brian Mackie," says Sticks, "my brakeman."

"Thank you for not throwing me off the train," Will says.

Mackie makes a noncommittal grunt.

For the first time Will takes in his surroundings properly. Beside the stove is a wooden table. A shelf underneath contains pots and pans, and paper sacks of rice and onions and potatoes. Above the small sink and water pump are two shelves with some cutlery and knives and tinned goods.

Farther forward against either side of the caboose is a small bed. Shirts and coats and trousers hang from pegs high up on the walls. In a far corner is a tidy desk, and above are a clock, a small mirror, and a bulletin board pinned with schedules and lists. At the very front of the car is a narrow door, which Will guesses must lead to the toilet—for he realizes these guards stay here for the duration of the trip. This is their home. Oil lanterns give the place a welcoming glow. There is a small square window on either side of the car, and even a couple of pictures pinned to the walls.

Most intriguing is what's right above him. When he looks straight up, he can see a little observation room with windows on all sides, and two swivel chairs on platforms reachable by ladders.

"That's the cupola," Sticks says, noting his gaze. "Where we sit when the train's entering and leaving station, or being shunted, so we can make sure the tracks are clear of obstruction."

Will thinks that if circumstances were different, he might ask to climb up and sit in one of those chairs.

"We were just settling down to our dinner," says Sticks. "Are you hungry?"

"Not what you're used to in first class," says Mackie sourly.

Sticks takes some bowls from the shelf. He lifts the lid of the largest pot and ladles out a stew thick with carrots and potatoes and onions and peas and parsnips and cubes of beef. He passes a bowl to Will with a spoon. Will holds it in his lap, just staring at it. Last night he ate lamb in first class, but right now he's not sure he's ever smelled anything this good. Greedily he begins to eat.

"Guess they're not feeding them too well up front," says Mackie.

"Quiet, Mackie," Sticks tells him with calm authority. He tears a big hunk of bread from a dark loaf and passes it to Will. "Mop up with this."

Will wipes the bread around and around the bowl and devours it all. He appreciates it with an intensity he didn't feel in the first-class dining car. He notices everything: the grainy texture, the yeasty flavor.

"Thank you," he says gratefully.

A few melodious notes float through the air, and Will looks up inquisitively.

"My wind chimes," explains Sticks. "Hanging out back. Now, William Everett, suppose you tell us why you're on my caboose."

With food in his stomach, Will feels restored. He begins to tell his story. He avoids Mackie's hostile eyes and looks at Sticks instead, who regards him patiently and nods every now and then—and even chuckles quietly when he hears about how he bought the sasquatch urine.

When Will comes to the part about seeing the drunken funeral car guard in the woods, he hesitates—and doesn't mention the dropped key. He knows what that key does, and he trusts Sticks, but not Mackie. He can feel the key, still in his pocket. Then he tells Sticks about the guard being stabbed. Will notices that Mackie is leaning forward slightly in his chair.

"This fellow with the knife," says Sticks softly, "did you get a good look at him?"

Will sees the knife in Brogan's clenched fist pulling back, wet, and he feels a queasy swell in his stomach.

"He was in brakeman's clothes. His name's Brogan."

"There ain't no Brogan on this train," Mackie says to Sticks.

"Are you sure he was in brakeman's clothes?" Sticks asks Will.

Will is less sure now. "Well, they were overalls."

"Anyone can wear those," says Mackie.

"Describe him," Sticks says.

"Big but not too tall, fair hair, and his nose had a kink in it, like a break that hadn't healed proper."

He knows he should have said "properly" but thought it might sound prissy alongside all the blunt talk of the caboose men. He likes that talk, the sound and shape of it.

He adds, "Blue eyes."

"You noticed the color of his eyes?" Mackie asks.

"I've seen him before."

Sticks's eyes widen. "When?"

"In the mountains. He tried to steal the last spike."

Mackie gives a caw of laughter. "And I suppose you drove the last spike too!"

"I did," said Will, tired of Mackie's sneering.

"Crazy and a liar," Mackie scoffs. "I seen that photo of the last spike, and you are not holding the hammer."

"I wasn't in the photo," Will says, "'cause—"

"Because Donald Smith bent the spike," Sticks says, nodding. "I've heard this story. They said a boy drove it in. So." He looks at Will. "That was you."

Will nods.

"And this Brogan," Sticks says, "what happened to him up there?"

"He got attacked by a sasquatch. Thrown over the cliff. Everybody thought he was dead."

"You believe all this, then?" Mackie asks Sticks.

"I do. I've been around people long enough to know a liar. This boy is not lying."

"We'll find out, I suppose," says Mackie.

"I doubt this Brogan fellow works on the train, though," says Sticks. "There's all kinds of rough sorts hanging about the Junction."

Will looks at the clock. "How will I get back?"

"Well," says Sticks, "the Boundless is more than nine hundred cars long, and it's a good five miles before you even get to colonist class. It's no easy stroll over the top of freight cars, unless you're partial to jumping in the dark."

Will knows the Boundless isn't scheduled to stop until tomorrow afternoon.

"If your father's the general manager," Mackie says, "why don't he just stop the train for you?"

"He won't even know I'm gone," Will says, realizing. "He's driving the Boundless."

"Then he'll know there's a freight close behind us, and the Intercolonial not far after," Sticks says. "Stopping's out of the question. We can't be blocking the whole track. And there's no siding long enough to hold us. Most likely you're stuck with us until tomorrow."

"Well, ain't that a joy," Mackie mutters.

"Mackie," says Sticks, "another unkind word from you, and you can sleep on the roof tonight."

"Might prefer it, the stink coming off that boy."

"Wash the dishes. After that I want you to take a note up and tell the fellows to pass it forward." To Will he says, "We can work a message to the front to the conductor. There's a brakeman every twenty cars."

"The fellas won't like it," says Mackie. "Not in the dark."

"We've got a straight stretch for a good while," Sticks says.

"Easy for you. You won't be the one up top. And it looks like there might be rain."

"Right now there's a full moon. Plenty of light. Anyway, this is important. If a guard's been murdered, they need to know about it. Especially if the killer's on board."

Will's insides clench. "You think he might be?"

"Could be. But there's a Mountie aboard who'll sort things out."

"It's Sam Steele," Will says, trying to make himself feel better.

"There you go. No one finer than Samuel Steele."

Sticks walks over to his desk, picks up a pen, and starts writing a note.

Reluctantly Mackie gets up and pumps some water into the sink, sluicing the dirty bowls and cutlery. Will remembers a sink like that in his old apartment, before they were rich. He sees a dish towel and steps forward to help.

"My father used to be a brakeman," he says to Mackie.

Mackie grunts. "Then you know it's pretty much the most dangerous job in the world, 'specially in bad weather. Them running boards get all slick. Rain drives into your face. You get a sudden rumble or curve in the track, you slip and get thrown."

Before he can stop himself, Will glances at the peg jutting from Mr. Chan's floppy pant leg. Then he looks away, but not before Mackie has caught him out.

"Nah, he didn't fall off," says Mackie. "He was blasting in the mountains with the nitro. Got his leg blown clean off. Least he survived. Gets to work inside now. Not like us. You know there's five brakemen killed every day cross this continent?"

"The boy doesn't need your sob stories," Sticks says sharply. "And neither do I. For every mile of track we laid through the mountains, four of my countrymen died."

Sticks hands a sullen Mackie an envelope marked with the Boundless insignia. "Get going and take that forward."

"I'll see if anyone's heard about this funeral guard," says Mackie. He pulls his jacket and cap from the pegs, takes a lantern, and leaves through the forward door.

"Don't mind him," Sticks tells Will. "He has indigestion of the soul. If he were my son, I'd have let wolves raise him."

Will smiles. He feels a lot better knowing his father will be getting a note about him, and the guard—and that Sam Steele will know too. He looks around the caboose, and up through the cupola windows, where he can see the full moon. The idea of spending a day in a caboose doesn't seem so terrible—in fact, he likes it. He could do without Mackie. But how many people get to cross the country in a caboose? It's almost as good as riding in the locomotive.

He isn't even aware that his eyes keep closing, until he hears Sticks say, "Why don't you get some rest?"

Will nods. He feels unaccountably heavy.

"You can have my cot," says Sticks. "But if you don't mind, have a wash first. That sasquatch urine is potent."

"Sorry," says Will, walking unsteadily toward the front of the car. Behind a small door he finds a tiny washbasin and a hard bar of soap. He scrubs at his face, especially behind his ears, until his skin is chafed.

"There you go," says Sticks, nodding at the cot. Will is touched that he's folded down the sheets for him.

Will takes off his shredded jacket and vest, then sits down and removes his only shoe. It feels strange settling into someone else's bed. His head sinks into the pillow; he pulls the blanket around his neck. Against his face gentle heat pulses from the stove. The sound of wind chimes wafts in from outside. The mattress is a bit saggy—nothing like the firm comfort of his bed in first class. But then the motion of the train, like some rough lullaby, works on him, and in moments he is asleep.

CHAPTER 6

AN UNSCHEDULED STOP

When Will opens his eyes, it takes him a moment to understand where he is. He hears the musical trill of wind chimes. Beyond the caboose windows it's still dark. He sees Mackie in his cap and jacket, lantern in hand, talking quietly with Sticks at the desk.

"Why've we stopped?" Will asks, sitting up.

Sticks and Mackie both turn.

"There's a slow freight ahead of us," Sticks says. "We're waiting for it to be shunted so we can pass."

"Did my father get the message?"

"It'll be working its way up," Mackie says.

Hopeful, Will asks, "Is there enough time for me to make it up front?"

"Could be. We were just going to wake you," Sticks says. "Mackie's going to walk you up to the next guard, and they'll take you from there. You might make it all the way; worst case, you bunk in a guard cabin. I'd take you myself"—he taps his wooden peg—"but I'm a bit slow."

"Get your shoe on," Mackie says to Will. "Be quick about it."

Hurriedly Will ties the laces of his single shoe. Without the blankets he feels the cold again and shivers as he pulls on his vest and jacket. He's vaguely disappointed to be leaving the caboose. It's cozy, and he likes Sticks. He was looking forward to the stories the old guard might tell. He tries to brush off the dried mud his trousers have left on the bedsheets.

"Never mind that, lad," Sticks tells him.

"Thank you very much for your kindness," Will says.

The caboose guard claps him on the shoulder. "You're quite welcome, lad. Quick now, and with a bit of luck you'll finish off the night in your own bed."

Mackie is already leaving by the forward door, and Will hurries after him, out onto the platform and down the steps to the gravel.

Despite the moon and stars, the night is startlingly dark. It takes him some minutes for his eyes to grow accustomed. His feet crunch in the gravel as he walks past one dark boxcar after another. Far in the distance he thinks he hears an impatient hiss of steam from the Boundless's engine—or it might just be the sound of the wind in the trees. He has no idea where they've stopped, or even what time it is; he forgot to check the clock before he left. He hurries to keep up with the sullen Mackie.

From the glowering wall of forest beside him emanates an oppressive silence, broken occasionally by a fierce scuffle of leaves. He thinks he catches the flash of eyes low to the ground. Mackie seems not at all concerned, and just keeps walking.

"Do you think there's bears in the woods?"

"Worse, probably." Mackie doesn't even glance at him. "Saw a Wendigo around here once."

Will's skin crawls. "Really?"

"Luckily, we was moving at the time. Threw itself at a cattle car. Nearly ripped the door right off."

Will walks faster. The train stretches ahead in a long, slow curve. At regular intervals red lanterns hang from its side. Will remembers from his father that the brakemen hang red lanterns when the train's been ordered to stop, to send a signal all the way down the cars. When the train gets under way again, the lantern lights are green.

After a few more minutes Will sees a bright white light up ahead. This one swings.

"There he is," says Mackie. "He'll take you on."

Will can't say he's disappointed exactly, but he feels a bit apprehensive about meeting a string of strangers in the darkness. The two of them pass a few more freight cars. Will can see the other brakeman's tall silhouette.

Will still isn't used to his lopsided one-shoed gait, and when he stumbles on the rail ties, Mackie takes his arm to steady him.

"This the young gent?" says the other brakeman, walking to meet them.

"The very one," Mackie replies.

In a sudden splash of lantern light, Will catches sight of a shadowed face with a nose that looks like it's been broken one too many times.

Will's throat clenches. "But—" He looks at Mackie in terror. He backs up, ready to run, but Mackie's grip tightens on his arm. "That's him!" Will cries.

Swiftly Brogan strides toward him. Something clenched in his hand flashes darkly. Will tries to wrench his arm free. Why won't Mackie let him go? And then some desperate instinct springs inside him, and he throws his full weight against Mackie. The brakeman staggers, nearly dragging Will down with him, but Will twists free. Half-blind, he runs back toward the rear of the train. He has no breath to shout for help. Brogan's boots crunch in the gravel behind him.

With his one shoe Will is clumsy, and he can barely see his feet.

"Key's all I want!" gasps Brogan. "Gimme that key, boy, I let you live!"

Will knows he's lying. He casts a wild look at the woods, five yards to his left, and doubts he'll make it in time before Brogan catches him. On his other side the train is an unbroken wall but for the gap beneath cars. The quick puffs of Brogan's breath are getting louder.

Will gives himself no more time to think, just throws himself under the train. The steel rails punch the breath from his belly as he lands atop them. Head against the gravel, he scrabbles furiously, the smell of creosote sharp in his nostrils. He's halfway through when a hand seizes his ankle and drags him back. He digs his fingers into the gravel, then grabs the rail and holds tight, kicking. His second shoe flies off, and he hears a curse as his foot connects with Brogan's face. Twisting, he kicks out again.

But Brogan grips his ankle and hauls him backward. Will plunges a hand into his jacket pocket and grabs the vial of sasquatch urine. With his thumb he forces out the cork. Half the contents slop onto his hand as Brogan gives another violent jerk, but Will splashes the rest of the liquid into Brogan's eyes. The brakeman curses and lets go to swipe at his face. Obscenities fly from his mouth. Will is free and hauling himself out onto the other side of the train.

He figures he has only a matter of seconds before Brogan comes after him or Mackie vaults over the couplings between cars. But for these few seconds Will knows he can't be seen.

He sucks in a breath, and in his stockinged feet runs full tilt away from the tracks. He hurtles through the wild grass and scrub and is among the trees. He crouches low.

Peeking out from behind a trunk, he sees a misty beam of lantern light stab the darkness. The beam sweeps up along the train, then down, and then Will hears a muffled curse. A second lantern joins the first. Mackie and Brogan murmur together.

Mackie, the scoundrel, knew all along! He and Brogan are in this together. And Sticks? How could he *not* have heard of Brogan? Unless Brogan changed his name. . . . Will holds his breath, praying they won't come looking. Mackie runs toward the back of the train, Brogan forward, both jabbing their lights like spears between and underneath cars, searching for him.

As swiftly as he dares, Will pads through the undergrowth, in the direction of the faraway locomotive, letting Brogan stay well ahead of him. Will wants to keep moving. Who knows how long the Boundless will stay here? If he can make it as far as the passenger cars, he can dash on board. Once he's among other people, he'll be safe.

Without his shoes he feels lighter, glad at least to be moving in the right direction. He's never known darkness could have so many shades: the sky, the train, the woods, the ground underfoot. He keeps an eye on Brogan's lantern up ahead and then throws himself to the earth as the beam swings suddenly toward him.

Will can't believe how far the lantern light reaches—and so powerfully. Like a living thing it seeps over the forest, and Will scuttles backward and presses himself against a thick tree. The swath of light edges closer, illuminating a rotted log, leaves, a crone-shaped bush that crooks a finger at him. The light is briefly eclipsed by the trunk Will hides behind, and continues on the other side before hesitating. Will holds his breath. The light seems to be getting more intense, joggling slightly, and then he hears the footfalls. Brogan is coming. Will doesn't dare make a run for it. All he can do is stay here and stay still.

Twigs crackle. A lantern handle creaks. Will thinks he can hear Brogan breathing; he imagines his lantern in one hand and the knife in the other. Abruptly the light goes out, and Will almost gasps. For a few agonizing moments he is completely blind, completely helpless. Silence. He needs to breathe but waits for retreating footsteps that don't come. He knows Brogan is just standing there in the darkness, waiting and listening.

Will must breathe. Through his mouth he inhales a small draught of air; to him it sounds like a wheeze. He bottles his breath, and listens harder, trying to divine the location of Brogan. His temples throb.

A single footstep, then a second. Will's pupils dilate. He can't tell if the footsteps are getting louder or softer, for everything in the night forest is amplified. Will sits forward, ready to bolt, already plotting with his panicked animal eyes a path deeper into the woods.

Farther away—the footsteps are getting farther away! He sinks back, tugging air into his lungs. He risks a peek around the tree, sees the killer's silhouette in the swinging light as he makes his way back toward the train.

Hunched low, Will hurries forward. He knows there are other brakemen posted along the train. There's a bunk cabin every forty cars or so. He could run to them, call for help. But how does he know he can trust any of them?

Another sickening thought breaks across his mind. The message to his father—Mackie wouldn't have passed it on.

There will be no help coming.

He keeps going, wanting to get as far as he can. In the distance come two short blasts. He knows the signal well: train leaving the station. He breaks into a run. He can't be left behind in the middle of nowhere! But what if he jumps aboard and meets another murderous brakeman?

Up ahead he sees a red lantern turn green. Then, one after another down the length of the train, all the lanterns go green. Couplings creak as the cars give a forward tug.

From within the forest something moves. Will looks over his shoulder and sees nothing. Undergrowth crackles. He remembers what Mackie said about the Wendigo, and runs.

In the moonlight the boxcars glide past, picking up speed. They have no platforms, no steps, only a set of rungs on the side, near the rear. Will locks his eyes on the closest set of rungs. With a burst of speed he grabs for the lowest one. The thin cold metal bites into his palms. Kicking off, he reaches higher and slams his feet onto the lower rungs.

When he looks back down the train, he catches a distant flash of light—a lantern held by someone leaning out from a freight car. Will pushes himself flat. If he hasn't been spotted already, he soon will be.

Just around the corner of the boxcar, on the back, is another set of rungs. If he can get to those, he'll at least be hidden in the space *between* cars. But moving is the last thing he wants to do. He grinds his teeth. What has he done? He can't cling on to a boxcar forever!

Cold wafts from the boxcar as though it were an icebox. His hands are numb, his limbs exhausted. But he knows he has to move. Releasing one hand from the rung, he reaches around the corner of the car. His fingertips find the rung and close around it. Then, swiftly, before his courage fails, he leans back and swings his whole body onto the other set of rungs. Gasping, he presses his face against the cold metal, willing his arms and legs to stop trembling before they shake him off the train altogether.

He waits, the judder and rumble of the train melding with his pulse. There is no door back here; it isn't like a passenger car. Sooner or later he'll be discovered. Or fall.

He has to move and keep moving until he reaches a passenger car or—Zirkus Dante! He remembers the circus train is back here somewhere, nestled amongst the freight. Eighty cars they have, that's what the conductor said.

The rungs lead up to the roof of the boxcar, and he can make out running boards jutting over the edge. Just hours ago he ran along them. But the train was still then, and now it's moving at forty miles an hour through darkness. Five men killed every day.

He climbs a couple rungs—one more and his head is sticking up above the roof. He takes a backward glance and his throat tightens. The lantern is a faraway white dot, and he can't tell how quickly it's moving, but he knows it's headed in his direction.

The train gives an unexpected jolt, and Will's feet are nearly jarred from the rungs. He faces forward, breathing hard.

Go!

On the roof of the boxcar is a single handle to the left of the running boards. He takes hold, heaves himself up onto his belly, and slithers onto the boards, gripping them tightly.

There is a constant shimmy to the train, an impatient forward surging. Will is afraid to stand, and drags himself forward on his belly. But it's no good. He'll be overtaken in minutes this way. He gets to his knees and crawls, slowly, for he's very tippy. The boxcar's roof slopes gently away on either side. It would be so easy to roll right off.

When he takes another backward look, his worst fears are confirmed. The lantern light is definitely bigger. Has he been spotted already? The train banks slightly, and he nearly loses his balance. *Look ahead. Never turn your back to the track.*

He has to get up. He plants one foot on the running boards, raises himself into a sprinter's start. Quickly he stands, knees bent, arms out. He will not look down to the sides, only forward. One step, then another, his feet mere shadows in the moonlight. The dark outline of the running boards is his only guide.

Cold air pushes against him, and he has to lean into it for balance. The faster he walks, the less he teeters. At the end of the car, he looks down into the noisy, churning gap. He's not ready to jump. He'll climb down, cross the coupling, and then go back up. But when he kneels and turns to descend the rungs, he sees Brogan's lantern, closer still. Its light is pale upon Will's clothing.

No time to climb. Once more he stands, and takes a few steps back. Squinting to check that the train isn't turning, he jumps. He locks his eyes to the running boards, lands, stumbles, but doesn't fall.

He keeps going at a steady jog now, his body parting the wind, the night forest hurtling past on either side. Brogan's powerful lantern beam hounds his legs like an attack dog. Will jumps again, keeps running, counting cars in his head. Five . . . six . . . seven . . . He squints, then blinks. It's like part of the sky is blocked out. Then he realizes that before him, rising like a wall, is a double-decker boxcar.

Will pulls up short, panting. How does he do this? He knows he's out of time. He steps back, takes a wild jump, and clumsily catches hold of the rungs. One of them strikes him hard on the cheek and sends bright sparks of pain through his head. He keeps climbing.

On the high roof he feels the train's sway more strongly. As it rounds a curve, he crouches for safety. He notices that the lantern light no longer dogs him—for a few moments he's invisible. But Will doesn't know how much longer he can keep this up. Eventually Brogan will catch him, and then what? A quick tussle, a thrust of the knife, and his body tossed off the train. The mere thought makes him feel faint—and he very nearly falls into the hole that suddenly yawns before him.

He jerks back. Cut into the roof is a large rectangular opening. No way can he jump across. On one side he sees a skinny running board, perilously close to the boxcar's edge. One false step and he'd be over.

He shuffles toward it. He really does feel like a tightrope walker now. Something thick and rough brushes his ankle. With a yelp he looks down and sees it slither past his leg and disappear into the darkness of the hole. A hot whiff of animal rises up to him.

He moves as quickly as possible, but suddenly a shape undulates before him like a giant cobra. It sways, its head a toothless gaping hole, and sends a snort of rank air into his face. Will staggers and falls. His hands uselessly claw the empty air—

And the dark snake hooks around his waist and plunges him through the hole in the boxcar roof. Even as Will hollers, he's aware of some vast shape in the darkness, and he understands finally that this creature twisted around him is no snake but the trunk of an elephant.

A thick layer of straw rustles beneath his feet as he's set gently down. The trunk releases him, and the tip prods his body inquisitively.

"Thank you," is all Will can think to say.

And then jubilantly he realizes: Zirkus Dante!

These must be the first of their animal cars! He's never been so close to such a large beast. It could trample him by casually lifting a single foot. Who's to say it won't? Will wishes he had something delectable to give it.

It pushes against his pocket, and Will remembers the sugared almonds. He takes out the mangled paper bag and holds it up to the elephant. Its trunk deftly slips inside, extracts the last few nuts, and carries them to the shadowy regions of its mouth. Will hears a satisfied chewing sound.

A beam of light plays across the hole in the roof. Will staggers into a far corner of the boxcar. Hastily he throws straw over his legs and torso and sinks back.

A figure appears at the edge of the roof. Light stabs down. Will holds his breath. For the first time he sees the elephant properly, its ancient mottled gray skin, and its big patient eye—dilating with the light shined into its face. It makes a disgruntled sound. Its trunk arches up and, with a flick, knocks the lantern from Brogan's hands.

"Cheeky beggar!" Will hears Brogan mutter. "I'll give that trunk of yours a hiding. I know you're down there, boy! And I'm coming for you!"

In the moonlight Will sees the elephant's trunk flex and shove the man. There's a thud against the roof and considerable cursing as the elephant pummels Brogan, barring his passage.

Will leaps up. At the front of the car he finds a low door. It takes him some time to figure out the latch, but he manages, and swings it inward. The noise of the track clatters against him. He steps out onto a narrow platform. There are no railings here, just a wooden gangway shuddering atop the great iron coupling.

It's just a few feet across, but Will hesitates. Somehow this is scarier than jumping across roofs. The tracks are so close. He steps onto the gangway, feels the deep vibration of the train's metal bone and sinew pass through him—and jumps the rest of the way. He grabs hold of the handle of the next car, opens the door, and ducks inside.

More animals—he can tell from the fug of straw and excrement. High up, a few windows let in starlight. Almost the entire car is an enormous cage, with only a very narrow corridor running down one side. He presses himself against the wall as he pads along, trying to keep away from the bars.

A low feline growl wafts up from the darkness, and he quickens his pace. From the corner of his eye he sees a shadow of movement—low to the ground, stripes. Bengal tiger.

Will reaches the end of the car, opens the door, and crosses again, noticing that the sky is starting to lose its darkness. The next car is divided into stalls, and he hears the comforting sounds of horses nickering. How far does he have to go before he finds people who can help him?

The following car holds monkeys, which set up a terrible shrieking when he enters. After that is a large open pen of camels, which smell terrible. There are no cages, and he has to walk amongst them. Most of them just sit and watch dolefully as he passes, but one stands up on its ungainly legs and produces an appalling rattling call.

When Will enters the next car, he knows right away there is something different about this one. There are no windows at all, only a few small grilled vents high up. Before he closes the door, he sees that the bars of the cage seem thicker and more closely spaced. The corridor is a little wider. The smell is different too, skunky, cloying.

He walks quickly. From the cage comes a surprisingly light patter of footsteps. Fear crackles across his back like brush fire. The train sways violently, and Will bumps against the bars.

A hand closes around his wrist.

Will chokes on his own cry, coughing for air. He tries to pull free, but the fist tightens. He's aware of something very tall on the other side of the bars. A face looms from the darkness. It's the eyes he first notices, far more intelligent than most animals'. The face is long and lined, bordered by dense hair. All the terror that has been dormant in Will since the avalanche is suddenly wakened.

Will pulls again, but the sasquatch tightens its grip and pulls too, so Will's face is smacked against the bars, right next to the creature's. He can feel the hot air expelled through its nostrils.

"Please," Will says.

"Get back!" a voice shouts, and Will looks over. A young man with a lantern and a stick walks toward the cage. "Let go, Goliath!"

Will feels the sasquatch's grip loosen but not release. He sees its hand clearly now, twice as big as his, the fingers long and leathery. It stands taller than Will. On its left shoulder is an angry line of raised scar tissue.

"Now!" The young man bangs the bars with his stick, and the sasquatch finally lets go.

Will falls back against the wall, his mouth parched with fear.

In the wash of lantern light, the sasquatch squats and rocks on its haunches, staring at the man balefully.

"That's good, Goliath," he says. "Good!" From his pocket he takes something and tosses it at the sasquatch. Almost dismissively the creature picks it up, sniffs it, and puts it into its mouth.

The young man turns now on Will. "What the blazes are you doing here?"

"My name's Will Everett," he says hoarsely. "And someone's trying to kill me."

ZIRKUS DANTE

Will is unceremoniously marched through one dimly lit car after another. The young man has yet to tell him his name. In fact, all he has said is: "Mr. Dorian will want to hear about this." Will assumes this young man must be one of the Zirkus's animal handlers. He seems grumpy, and Will supposes he's to blame for waking him up—that camel's rattle was certainly loud enough. The animal trainer wears loose-fitting trousers and a vest. He can't be much older than Will. Though he's not as tall, the trainer's shoulders and arms are more muscled. On his left forearm are twin scars that look like claw marks.

"That sasquatch," Will says. "Is that the one Mr. Dorian caught in the mountains? When it was just young?"

The young fellow glances at him. "How d'you know that?"

"The scar on its shoulder," Will says. He's so relieved to be with someone who isn't trying to kill him. "I was there. I saw it get stabbed. Are you the animal trainer?"

"Assistant animal trainer," the fellow mutters.

"What's it like?" Will asks. "The sasquatch."

"Smart."

"Are you training it?"

"You don't exactly train a sasquatch. He lets you *think* you're training him sometimes. He's cooperative—so long as you don't annoy him. Sometimes I think all he wants is escape."

Will has lost track of how many cars he's passed through. He looks about. On either side of the corridor, thick burlap curtains conceal berths. The hallway is humid with the smell of people sleeping. Clothing hangs from any old place—pegs, hooks hammered into the ceiling, makeshift clotheslines.

"Something smells . . . *bad*," rumbles an angry voice from one of the lower berths. "*Really* bad."

A curtain pulls back, and from the berth emerges a body so huge that it seems impossible it could all fit inside. When the man stands, his head nearly hits the carriage roof, so he hunches forward, making his shoulders and chest seem even more massive. The giant points a carrot-thick finger at Will.

"He must be thrown off the train," the giant says matter-of-factly. He tilts his head, as though pondering how best to fold Will up. "I cannot bear that stink. I will throw him off now."

"No, wait! It's just sasquatch urine!" says Will as the giant steps toward him. "I can wash it off!"

"Mr. Beauprey has a very sensitive nose," says the animal trainer without any apparent concern for Will's welfare.

"Let's just wait a moment, Mr. Beauprey, shall we?" says a compact fellow springing down from the upper berth. A handlebar mustache is the only hair on his bald head, and he is dressed like he's ready to do gymnastics. He winks at Will. "There'll be plenty of time to throw him off the train. But maybe first we should find out a little more about him."

"I see no point in waiting," Mr. Beauprey says, brow furrowed.

"Where'd you find him, Christian?" the small man asks the animal trainer.

"Holding hands with Goliath." Christian nods at Will. "That sasquatch urine probably saved your life. He might've bit off your arm, but I think he was confused."

Will nods weakly. "Lucky."

More people are slipping out from their curtained berths, gawking at Will, as if he were a circus attraction for all to see.

"How'd you get into our cars?" the short man asks.

"I ran over top. Your elephant lifted me down."

"Elfrieda," says Christian fondly.

"You jumped cars at night?" Mr. Beauprey asks.

Will nods, and sees a slow spread of admiration across the giant's features.

"Says there's a man trying to kill him," Christian says dubiously.

A wiry fellow in an undershirt rushes in from the rear of the car. "Brakeman coming," he whispers urgently. "Seems angry."

Christian frowns. "They're not supposed to come in here. What've you been up to?" Before Will can protest, Christian grabs his arm and pulls him forward. Hurriedly they cross to another car. This corridor here has no curtains, only doors. As they approach one of them, it opens before Christian can raise his knuckles. The dignified form of Mr. Dorian emerges, wrapped in a silk robe.

"Mr. Dorian!" Will exclaims with a rush of relief.

The ringmaster ignores him and says to Christian, "Bring him inside."

Will is pushed roughly into the stateroom. Even compared to first class, it's impressive. Velvet drapery hangs from the windows. Resting on a thick Persian carpet are two armchairs, a small desk, and several crammed bookshelves. Mostly concealed behind a screen is a large four-poster bed. A tall steamer trunk stands upright in one corner. Mounted on the walls is a dizzying collection of oil paintings, and all sorts of Native handiwork: a pipe with a beaded stem, a decorated goose head, some kind of tool with a wickedly sharp triangular blade.

"Where's your bloody ringmaster?" shouts Brogan from the corridor. "Someone who isn't a freak!"

Will turns to Mr. Dorian in alarm. The ringmaster seems untroubled.

"You can see the mayor if you like," the cavernous voice of Mr. Beauprey replies. "You address him as 'Your Lordship.'"

There's a sober pause before Brogan replies: "Fine. You just get me to him."

"Christian, go show our guest in, please," says Mr. Dorian. Then he swings open the lid of the steamer trunk and nods for Will to step inside. Will does as he's told, and the lid swiftly closes and latches, leaving him in total darkness. He can, however, hear everything.

"You the man in charge?" demands Brogan.

"That would be me, sir. Mr. Dorian, at your service." He speaks with a quiet elegance that carries a weight of authority. "I don't believe we've been properly introduced."

"Name's Brinley. I'm head brakeman."

So he has *changed his name*, Will thinks from inside the trunk.

"There's a boy hopped the train. You seen him?"

From outside the door Mr. Beauprey bellows, "Is he addressing you as 'Your Lordship'?"

"It's quite all right, Mr. Beauprey, thank you," replies Mr. Dorian. "Now, Mr. Brinley, we've barely woken, but no, I have not seen any such youngster. I will, however, tell my people to keep an eye open."

"You all look pretty awake to me," Brogan says unpleasantly. "And I can smell him. I know he's around here somewhere."

"With respect, sir," says Mr. Dorian, "are you certain the odor does not originate from you?"

"Only 'cause he splashed me with it when I was trying to catch him!"

Mr. Dorian makes an understanding sound. "It is a powerful smell."

"It is a very, very *bad* smell!" rumbles Mr. Beauprey from the corridor.

"Well," says Brogan, "I'm sure you won't mind if I take a little look around." It does not sound like a question.

"I must kindly ask you to leave our carriages," Mr. Dorian tells him. "These are the private property of Zirkus Dante, and you have, alas, not been invited to enter."

Brogan scoffs. "Don't take that tone with me. You're connected to the Boundless, and you need our engine and our brakemen, and you follow our rules, or there'll be hell to pay. If it turns out you've been harboring this hooligan, we'll shunt the whole lot of you at the next siding, and you can give your show to the mosquitoes."

"I hardly think you have the authority to do such a thing," Mr. Dorian replies calmly.

"You'd be surprised. And I don't take my orders from circus folk—especially half-breeds like you."

"How perceptive you are," Mr. Dorian says placidly. "I prefer the term 'Métis,' however."

Inside the trunk Will is amazed at the ringmaster's restraint.

Having grown up in Winnipeg, Will is familiar with the Métis—the offspring of French settlers and Cree Indians—and the insults they endured, especially after their failed uprising.

Will hears Brogan moving about the carriage, shifting things. He's coming closer to the trunk, and laughs. "This would be a daft place for someone to hide, wouldn't it?"

Horrified, Will hears Mr. Dorian say, "Be my guest."

Will nearly chokes. Involuntarily he takes a step back, but there is nothing to conceal him, no heavy furs, no garments at all. He hears the clasp open. Swiftly the lid swings wide, and Brogan stands before him with his busted nose, staring directly into his eyes. There is not two feet between them. Mutely Will stares back. Brogan's blue eyes dart about quickly; then his mouth compresses in sour frustration. Turning his back, he slams the lid shut.

Only now does Will's heart pound—with equal measure terror and wonder at his escape.

"If you're quite done now, Mr. Brinley," comes Mr. Dorian's voice. "I'll have one of my men escort you out."

"I don't need no escort. You remember what I said. We want that boy. The Mounties want to question him."

"Intriguing," says Mr. Dorian.

"For murder. You find him, you tell me or my men. We'll be keeping an eye on your cars, you can count on that."

"Thank you, Mr. Brinley. Mr. Beauprey, please show our uninvited guest to the nearest door."

"Shall I throw him off the train?" Will hears the giant say.

"No, Mr. Beauprey, that won't be necessary."

Will hears a heavy sigh of disappointment from the giant, then the sound of Brogan's retreating footsteps. The stateroom door closes. After a few more moments the lid to the trunk opens and Mr. Dorian smiles in at him.

"You can come out now, lad."

"How?" Will asks, turning to look back inside the trunk. "Why didn't he see me?"

Mr. Dorian steps nimbly inside. "Close it," he tells Will, who does so. From inside he says, "Now open it."

Will opens the lid to behold an empty trunk. "Where are you?" he asks in awe.

"Reach out your hand."

Will stretches his hand out into the emptiness, and gasps when he touches an invisible shoulder. Mr. Dorian steps into full view.

"It's a very simple trick. Mirrors spring into place when the lid opens, and show you a reflection of the side of the trunk. You think you're seeing the back. It's hardly foolproof—you need but reach inside—but people are easily fooled by their eyes."

"Thank you, for hiding me."

"You don't look like a murderer to me, young Mr. Everett. Nor did you when I first met you three years ago."

"I didn't know if you'd remember me. Your Lordship," Will adds hastily.

Mr. Dorian chuckles. "You needn't bother with that. And certainly I remember you. It was an eventful day. Especially for you, by all accounts."

After the avalanche Will didn't see Mr. Dorian again. The company train made many trips back and forth between Farewell, carrying the injured out, bringing back supplies for the men waiting their turn for transportation off the mountain. It was two days before Will and his father got back to town. By then Maren and the Klack Bros. Circus was gone—and Will's life had changed forever.

"And now you've been accused of murder by this Mr. Brinley."

"His real name's Brogan. He was up in the mountains too. He tried to steal the golden spike."

"Good stories seem to have a habit of finding you, William."

"I've never thought of it like that," Will says. "I always thought . . . well, I was just there when they happened to other people."

Mr. Dorian smiles. "Well, I'd like to hear this particular story from the beginning, but first—"

"I'm sure he'd like a bath," says a voice behind Will.

He turns to see Maren standing in the doorway in a simple green dress. Without her makeup or vibrant clothing she looks younger, much more like the girl he met three years ago. He can't help smiling, like he's just found something important that's been lost a very long time.

"I was looking for you!" he blurts out. "In the Junction. I was really hoping . . ."

All the words fly out of his head, and his face reddens. Babbling like a little kid. He wishes he'd kept his mouth shut. He realizes how bad he must smell, and how generally shabby he looks. He glances down at his tattered socks, wondering how long she's been there.

"I guess I have a habit of just showing up," she says.

"Did you know, William," says Mr. Dorian, "that it's because of you that Maren is now part of our show?"

"Really?"

"On that train into the mountains, you told me how fine the Klacks' wire walker was. I made inquiries, and indeed you were right. And here we all are. No doubt you'd like the chance to bathe. Maren, can you please show him to the washroom? And on the way pick out some clean clothes for him in the wardrobe car—he'll need to launder his own."

"I'd just like to apologize for the sasquatch urine," Will says, and sees Maren bite back laughter.

"Come with me," she says.

He hangs well back as she leads him down the corridor.

"It doesn't help, you know," she says over her shoulder. "I can still smell you."

"I can't smell it anymore," Will admits.

"It's not so bad. After a day with the animals, Christian smells even worse."

"You know him?" Will asks with a pang of jealousy.

"He's my brother."

"Oh." He falls silent a moment. Over the years he's often had conversations with her in his head. Now he struggles to find a place to start. She beats him to it.

"You never came to the circus," she says.

It takes him a moment to understand what she means. "Oh, I really wanted to. But, well, there was an avalanche, and you were gone by the time I got back down."

"You're all rich now."

Will laughs. "I hardly *look* rich."

She regards him carefully. "You talk differently too."

"I suppose so. I don't use 'ain't' as much. I miss 'ain't.'"

"Are you still drawing?"

He smiles. "Yes."

"Do you have any with you?"

"Just a sketchbook."

"You'll show me later?" She seems touchingly excited.

"If you like. Have you crossed Niagara Falls yet?"

She shakes her head. "Not yet. But one day, absolutely."

"You've mastered the disappearing act."

"Thank you. It went pretty well the other night, I thought."

"Did Mr. Dorian hire you right away?"

"No. I stayed with the Klacks for another year almost. My whole family did. But then my pa had an accident and broke his leg in two places. The Klacks didn't want him like that, so we all left. It was a bad show anyway. I wrote to Mr. Dorian, and at first he said he wanted only a wire walker. But he agreed to take on my brothers if I signed a five-year contract."

She leads him into another car, which is entirely filled with long racks of costumes and steamer trunks spilling over with gloves and scarves and bracelets. Skinny paths run through the rolling hills of fabric and color.

Maren casts a critical eye over him and then begins sifting through the piles.

"Here, these should fit."

Will takes them. "These are . . . clown clothes."

"Clown's assistant, actually."

Just by looking at the denim overalls, Will can see that the legs are too short. The white shirt has puffy sleeves and ruffled cuffs.

"You'll look like a pirate," she promises with mischief in her eyes. "You never wanted to be a pirate?"

Will doesn't tell her he used to dream about it all the time.

"How about that other, normal shirt, there?" he asks, pointing.

She shrugs. "If you must. You need shoes, too." She rummages through a box on the floor and extracts a pair of fat white shoes that are twice as big as Will's feet. "Here."

Will looks at them in mute dismay. "These are definitely clown shoes."

Maren begins laughing, a surprisingly hearty sound to come out of such a slim person.

"I suppose there's these," she says, pulling out a pair of ordinary black shoes.

Will takes them gratefully. From another mound of clothing she picks out some socks and underwear without a hint of awkwardness. Will is embarrassed and turns so she won't see him blushing.

"And this, too," she says, and when he looks over, she's holding out his sasquatch tooth.

He takes it from her. It's warm, like it's been in her pocket a long time. "Thanks."

"I stole it, kind of."

His eyes widen. "I thought you just forgot!"

She clears her throat. "No, I wanted to show you how clever I was. I was going to give it back when you came to the circus. Sorry I've had it so long."

He smiles. "That's all right." He likes the idea of her having it. He wonders: *Has she been keeping it in her pocket all these years? Did she ever think of me, sometimes?*

"Come on," she says, leading him to a door at the end of the car. "This is the men's washroom."

Strings crisscross the room, draped with all manner of clothing. The single window has been soaped, so no one can see in. There are a couple of big, circular metal tubs. Through a drain in the middle of the floor, Will sees the dark flash of passing rail ties.

Maren walks to a cistern bolted to the wall. Attached to the spigot is a length of rubber hosing. She picks up the end and turns a tap, and a gush of water pounds against the bottom of one of the tin tubs. After mere seconds she turns the water off.

"That's all?" Will asks.

"That's what you get. The water's got to last a long time."

"Is it hot?"

She shakes her head. "It's very, very cold. You can wash your clothes in the tub after you've bathed."

"Bathed" seems a very fancy word for what takes place here. Even when they lived in that cold-water flat in Winnipeg, he had hot water when he bathed—which was seldom.

Maren closes the door behind her. Will is dismayed that there's no lock. He looks at the thin layer of water in the tub, which itself seems none too clean, and strips off his torn, reeking clothes. He begins to fold them, then realizes it's pointless. He steps quickly into the tub. The chilly water scarcely reaches his ankles. On the tub's rim is a mottled lump that he assumes must be soap. He crouches and dips it into the water, wondering how many people have used this soap, and this tub.

The door flies open, and Will looks over in horror. A burly man strides in with hardly a glance at him.

"Um, I'm having a bath," says Will.

"I ken see that!" says the fellow in a thick Scottish burr. "Kerry on!"

"But . . . isn't it my turn?" Will asks, and feels immediately childish.

"Lad, how many tubs do you see in here?"

"Two," he sighs.

"That's right!" The man takes the hose and fills the second tub, strips, and hops into the cold water with great satisfaction. "Ah! That's a *treat*, that is! Haven't bathed since I don't know when!" He lathers himself up. "Nothing like a good invigorating wash and *scrub*!" He stops to sniff in Will's direction. "I think you might scrub a little harder!"

Will sighs. "Yes, it's just some . . . sasquatch urine."

"Nasty stuff!" the fellow remarks.

Will tries to wash himself as thoroughly and quickly as possible. He keeps glancing back at the door, terrified it will burst open again and a troupe of gymnasts will somersault in. Maybe the giant, too.

He remembers the sandpaper rub of soap from childhood, and finds it strangely comforting. The water turns an unappetizing shade of gray. He steps out and looks around for a towel. Hanging from a nail is a piece of something so threadbare and stained, Will can only imagine it has been there for the last twenty years. It's dry at least. Gingerly he pats himself fast all over.

He dresses in his new circus clothes. From his soiled jacket he carefully removes his watch, his sketchbook and pencil, his muskeg spectacles, money, his sasquatch tooth—and the funeral car key. He swallows, and covers the key with his sketchbook. He glances at the Scottish bather, but he's taking no interest.

Will dumps the whole lot of his soiled clothing into the tub. He pummels them with the bar of soap, then twists them dry and hangs them from an open stretch of clothesline. He's probably ruined the jacket.

For a moment he feels heartsick, thinking of his father on the same train but miles away—probably with no clue what's happened to Will. And if he did know, what could he do? Would he stop the entire train and search it front to back? Would he rescue him? Will frowns as he suddenly realizes that he doesn't want his father to rescue him.

When he opens the washroom door, he finds Maren talking to Mr. Dorian.

"Did you enjoy your bath?" she asks, a smile pulling at the corners of her mouth.

"Very much, thank you. It's always nice to have some company."

"Would you care for some breakfast, William?" Mr. Dorian asks.

Breakfast. He looks at his watch. Just past six o'clock. From somewhere comes the smell of bacon, and his stomach gives a long noisy gulp.

"I heard that," says Maren. "I'll take you to the dining tent."

"Tent?"

"We call it the tent even though we're on the train. Habit."

"I'll join you shortly," says Mr. Dorian.

Will follows Maren through several cars. There are humbler

berths here, and long communal washbasins where men shave in their suspenders, or splash water on their faces. The air is muggy with colognes and perfumes. People are hoisting up trousers, fastening belts, combing hair, pulling on stockings, squeezing past one another in the narrow corridor, too early yet to grunt more than a hello. A whole village of people getting ready for their day.

"It's very . . . cozy," he says.

She nods. "Home away from home."

The first thing Will sees passing into the next car is a man and a woman on what looks like a giant tandem bicycle, pedaling hard. The bicycle isn't going anywhere because the whirling wheels don't touch the floor. Thick cables sprout from them and disappear into the ceiling.

"What are they doing?" Will whispers as he and Maren walk by.

"Making electricity for the cars," she replies. "Everyone does twenty-minute shifts during the day."

"That's incredible!" he says.

"And you thought only first class had electrics!"

She opens a door, and Will is nearly bowled over with the sound of hundreds of people talking, laughing, bawling out to pass the eggs or fetch the coffee. Long trestle tables run the length of the car, leaving narrow aisles that are crammed with people carrying platters heaving with pancakes and roasted potatoes and rashers of bacon and cornmeal muffins and baked beans and pitchers of milk. Will isn't sure he's ever seen so many people seated in one space. As soon as one person leaves, another slips into his seat, and the eating begins again.

Will tries not to stare. But he can't help noticing all sorts of people, the likes of which he's never seen. Mr. Beauprey, of course, is impossible to miss, given his immense size. ("I wanted to throw him off the train," Will overhears him saying to the fellow next to him, "but they said no!") Across from the giant is a pair of slim Asian gentlemen who appear to be joined together at the hip. A large woman mops her beard daintily with a napkin. And then Will absolutely *does* stare, because running across the top of a table, carrying a small stack of dirty dishes, is a gray monkey. White fur grows around his face, making him look like a solemn waiter with muttonchop sideburns. And he's not the only one. Across all the tables now Will sees more monkeys hustling about, bringing people cups and pots of tea.

Dazed, he says to Maren, "There are monkeys."

"Japanese macaques. They're very helpful."

She takes his hand matter-of-factly and leads him through the crush to a smaller table with a linen tablecloth and a small vase of flowers in the center. When she releases his hand, he looks at it, like it might be transformed. A girl has never taken his hand before.

"Help yourself," she says, nodding at the platters of food.

Will takes a clean plate and piles it until there is no room left. He's never been so hungry. Where to start? In the end he pours maple syrup over his stack of pancakes and carves himself an enormous wedge. But before he can cram it into his mouth, a monkey taps him on the arm.

Will looks down and sees a macaque expectantly holding out a steaming towel.

"To wash your hands," Maren says with a grin.

"Oh," says Will, taking it. "Thank you."

He washes his hands and then digs in. Fifteen minutes later he's finishing off the last strips of bacon and bits of fried potatoes. As if from nowhere Mr. Dorian sits down opposite him.

"Well, William Everett, it seems as if you've replenished yourself. Are you in a talkative mood?"

A monkey comes and takes Will's plate and cutlery away. Will holds on to his glass of milk. He takes a drink and then launches into his story. He can't explain it, but he trusts Mr. Dorian, and he leaves nothing out. It is a long story, and Will isn't sure he's ever talked so much all at once. But it passes quickly, and he realizes he rather likes telling it. He likes seeing how they listen—more than that, how they sometimes seem *captivated*—and he wonders now if he isn't as bad at talking to people as he thought.

"That is quite a tale," Mr. Dorian says. "You're a man of hidden talents."

Will feels his face warm, and knows he's blushing.

"Jumping those trains at night is no mean feat."

"I think he would've killed me otherwise," Will replies.

"Quite likely," Mr. Dorian says. "You're the only witness to a murder. If he's killed one man, he can kill two."

Will's breakfast suddenly feels unpleasantly heavy in his stomach.

"He wants the key," says Will, remembering how Brogan's eyes locked onto it, how he offered to spare his life if only Will gave up the key.

Maren nods. Will keeps looking over at her, even though she's not talking much. He likes looking at her.

"May I see it?" Mr. Dorian asks.

Will takes it from his pocket and hands it to the ringmaster, who peers at it carefully, both sides, before returning it.

"The last spike's in there," Will whispers. "The one made of gold."

"Is it?"

Will wonders if he's made a mistake. But he wants to impress Maren. And he'd like someone to tell him what to do now.

"We may be getting another visit from Mr. Brogan," says Mr. Dorian, "and he probably won't be alone this time."

"There's Mackie," Will says. "He's in on it."

"And possibly more. Right at this moment there are brakemen sauntering about overhead, watching the couplings between our carriages."

"There are?" Will says.

"They suspect you're here, and they expect you to bolt."

"There's a Mountie on the train," Will says. "Samuel Steele."

"Alas, we're a little island unto ourselves back here," says Mr. Dorian. "There are miles of freight cars between us and colonist class. And we're not scheduled to stop until late afternoon."

"How about the pigeons?" Maren asks. "We could send a message forward."

"They're swift but not swift enough to outpace the Boundless at forty miles an hour."

"Can I stay here until the next stop?" Will asks.

"Of course," says Mr. Dorian with a kind smile, "but I don't think your problems will end there. They'll be watching for you. If Brogan's as intent on this key as we think, I don't think you'd make it very far without being caught."

"He could if he joins the circus," Maren says.

Will thinks she's joking, until he sees Mr. Dorian nod.

"I see exactly what you mean," the ringmaster says, turning to Will. "We have an agreement with the Boundless to give a number of performances during the journey. You saw the first the other night. When the train stops this afternoon, we're to walk up to colonist class for our second show. Then we're to remain on the passenger cars and make a performance in every class. The finale is in first class on our last night of the journey."

"You can be part of our show," Maren says.

Will frowns. "But if Brogan's watching, he'll recognize me!"

"You'll be disguised," Maren says. "Obviously."

"Completely unrecognizable," adds Mr. Dorian. "Madame Lamoine is one of the finest makeup artists in the world."

Will's eyes have fallen to the tablecloth, his fingers tracing part of the pattern in the embroidery. "But I can't *do* anything."

Mr. Dorian waves his hand. "Nonsense. Everyone can do something."

"Not that Winston lad," Maren remarks.

Mr. Dorian purses his lips. "Well, no, he was completely hopeless—but we still worked him into the show."

"What did he do?" Will asks.

"We cut him in half every night."

"Twice on Sundays," adds Maren.

"Until the accident," says Mr. Dorian, wincing.

Will stops breathing. "You didn't really . . ."

"Heavens, no," says Mr. Dorian with a rare chuckle. He looks at Maren. "He thought we actually sawed him in half! No, no. He was trampled by the camels."

"It's true," Maren says soberly.

Mr. Dorian takes a drink of his coffee. "I can already tell that you, Mr. Everett, have many talents. What do you say? I think it's the safest way to get you up to the passenger cars."

"And you'll both be going?" Will wants to make sure.

"Absolutely. It will be the three of us."

He likes the idea, as much as it makes him nervous. Mr. Dorian seems to have more faith in his abilities than he does. He hopes he doesn't disappoint him—or Maren.

"Yes," he says. "I'll do it."

"Excellent. Maren, why don't you take Will to the rehearsal hall and see what grabs his fancy. Take care crossing between cars. Make sure there're no brakemen lurking about. I'll go find Madame Lamoine and let her know what we have in mind."

"I never thought I'd run away to the circus," Will says.

"Isn't it every boy's dream?" Maren asks.

Mr. Dorian gets up to leave, and then as an afterthought leans closer to Will. "I'd not tell anyone about the key you carry. For your own safety, you understand."

"This ain't the way it was supposed to go," Mackie says nervously.

"No point whining about it," Brogan snaps, and takes a snort of whiskey. He's battered his share of men, but this is the first he's killed, and he wants to burn away the memory of the guard's face. "Damn fool got all high and mighty. Started hollering." He shakes his head bitterly. "Could've had a share."

The brakeman's cabin shudders over a rough patch of track. There isn't much by way of suspension. Spaced every forty freight cars, they are tiny shacks on wheels, meant to sleep two men. The place smells like creosote, food that was best eaten a week ago, and man stink. A couple of hammocks crisscross the room. There's a small stove, a table, a hole in the planks for doing your business, and so many pegs and hooks jutting from the walls that it's a danger to lean anywhere. It makes the caboose look like first class.

Right now Brogan's cabin is crammed with the eight other brakemen he chose for his job. At some time or another he's worked with all of them. He might not exactly trust them, but he's got dirt on each and every one—and that wins a man's loyalty. Anyway, he's relying on their greed to keep them in line. And on this job there's a lot to be greedy about.

"What do we do now?" Chisholm asks. He's got buggy eyes that make Brogan think of boiled eggs.

Brogan looks around at the weathered faces of his other men—Peck, Richter, Strachan, Delaware, Talbot, Welch—and knows they're all tense and waiting for him to lead.

"Nothing happens without that key," he says, laying it out. "The boy has the key, and the boy's in those circus cars. That half-breed ringmaster's hiding him. We get the key, we're back in business."

"You sure he didn't just fall off?" Mackie asks. "Hard to believe a kid could make it across all those cars at night."

"His father was a brakeman," Brogan says, "and a damn fine one. I saw that boy up in the mountains. Survived an avalanche. He's got grit. If the kid fell, it was into the elephant cage."

"If he's alive, he's blabbed by now," says Welch.

"Don't matter if he has," says Brogan. "Who's he gonna tell? You think anyone's gonna take the word of some circus freak?

Anyway, if he's in those cars, he ain't leaving them alive."

There is a brief, heavy silence.

"You sure you want to be killing the son of the general manager?" Chisholm asks, looking around at the other men anxiously.

"Can you think of a better way to keep someone quiet?" Brogan demands fiercely. "You boys can step off at any time. When the stakes are this high, you're gonna have to dirty your hands some. This job is once in a lifetime—and you'll have more money than you can spend during it. Or would you all rather keep working the rails? Peck, you lose any more fingers, you're no good for even the mail car. And, Richter, remember what happened to your buddy McGovern? Who's gonna take care of *your* family if your legs gets sliced off during a flying switch? No one'll sell us insurance, boys. We got nothing. We're slaves. This is our chance to bust free."

He watches his men and knows he has them.

"We're going back to the circus, all of us this time," he says. "And we're going to take that boy."

CHAPTER 8

JOINING THE CIRCUS

Zirkus Dante's practice room is a long, narrow gymnasium, filling an entire double-decker train carriage. Light pours in from the windows and skylights, all of which have been covered with rice paper to keep spectators from gawking inside when the train is at rest. Colorful handbills plaster the walls, advertising wild animals, death-defying feats, and miraculous marvels.

Two stilt walkers waltz across the room—and Will realizes they're the Siamese twins he saw earlier in the dining car. Both men are perched atop three stilts and work together so seamlessly that Will can only stare in wonder.

"Those are the Zhang brothers," Maren tells him. "They're one of our most popular acts."

"They're incredible!"

"It's too bad they don't get along better."

"No?"

"They hate each other. Well, who wouldn't, being attached to someone their whole life. Li actually tried to stab Meng once. Luckily, his sight's terrible. He needs Meng to see."

Farther down the room an acrobat flings himself from his trapeze, tumbles through the air, and lands on a seesaw that launches a second acrobat up to a high set of rings. Both men are lean and muscular. Their heads are bald except for a tuft of long hair at the back, which is gathered into three braids.

"Are they—" Will begins.

"Mohawks, yes," says Maren. "The best acrobats I've ever seen. Heights mean nothing to them. They're fearless."

Across the carriage, against a mirrored stretch of wall, a trio of leggy milk-haired ballerinas is limbering up.

"Mr. Dorian thinks ballet lends the circus an air of distinction," Maren says, catching Will looking at the dancers. "Don't fall in love with them. They're not quite as angelic as they look."

"Really?" Will asks, intrigued.

"You should hear them cuss."

Elsewhere a few performers are practicing a complicated three-way juggling routine. Will feels like he's part of something rare and exciting, but all the activity in the room is a bit overwhelming, and he can't imagine what he might be able to do.

"Look," Maren says, "don't worry. No one expects you to do

anything like this. It would just be good if you had some little thing you could do during the show."

"And if nothing works out, you can just saw me in half," he says.

"Exactly. Maybe you can help me with my tightrope act."

She leads him over to a long stretch of wire suspended a couple of feet off the floor. Even if he slips, he doesn't have far to fall.

Maren disappears behind a curtain and comes out in a leotard. She is very slim, but her legs look strong.

"Here," she says, handing Will a small cloth sac. "There's some things in there I'll ask for later."

After some stretches she takes up a long balancing pole and steps onto the wire. She walks across a few times effortlessly, then does a somersault. A small furrow appears in her forehead as she reclines on the wire. Her lips compress on one side and then the other. She lets go of the balancing pole and does a backward somersault. Then she lies flat again and uses her feet to push herself headfirst along the narrow wire. Will can only marvel at her skill.

"All right," she says, still balancing on her back. "Throw those four balls my way. Fast!"

Will takes them from the sac and fires them at her. One bounces off her knee; another sails beyond her reach.

"I meant throw them in the general direction of my hands," she says, laughing.

He runs around, gathering up the balls and trying not to get crushed by the Zhang brothers on their stilts.

KENNETH OPPEL

"Get out of our way, little bug!" Li shouts down at him.

When Will throws the balls a second time, Maren catches them all and instantly juggles them.

"That's amazing!" Will cries.

After another few seconds she tosses back the balls and says, "Now the padlock!"

He finds it in the bag and tosses the heavy piece of metal to her.

After catching it in one hand, she cajoles some tools from her sleeve, inserts them into the lock, and teases until it springs open.

"I can't believe it," Will exclaims.

"It's still taking too long," she says. "Again, please."

They run through the padlock bit once more, and she's faster this time. Will chews his lip. "I don't feel like I'm doing very much."

"It would be great if you could get up on the wire with me," she says, hopping down to push a stepladder closer. "Take off your shoes and give it a try."

He strips his feet bare and climbs the ladder.

"Step on with just one foot," she instructs him. "Make sure the wire's centered—right between your big toe and second toe. . . . That's it! Now arms out! Looking dead ahead. Keep your balance!"

He loses his balance immediately and jumps clumsily to the floor.

"That's okay," she says. "Everyone's like that at first. Again."

He tries again, and again—and again. He feels like an idiot, windmilling his arms around, bucking back and forth.

"I don't think I have the knack," he says.

She doesn't disagree with him. "Maybe I can help. Come back up."

Once more he steps onto the wire, and this time she's right behind him. She puts her hands firmly on his waist. His breath catches, and for a second all he thinks about is the pressure of her fingers against him.

"You're doing it!" she says.

Immediately he's thinking about his balance again, and starts wavering. His arms tilt wildly, but Maren's hands nudge him from side to side, guiding him. He stays on the wire.

"I don't like your doing it for me," he says.

"I'm just helping you."

"Let me try it alone."

She nudges him to one side. "You're not ready yet. Focus now!"

He tries to take a step away from her, and immediately topples off.

"Suit yourself," she says, exasperated. "Go try something else if you want."

She goes back to her practicing. He wonders if he's hurt her feelings. He didn't mean to be rude. He just felt ridiculous, flapping around like a baby bird. He doesn't want people doing things for him, especially not her.

148   KENNETH OPPEL

He looks around the gymnasium. What *can* he do? He sees a short pair of practice stilts leaning against the wall. Even though they put him only inches off the floor, it takes him a long time just to stand upright for two seconds. He takes one step and then topples onto the sawdust floor. He picks himself up and tries again, and this time manages three careening steps before sprawling flat again. It's easier than tightrope walking, but just.

Across the rehearsal car a clown is watching him. White face, huge painted mouth, eyeliner, a curly wig, a red ball for a nose. He's just standing there dejectedly, arms hanging long by his sides. Then, as if every bone has suddenly dissolved, he collapses onto the floor and is nothing but a large puddle of puffy clothing. When he springs back up, fully formed again, Will smiles.

The clown crooks a finger at him. Will puts down the stilts and walks over. The clown's mouth widens in silent glee. They regard each other. The clown pats Will's cheeks gently with both hands. Will chuckles a little awkwardly. The clown pulls a pickle out of Will's ear, then puts both hands on his hips and tilts his head back in silent, raucous laughter.

"It's not that funny," Will says.

The clown stops and assumes such a tragic expression that Will can't help but laugh.

"All right. You're funny!"

Eyes wide, his grin wider, the clown takes Will by the shoulders and guides him back against a wall. He pats Will's head and motions for him to stay put.

"Okay," Will says.

The clown walks away, stopping every few steps to look back over his shoulder and make sure Will's still there. Will has to laugh. When he's a good twenty paces away, the clown stops, turns, and gives a big smile. Then he pats his hands in the air.

"You want me to stay here?" Will asks.

The clown clenches his fists and makes his body rigid.

"You want me to stay *very* still."

The clown gives a hop of joy.

"Okay," says Will.

The clown turns his back on him. In one swift movement he ties a scarf over his eyes. He bends down and opens a slim case. He draws out three knives. He hurls one back over his shoulder. Before Will can say a word, a knife impales itself in the wood next to his neck.

Will dares not swallow; he dares not even blink. The clown proceeds to hurl another knife backward at Will. The blade streaks toward him and thunks into the wood over his head. Before he can breathe, a third knife buries its tip on the other side of his neck, so close, he can feel the cold steel.

The clown turns around with the biggest smile of all and jumps up and down with jubilation.

Everyone has stopped what they are doing and now gives a rousing round of applause, except Maren, who strides over to the clown and smacks him on the shoulder.

"Roald!" she cries. "That was cruel!"

Will gingerly steps away from the wall, afraid of leaving some part of himself behind.

"I rarely miss!" the clown insists, speaking for the first time. He has a slight accent.

"You terrified him!"

"I'm fine," says Will, and strangely he is. He feels oddly immortal. He's survived a murderer and a sasquatch. Nothing can touch him. "You're a clown *and* a knife thrower."

"And my brother, sadly," says Maren.

"How's the little baby girl?" Roald asks, grasping her tightly by the shoulders. She expertly twists to escape his grip.

"Oh ho! Very good." His gaze turns on Will. "Is this the criminal?"

"My name's Will. I'm not a criminal."

"I heard you were a murderer."

"No."

"I'd deny it too. Well, criminal or no, I'm happy to meet you." He extends his hand, and when Will grips, it collapses like a rotten peach. With a gasp Will looks down to see the fake hand that Roald holds from inside his sleeve.

"That is so childish," Maren tells her brother.

"Many children come to the circus," he retorts. He peels off his wig and red nose. He has hair the same color as his sister's.

"How did you do the knife trick?" Will asks.

"With a great deal of practice," Roald says.

"And the help of a mirror," Maren adds, pointing. "Look."

For the first time Will notices the small mirror attached to the wall in front of where Roald stands.

"Still," Will says, "you did it all backward!"

"Yes. I confess I am a bit out of practice. But it went well."

Will decides not to think about this.

"So we are harboring a murderer," Roald says, swiping off his face paint with a rag.

"He's not a murderer! And he's coming with me and Mr. Dorian to perform on the train. We need to work him into the show."

Roald chews his lip. "I'm not sure he's very coordinated."

"He's not."

"Hey!" objects Will.

"Can you teach him some tricks?" Maren asks her brother.

"How long do I have?"

"Six hours."

"I don't think so. Do you have any skills, Will?"

"Not really," he says.

"Yes, you do!" Maren says, as if remembering suddenly. "You can draw! Show him!"

Reluctantly he pulls the sketchbook from his pocket. She takes it from his hands, in the same familiar way as she did three years ago. It bothered him then; now he likes it; it's as if they're old friends. "Look at these!"

"This one's of you," Roald tells her with a grin.

Will's face heats up.

"Just look how good they all are," Maren says quickly, flipping pages. Will sees the color rise in her cheeks too.

"Yes," says Roald with a shrug. "This is very pleasant, but . . . Well, can you do one of me?"

"I'll try," says Will.

Roald picks up a knife and holds it back over his head, ready to throw. "Like this!"

Will locks onto him with his eyes and does a quick gesture drawing. It makes him nervous with Maren watching him.

"Roald, come see!" she says when Will is done.

"Is that me?" he asks.

"Of course it's you," says Maren impatiently.

Roald looks at Will for corroboration. Will nods.

"But my hair doesn't look like that."

"It's a sketch," Will says. "Just to capture your movement."

A smile spreads across Roald's handsome face. "I look *massive*. Like a giant about to throw a boulder. I would like this picture. May I?"

Without waiting for an answer, he rips the page out.

"Roald!" says Maren. "You can't just rip a page out of an artist's sketchbook!"

"Oh. I'm sorry."

"No, no, you should have it," says Will.

"Look at this!" Roald says to the other performers, holding the drawing up in the air, grinning.

Before Will knows it, a small crowd has gathered around him.

"Could you do one of me?" asks the prettiest of the ballerinas, batting her eyelashes.

"I would like one as well," says Meng from his stilts.

"I'm the eldest. I should be first," Li says.

"You're practically blind," Meng replies. "It would give you no enjoyment."

"I will bite you, Little Brother."

"I'd love to do all of you," Will says hurriedly to the crowd.

"I want a proper portrait," demands a portly woman in a riding outfit, pushing to the front. "Not these little scribbles. Can you do that for me?"

"I'm not sure, ma'am."

"You call me Duchess Sabourin," she says. "My family is royalty in Luxembourg. You must do a portrait in oils, in the finest style of the old masters. For this I will pay you a hundred dollars. You will start after lunch."

With this the duchess walks off to the muffled laughter of the other performers.

"She doesn't have a hundred dollars," Maren tells him.

"Do I still have to do it?" He's fine with drawings but has never been happy with proper portraits. The people always come out wrong.

Maren shakes her head. "She once offered someone a thousand dollars for their hair. Don't worry. She'll have forgotten the whole thing before lunch. Still, you could turn a good business with this. Maybe Mr. Dorian would let you have a sideshow. We could dress you up and . . . That's it!"

"What?" asks Will.

"Your act," says Mr. Dorian.

In surprise Will turns to see the ringmaster standing behind him.

"People love having their portraits done," Maren says.

"These aren't proper portraits . . . ," Will says, alarmed.

"And it's not a circus act," Roald says.

"It is if he does them blindfolded," Maren says, taking the scarf from around her brother's neck.

Mr. Dorian nods. "Intriguing."

"Blindfolded?" says Will with mounting panic.

She ties the scarf tightly around his face, and to Will's amazement he can see right through it, almost as if nothing obscures his eyes.

"How does it work?" he asks, unwinding it and peering at it up close.

"Tie it one way, and you can see through. The other way . . ." She holds it against his face, and it's as if the room has been blacked out. "If someone in the audience is suspicious, we tie it on them this way, and then we wrap it on you the other way.

But you'll also have your back to them. You'll never set eyes on them."

"I can't do that!" he protests.

"Of course you can. Because I'll be standing in front of you, with a small mirror attached to my dress. You'll see the person. You'll draw them. They'll walk away with a lovely picture, and everyone's happy."

Mr. Dorian grins at her. "You'll be ringmistress of your own show one day. And here's Madame Lamoine to help us with your disguise."

A short, tent-shaped woman walks dolefully across the room.

"We need to transform William . . . into an Indian lad, I think," Mr. Dorian tells her.

Madame Lamoine glances at Will, lifts her fleshy hands, and sighs.

"Excellent," says Mr. Dorian.

Madame Lamoine shrugs and walks away.

"What just happened?" Will asks Maren.

"We're supposed to go with her. She's not a big talker, Madame Lamoine."

Will and Maren follow her to the next car and into a room cluttered with wigs and colorful jars and brushes and mustaches and noses and other little bits of people. Stools are set up in front of a long mirror. Madame Lamoine motions Will to a chair before a stained metal sink.

"Hair first," she says, sounding incredibly depressed.

She wraps a ratty piece of burlap around his shoulders and pushes his head back. She soaks his short hair, then slides on gloves. She opens a jar containing some foul-smelling black goo.

"What's in it?" Will asks, recoiling.

"Never you mind."

Without further ado she starts slapping it on. She's none too gentle. Her meaty fingers poke and shove at his face. He looks at Maren, who smiles encouragingly.

"Eyebrows, too," says Madame Lamoine, handing Maren the jar.

"Close your eyes," Maren tells Will.

She is much gentler. He concentrates on her fingertips stroking his eyebrows. It feels a bit tickly, but surprisingly nice—especially now that Madame Lamoine has stopped smacking his head around. When Maren's done, she daubs carefully around his eyebrows with a moist cloth to clean away the dye.

"You can open your eyes now," she tells him.

Sitting up, he asks, "How long do I have to leave it in for?"

"An hour."

When Will first glimpses himself in the mirror, he gasps. His eyebrows and slick hair are startlingly black against his pale face.

"It doesn't look right," he murmurs.

"Wait until the face," says Madame Lamoine. "Don't touch! Go and come back. I prepare paint now."

Maren leads him out of the compartment.

"I feel like a freak," he says.

"That's not a word we use around here," she tells him.

"Oh. Sorry."

"We call them marvels. That's nicer, don't you think?"

Will nods. "Much nicer."

"Speaking of marvels . . ." She trails off, as if reconsidering. "Outsiders aren't supposed to go in there, but you're practically one of us now."

Will smiles to himself. What would it really be like to be part of Zirkus Dante? What a huge and very odd family it is.

"You'll like this, I bet," she says. "Come on."

Will follows her, swept up by her enthusiasm. Across another set of couplings to the next car, she opens the door and ushers him inside. Black blinds cover the windows. From the ceiling hangs a single pale oil lamp. The room is like a shadowy museum, all the tables and display cases shrouded with curtains and cloths. Cabinets and steamer trunks are everywhere, some open and revealing lurid masks, or a collection of bones. Down the carriage a dozen life-size marionettes sway from hooks in the ceiling, jerking as the train rattles over a rough section of track.

Will hesitates at the sight of a narrow table with a body atop it, covered by a sheet. From the bottom protrudes a pair of large yellowed feet. A nearby workbench glints with sharp metal instruments. The body gives a sudden tortured gasp, its skeletal ribs pressing against the sheet.

"Who is that?" Will says, jerking back.

"Dying Zuoave," Maren says, placing a cool hand on his arm. "It's just a mechanical."

She pulls back the sheet to reveal a frighteningly lifelike mannequin, its mouth agape, eyes rolling. "He's supposed to be in his death throes."

"How does it work?" Will whispers.

"It's a windup toy."

"Who's been winding it up?"

"Well, that's the thing. You need to wind it only every few weeks. It sort of keeps going. It's unpredictable."

Will swallows. "It's awful."

"I know. That's why people pay a dime to see it!"

Will grimaces as the mechanical figure gives another choking gasp. Maren covers it and moves to another narrow table. She draws back the sheet to reveal a beautiful woman with long raven-black hair. Her eyes are shut, but she looks utterly alive. The faintest whisper of breath escapes her ruby lips; her chest rises and falls gently.

"We call this one Sleeping Beauty."

Will doesn't know which is eerier, the gurgling death gasp or the ghostly sigh of the eternal sleeper. Suddenly Sleeping Beauty gives a very loud hiccup. Will laughs.

"She's not supposed to do that," Maren tells him. "Mr. Dorian's trying to fix her. He made a lot of the things in here."

Maren takes his hand and draws him deeper into the shadows

of the room. Something murmurs inside a sealed trunk, and Will pauses.

"What's in there?"

"Indonesian night puppets. They're quite active. Not even Mr. Dorian's sure how they work. Don't open the lid! It's impossible to catch them once they start bouncing all over the place. Here, look at this."

She parts a curtain to reveal a large tank filled with murky green water. Bobbing inside is a bizarre skeleton. Some scales still cling to the ragged remains of a tail. Atop an algae-coated rib cage and crooked spine is a terrible skull with its lips pulled back. Abundant hair undulates in the water. Withered eyeballs cling to their sockets. A sign on the case says: THE FEEJEE MERMAID.

"Is it real?" Will breathes.

"It's pretty hard to know what's real and what isn't sometimes. Especially around here."

In a cabinet's open drawer Will spots a large meaty hand with a bloody stump of a wrist.

"What's that?"

"Hm? Oh, that's just to scare the kids. Touch it if you want."

Will pokes at it, and the hand immediately flips over and grabs his wrist. With a yelp Will shakes it loose. The hand falls to the floor and scuttles about like a spider. Will's about to stamp on it when Maren pulls him back, laughing.

"Sorry. I couldn't resist." Her voice takes on the tone of a circus spieler. "This here is the hand of none other than Attila the Hun. Yes, Ladies and Gentlemen! Preserved in a glacier in the mountains of China! Possessed eternally with the spirit of the savage warlord! Beware! Never turn your back, for he'll tighten his fingers around your neck!"

The hand leaps out of sight.

"Oh no. Can you see it?" Maren asks.

Will drops to the floor with her, but the hand has journeyed off underneath dusty crates.

"Lord knows where it'll end up now," she says. "Never mind. We'll get it later."

There's a thud on the roof. Will looks up in alarm, following the footsteps from one end of the car to the other. After a moment another person tramps overhead.

"Brogan," Maren says.

"There's lots of them," Will says as yet more runners traverse the cars. He knows his disguise isn't finished. The black hair won't fool anyone.

"It's all right. They'll never find us in here," says Maren. "This way."

She hurries toward a tall mannequin dressed like a boxer. His arms are cocked, his fists raised protectively before his face. His jaw juts aggressively, eyes squinted.

Maren lifts his shirt and turns a crank in his breastbone.

"What does he do?" Will asks.

"What do you think?"

On the boxer's heavy metal base is written: BEAT OUR BOXER AND WIN A DOLLAR!

From within the boxer's chest comes the faintest ticking—which is quickly blotted out by more heavy footsteps on the roof.

Maren turns down the wick of the hanging lamp and leads Will toward the tangle of life-size marionettes. They settle down amongst them, weaving their arms and legs around the wires, draping bits of fabric and shredded packing paper over themselves.

There's a squeak of a turning knob, and in the doorway stand the silhouettes of two men.

"Get some light in here!" one of them barks.

Will watches as a man wades across the cluttered car and raises the nearest blind. In the pale light Will recognizes the short, wiry brakeman with pouchy eyes. And now the second man is unmistakable: Brogan. Will's pulse jerks like a restless train.

Together the two brakemen slowly make their way down the center aisle. Clenched in Brogan's fist is a knife.

The Dying Zuoave gives an agonized gasp.

"What the hell's that?" the pouchy-eyed man hisses.

"A blinkin' toy," Brogan says, flipping back the sheet with his knifepoint.

"This place has a bad feel to it," says Chisholm. "My ma says circus folk traffic with the devil."

"Quiet down."

"You ever think the kid just fell off the train?" Chisholm says.

"We need that key."

"Didn't that guard say there was another one?"

"There is," Brogan says, "but it might be trickier to get. Anyway, we need the boy quiet."

Will feels faint. In a few moments the two brakemen will come abreast of him and Maren. He makes sure his limbs are loose and his head lolling forward.

"You figure this is real, this mermaid?" Chisholm asks.

"Dunno."

"Wouldn't mind meeting a real mermaid. Not this old rotted one."

From some corner of the carriage comes a scuttling sound.

"Hear that?" Brogan says.

Will does: the erratic gallop of five brawny barbarian fingers, then silence.

"A mouse probably," says Chisholm.

"Too loud," says Brogan. "Go have a look."

Reluctantly Chisholm slouches off, muttering, "Some kind of freak of nature, like the rest of the folk here. Two-headed rat or something . . ."

Brogan stops before the marionettes. With his knife he pokes distastefully at the closest ones. Will tries not to blink. He doesn't even breathe. His eyes start to water. Why won't Brogan move along?

"I can't find nothing," says Chisholm, returning. "Look at this fella here."

He leans toward the boxer to read the instructions, then stands with a chuckle. He throws a punch at the boxer's head, and the automaton's left hand instantly rises to block it.

"Feck it!" says Chisholm, jerking back with surprise. "That gave me gooseflesh."

"Don't bother with it," Brogan says impatiently.

But Chisholm is clearly entranced by the boxer. He raises both fists, facing off. He throws a right hook and is blocked, and follows up with a jab with his left. The boxer lowers his glove to deflect the blow.

"How's he do that?" Chisholm mutters.

"It's just a machine," says Brogan.

"One hell of a smart machine."

Will wishes they'd just move along.

Chisholm punches faster and harder, and Will can hear him puffing and grunting as the automaton effortlessly blocks him.

Then, from the corner of his eye, Will sees Attila the Hun's hand crouching in the shadow of a crate right near him. There is something expectant in the flex of its fingers. It steps closer.

Chisholm backs up, taking a breather.

In horror Will watches as the hand scuttles closer still to him.

"Hear that?" Brogan says. "That same rustling sound." He steps toward the marionettes.

The hand touches Will's shoe tentatively, tapping with its fingertips. Will forces himself to look away. He doesn't want to encourage it. He swallows when he feels a weight on his shoe and knows the hand has climbed on.

"Somewhere around here," Brogan's saying, not five feet from Will.

Will stays very still. The hand moves up to his ankle, and its fingers tighten in a grip so painful, he starts to sweat.

"It's a hand," says Brogan, "on that puppet's leg."

"Those dolls give me the creeps," says Chisholm, looking directly at Will, who tries to make his eyes glassy. "There's something not right about that one." Leaning forward for a better look, the brakeman puts his hand on the boxer's shoulder.

The boxer's left arm delivers an undercut that snaps Chisholm's haggard head back. He hits the floor like a bag of flour.

"Bloody idiot!" says Brogan, turning. He kneels and slaps Chisholm's face.

"What . . . what . . . ," the brakeman moans.

The severed hand hops onto Will's knee, and his leg involuntarily jerks.

Brogan looks over—and then up to the sound of running on the roof. There seems to be shouting, but Will can't make out the words. A second set of swift footsteps is followed by a third.

Will can't see it, but he hears the rear door of the carriage suddenly open—and someone wailing:

"They got a fecking sasquatch!"

From the doorway comes a blood-freezing animal wail, and Will sees Brogan's body tense.

"Dear mother of . . ." Chisholm squeaks, scrambling to his feet.

Will senses a large presence enter the car, and at the same moment the smell reaches him—that strange curdled smell that no other creature in the world has.

"Don't run!" calls a voice from the rear of the carriage. "You'll make him charge!"

Nonetheless Brogan and Chisholm take a few steps back as the sasquatch looms into view, restrained by three trainers holding chains. Goliath is six feet tall, and though his body is lean, it seems like it can barely contain the power and fury beneath the skin. The sasquatch stops and stares long and hard at Brogan, exhaling through his nostrils in hoarse, angry bursts.

"Easy, Goliath," says one of the trainers, whom Will recognizes as Christian.

Without warning Goliath lunges, his chest and muscle-knotted arms straining. The trainers lean back with their full weight. Will can almost feel the heat pouring off the sasquatch.

"Get that thing away from me!" bellows Brogan, his face gray with terror.

"I'd drop that knife if I were you," says Christian.

Will watches as Brogan lets it clatter to the floor.

"Goliath seems to know you," Mr. Dorian remarks, stepping out from behind the trainers.

Will remembers how, in the mountains, Brogan stabbed

KENNETH OPPEL

the young sasquatch in the shoulder. Clearly Goliath has not forgotten.

"Perhaps I didn't make myself clear the first time we met," Mr. Dorian says, and suddenly his polite calm disappears, and Will jerks in surprise at the ringmaster's rage. "You and your men are *not* welcome aboard my train, *sir*! The boy you are looking for is *not* on these carriages!"

Goliath gives an unearthly wail as if to emphasize the words.

"Let this be your last trespass!" Mr. Dorian seethes. "If I see you or any of your men aboard my train again, I will loose Goliath on you. And my enjoyment will match his as he rips your limbs from your body! Do I make myself clear, Mr. Brogan?"

"Name's Brinley," the brakeman mutters.

"Is it?" says Mr. Dorian. "I bid you good day, sir. Now get out!"

Brogan and Chisholm beat their retreat to the far end of the car. Will waits for the sound of the closing door.

After a moment Mr. Dorian looks directly at Will and says, "You can come out now."

Maren reaches over and flicks a little switch on the back of Attila the Hun's hand. Its grip relaxes instantly, and it falls off Will's leg. He stands uncertainly, keeping his eye on the sasquatch.

"You all right, Sis?" Christian asks Maren.

"Of course," she replies.

"I'd give you a hug, but Goliath might get jealous."

"Thanks for saving the day."

"You can take Goliath back to his cage now," Mr. Dorian tells the trainers.

"This way, Goliath," Christian says, with a tug on the chain.

Will feels a pang of sympathy for the sasquatch. It was born in the mountain wilds, and is now forced to live in prisonlike confinement, with none of its own kind for company. It shrugs against the pull of the chains and turns to stare right at Will with its fathomless eyes. Will stands very still.

"He remembers you, too," says Mr. Dorian.

"In a good way, I hope," Will murmurs.

After what seems like a long time, Goliath snorts and follows his trainers out of the car.

Mr. Dorian's expression is so severe that Will worries the ringmaster might be angry with him.

"I'm sorry for all the trouble—" Will begins.

"Don't be absurd," says Mr. Dorian. "None of this is your fault."

"How many were there?" Maren asks.

"Nine this time. It was all I could do to keep our people from fighting." The ringmaster looks thoughtful. "Nine men. It must be quite an undertaking Mr. Brogan's planning."

"Maybe he's ready to give up searching," Maren says hopefully.

Will swallows. "He knows there's another key."

"Your father's," says Mr. Dorian.

"We have to warn him! They're planning something big. And if Brogan's willing to kill a guard . . ."

"Your father's no man to be trifled with," Mr. Dorian says

calmly. "I very much doubt our Mr. Brogan would risk such a confrontation. If your father's in the locomotive, he's got people around him all the time. Brogan wouldn't attempt it."

Will wishes he were more reassured.

"As it is, we're leaving in a matter of hours," Mr. Dorian says, clapping him on the shoulder. "But first we have to finish your disguise. Madame Lamoine is ready for you."

Stroke after stroke, the paint goes on, thick and greasy. Will doesn't like the feel of it on his skin.

"It dries," says Madame Lamoine ambiguously.

She's done with his face and neck and is now finishing off his hands.

Maren returns with some clothing draped over her arm.

"We have an Indian fortune-teller costume that might fit," she tells Mr. Dorian, who's overseeing Will's transformation.

There is a loose-fitting white shirt with beadwork around the collar and buttons, a pair of white cotton trousers, and a brown leather vest.

"Stand," says Madame Lamoine, and steps back to look at him. She slaps him here and there, moving him around so she can examine him from every angle.

"Don't touch face," is all she says.

He thinks he understands what she means about it drying. The paint doesn't feel quite so wet and heavy.

"Try them on," Maren says, holding out the clothes.

Will takes them behind a faded Japanese screen. He's worried about where he'll put his things—especially the key. But he's relieved to find that the inside of the vest has many ingenious pockets sewn into it. He transfers his items and takes off his borrowed clothes. He's glad to be rid of them. These new ones fit much better.

When he steps out, Maren gives a melodramatic gasp. "What have you done with William Everett?" she demands.

Mr. Dorian nods his approval. "This will do nicely."

Will goes to the mirror and stares. He feels like he's inside a complete stranger, peeping out through their eyeholes.

"I don't recognize myself at all."

"Excellent to hear," says Mr. Dorian.

Will looks older, and somehow fiercer. His teeth are startlingly white, his eyes piercing in his pale brown face. A sense of liberation floats up within him. He's just performed his own personal disappearing act.

CHAPTER 9

THE PLAYERS

They don't look like circus performers as they step off the train in Kirkton. No clown makeup, no sparkly clothes. Will thinks they must look as solemn as a funeral party. There is Mr. Dorian, a sleek raven in his suit and top hat and silver-tipped cane; Maren's braids are tucked modestly inside the collar of a navy-blue greatcoat that goes to her ankles. And Will himself wears a dark wool jacket over his shirt and trousers, and a cap atop his black head of hair. Only Mr. Beauprey stands out, on account of his awesome size. Even though he won't be performing with them on the Boundless, the giant insisted on walking them up to colonist class, and carrying their bags. Will wonders if he's secretly hoping for the chance to throw someone.

If he is, it looks like he'll be disappointed. As they tramp along the gravel, Will spots several brakemen smoking atop boxcars, or inspecting the couplings—but they keep their distance.

The afternoon air carries the cold promise of snow. They're farther north now, and the trees are spindlier. The ground is rocky and grudging. There's no sign of a town in the distance—or the noise of a trackside market. Will figures the stop is too short, or there just aren't enough people in Kirkton.

With Maren at his side, Will walks after Mr. Dorian, trying not to appear too hasty. One car after another they make their way forward. Even with Mr. Beauprey nearby, Will worries they'll be confronted by Brogan and his cohort any second.

It seems incredible to him he hasn't been recognized. His face is the same shape, his eyes the same color. But he supposes people never look that closely at things. As Mr. Dorian might say, *We're easily fooled by our eyes.*

Still, Will is pretty sure some of the brakemen are staring hard at him as he passes. Maybe they're just curious about all the circus performers. The brakemen can't *all* be working for Brogan, but judging by the crew that broke into the circus cars, there are plenty—and how can Will tell the honest from the wicked?

His disguise isn't the only thing he's worried about. He has to remember not to speak when they're around other people, which will be pretty much all the time. He's quiet by nature, so maybe it will be easier than he thinks. But he's not so shy around Maren, which is one of the reasons he likes her so much.

As they make their way, Mr. Beauprey cheerfully bellows out the names of all the different types of trees, and the birds flitting between their branches. From the roof of a livestock car, a brakeman wolf-whistles at Maren.

"Come whistle for me, you brazen fiend!" Mr. Beauprey roars up at him. The brakeman cringes and slinks away.

Maren doesn't seem at all bothered. Will realizes she must be used to this kind of attention. For the first time he understands what a rough world this must be for a girl. Without her parents, too. At least she has her brothers, but they won't be with her for the next few days. Just Mr. Dorian—and him—but it seems little protection against the rough men along the steel road.

He glances over at her. He has no doubt she's good at taking care of herself, but the thought comes into his head suddenly: *I would like to protect her.* He almost laughs at himself. Isn't she the one protecting him? He wishes he could talk to her. There are still a lot of things he wants to tell her, and ask her. Three years' worth of questions. He contents himself with studying her profile. She has a very interesting nose.

They round a bend in the track, and up ahead Will sees a huge crowd. There are no vendors or stalls, just colonists stretching their legs and taking the air alongside the train.

From the rear of the last colonist car, a handsome young

porter appears on the steps. Will feels a surge of relief at the sight of him, looking crisp and official in his Boundless uniform.

"Would you be Mr. Dorian?" he asks the ringmaster.

"I would."

"My name's Thomas Drurie. We're expecting you. If I might just see your passport, sir."

"Of course." Mr. Dorian produces a paper booklet and hands it to Drurie.

The porter glances up at Maren and Will.

"And what're your names, please?"

"Maren Amberson."

Drurie looks at Will with some suspicion. "And you?"

Mr. Dorian says, "That is Amit Sen, our spirit artist. He understands a little English but speaks none."

"What does he speak?"

"Hindi," says the ringmaster.

"मैं माफी माँगता हूँ, लेकिन मै नही अंग्रेज़ी बात नही करते," says Will politely, just as he was coached by one of the performers an hour before.

Drurie's eyes widen. "What did he just say?"

"He apologized for not speaking English," says Mr. Dorian.

"And the . . . *large* gentleman?" Drurie asks with some concern.

"Mr. Eugene Beauprey. He won't be accompanying us."

"Excellent. Please come aboard."

"Thank you, Mr. Beauprey," Maren says, and gives the giant a hug around his trunklike waist.

"I will see you in Lionsgate City, Little Wonder," he replies fondly. He gives one last fierce look around, as if daring anyone to bother her, then starts back to the Zirkus Dante cars, whistling.

Will boards. He remembers being squished into third class when he was younger, but he's never seen anything quite like this. At first he thinks it must be the baggage car, for there are so many *things* everywhere, suitcases and sacks and oddly-shaped bundles trussed up with twine. But amongst it all there are people—far too many to count! Even though many passengers are still outside, the place feels impossibly full.

The smell barrages Will. Sausage and unlaundered clothes, and the reek of an overused toilet. Pickles, sweat, wet boots, and incense all add to the din of smell.

On either side of a narrow aisle are rows of bare wooden benches. An old man bounces a crying baby on his knee, singing a nursery rhyme in another language. Four men have their heads bowed over a game of cards. An anxious woman counts rosary beads. Between two fellows is spread a map, and they are stabbing their fingers at it and arguing.

And above these wooden benches are two levels of pull-down berths. On one a mother and a baby sleep curled up together; on another a burly man picks at his big toe. Two boys leap between berths while a mother hollers at them from the floor. Threadbare blankets and lumpy makeshift pillows are scattered everywhere. There is scarcely room to move. More children bound down and up the aisle, and clamber over the backs of the bench seats, making a playground of the carriage. The only light comes from narrow windows, high up near the ceiling, and a few oil lamps secured to the walls.

Slowly at first, and then more quickly, people start to notice Will and the others.

"Circus . . ."

"*Zirkus* . . ."

"*Sirkuksen* . . ."

"*Cirkuszi* . . ."

The word whispers and slithers itself through the car in all different languages. Most of the people look glad. A few shrink back as the trio passes. A small girl cries at the sight of Mr. Dorian in his severe black top hat and coat—until the ringmaster pulls a lollipop from his pocket and hands it to her. Suddenly the performers have a trail of children, their hands tugging, eyes imploring. More lollipops and jawbreakers appear from the ringmaster's bottomless pockets. Applause and cheers ring out from the passengers.

"You'll need to clear this aisle," Drurie calls out pointlessly, for no one heeds him. "You can't have all this here! It must be cleared of obstructions! Is that a chicken?"

A stove blazes in the center of the car. No fewer than seven pots sputter atop it. Will supposes this is how they eat: You cook when the stove's free and take your meals whenever you can.

"Is there just the one stove?" Maren asks Drurie.

He looks at her with a confused smile and ignores her question as if it isn't even worth consideration.

"I'm sorry you have to pass through all this," Drurie says to Mr. Dorian. "It's rather ripe in here."

"Not surprising," Mr. Dorian remarks tartly, "as it seems they have only one washroom per car."

As Will makes his way, he realizes these people have less room to themselves than the Zirkus Dante animals. It can't be right to have such cramped quarters when there is such luxury farther up the train. Does his father know how terrible it is back here?

"These people are fortunate to get passage on the Boundless at all," Drurie says with a sniff. "They're the poorest of the poor, and they've washed up on the shores of our country to claim our land."

"Interesting," says Mr. Dorian. "My mother's people are Cree Indian. Perhaps it's people like *you* who have washed up on *our* shores. A stimulating thought, don't you think?"

Drurie clears his throat and keeps walking. "There's rumors we may have a murderer aboard," he says, "and I'd bet anything it's one of these folks. I'd keep your eyes peeled."

Mr. Dorian lifts his hat to a large woman in a colorful headdress. "Good day, ma'am. Now, Drurie, if you could show us to where we'll be performing."

"We've made space for you a few cars up," he says. "I hope it's adequate."

"I'm sure it's more than adequate," says Mr. Dorian.

They cross several more carriages before they reach a car with an entire section that's been curtained off at the back.

Will expects this must be the stage, but when Drurie parts the curtains, Will sees what appears to be a small shop with many shelves: loaves of pumpernickel bread, cooked hams, tins of vegetables, some fresh fruit, bars of soap, towels, various corked bottles of different shapes and colors. A finely turned-out gentlemen sitting on a cushioned bench looks up as they enter.

"Ah, you must be the entertainment for the day," he says in what sounds to Will like an upper-crust English accent. "I'm Mr. Peters."

Right away Will notices how amazingly clean his fingernails are—and not only clean but buffed and shaped in a perfect curve.

"You're the chief porter?" Mr. Dorian inquires.

"No, no, just a paying passenger. Isn't that right, Drurie?"

"Yes, Mr. Peters, sir," says Drurie.

He certainly does not look like the other passengers. He has an entire corner of the carriage, the equivalent of three rows of seats, curtained off with thick drapery. At each entrance, front and back, sits a bearded man in a bulky coat, a rifle tilted against his seat.

KENNETH OPPEL

"You're a merchant, too, by the looks of it," says Mr. Dorian, surveying his goods.

"Well, as you know, the Boundless doesn't provide a meal service to these poor people, so I do my bit," says Peters.

"Two dollars for a loaf of bread," says Maren, reading the sign.

"Yes, miss."

"It seems a lot for a loaf of bread," she remarks.

"That's the fair market price aboard the Boundless, young miss. And before you get all holy on me, how many people of my sort do you think would choose to ride with this class of people? I do it so I can help them."

"Ah," says Mr. Dorian. "That is very noble of you."

"We're just in the next car," says Drurie, eager to lead them on.

"It's disgusting," mutters Maren when they've left.

"Is the conductor aware there is a profiteer aboard the train?" Mr. Dorian asks Drurie, who looks distinctly uncomfortable.

"He's paid for all those seats fair and square," says Drurie. "The passengers are happy enough to have him aboard when they need something."

To Will it sounds like a speech he's made before. He wonders again if his father knows this is going on aboard the Boundless.

"We've had the passengers clear an area here," Drurie says curtly, leading them into the middle of the car. Will can just imagine how the likes of Drurie would go about getting people to leave their seats. But he's surprised to be greeted only by grins, excited smiles, and more applause by all the people they've displaced.

"Thank you, thank you," says Mr. Dorian graciously. "*Vielen Dank. Merci. Grazie.* We promise you a good show, and you shall have the best seats in the house. We begin in one hour!"

Sheets have been pegged up to form a curtain and backstage area around the several vacated rows of seats. Drurie bids them good day and exits through the door at the front of the carriage.

Will's eyes linger on that door. Beyond it there is another colonist car, and hundreds more, leading to third class, then second class and finally first. The journey is right there, ready for him to take.

"The pair of them are disgusting," says Maren, setting down her bag behind the curtains. "Peters and that cowardly porter. It shouldn't be allowed."

"It has always been thus," says Mr. Dorian. "I don't see it changing."

All around them is the din of the passengers, so Will feels he can speak in a whisper without danger.

"I'm going to tell my father. He's a fair man. He won't stand for it."

Mr. Dorian smiles faintly. "You of all people should know how the railway was made, William. On the backs of poorly paid laborers. A dollar a day to risk your life. Less if you weren't a white man."

"Well," says Will stubbornly, "my father was one of those laborers. He wouldn't want to see them badly treated on his own train."

Mentioning his father makes Will all the more impatient. "I've been thinking. . . . I can find my way from here."

Maren looks at him in surprise. "What do you mean?"

"You don't need me. I can make my way up front."

"But that's not the plan!"

Mr. Dorian regards him calmly. "I wouldn't advise it, William. You have no ticket, no passport to get between cars. They won't let you through. Even if they did, you can be sure Brogan's men are watching—and it seems to me he's been talking this up with Drurie, and maybe other porters too. They're on the lookout for a murderer, and they'll report anything suspicious back to Brogan. You're safest to wait with us until we reach first class."

"It's only two more nights, Will," Maren reminds him. She seems genuinely concerned. "You're safest with us."

Chewing his lip, Will looks again at the door. What if Brogan tries to steal the key from his father and there's a fight? His father is strong, but how good is he with his fists—or against a knife? In his stories he mentioned breaking up plenty of fights. If he could survive three years working the rails, he can handle the likes of Brogan.

"All right," he says, dragging his eyes away from the door. He's still worried about his father, and he's also terrified of performing.

Never in his life has he done something like this. In school when he had to speak before the class, he dreaded it for days beforehand. And on the day itself he felt such intense horror walking up before the other students that he thought he might pass out. Every useful thought and word flew from his head.

"It'll be fine," Maren whispers as though reading his mind. "You're not Will Everett anymore. You're someone completely different. That's the wonderful thing about performing—it's not even you up there. It's someone who has amazing skills and power you never dreamed you could have."

For a flash he feels it again, the freedom of inhabiting another body that isn't quite his own.

"You're going to love it," Maren tells him.

Brogan strides with ease across the tops of the cars, heading forward. This is his terrain, this constantly moving, jostling road, and he knows its every landmark. He's as sure-footed as a mountain goat, despite a limp.

The limp's not from blasting or laying steel. Years he spent working the railway. Men died around him all the time, especially the Chinamen, but he was charmed. He was the best blaster around, and he wasn't injured until the very last day when the sasquatch grabbed his leg and hurled him into the gorge. He should have been killed. But there was a bit of scrub on the cliff face and he grabbed hold and stayed put, invisible, until the coast was clear. Then he climbed back and limped his way over the mountain to make a new identity for himself. A new name was all it took.

Brogan doesn't know if the Everett boy is on or off the train. Maybe the kid did fall off that night. All Brogan knows is there's no way he's going back into those Zirkus cars with that sasquatch around. There's not much he's afraid of, but those beasts turn his insides to liquid.

It doesn't matter, though. There's another key. The drunken fool of a guard told him so.

Brogan reaches the front of first class and drops down onto the platform. Brakemen aren't supposed to enter first-class cars. He stands out; he's not dressed pretty, but he'll be quick.

He steps into the elegant carriage and sticks his head into the steward's office. Empty. On the wall is a board of stateroom keys, all neatly labeled for the trip. He sees the one marked EVERETT and takes it. The stateroom is the first one down. He's inside in two seconds.

He listens, but there's no one moving about upstairs. He moves to the rolltop desk and starts pulling open drawers, sifting through papers. Nothing. Checking every surface, every shelf and cubbyhole, he moves through the parlor and then upstairs.

The main bedroom looks as though it hasn't been slept in. He checks through the chest of drawers without any luck. Then the boy's room. Same.

He's in a rage, wanting to slam and break the room apart. He takes a moment to calm his breathing.

The only other key must be on James Everett's body.

He leaves the room as he found it, exits the car, and climbs to the roof.

It will be bloodier. But there's no going back now.

His new plan assembles itself with each step of his long journey back.

Will peeks through the gap in the curtains.

The Boundless is moving again, and with all the passengers back aboard, the car seems impossibly full. On either side of the makeshift stage, people are sitting on the floor, in one another's laps, perching on one another's shoulders, dangling off the dangerously sagging berths.

Onstage Mr. Dorian has just mesmerized a fellow who chirps like a bird. The crowd laughs uproariously.

Will lets the curtain fall into place, and swallows.

"You all right?" Maren whispers to him.

He nods. He doesn't want to talk.

Four portraits—that's all he has to draw. But he feels like he might throw up. In his pocket his hand finds the sasquatch tooth, and he rubs its pitted surface.

"I'll be with you the whole time," she says, and gives his hand a squeeze. For a moment he's distracted by the touch of her skin against his, but then Mr. Dorian's voice rings out his cue.

"And now, Ladies and Gentlemen, you are about to witness a

most curious thing. Throughout history there have been gifted artists who can draw a portrait—but could any of them draw a portrait without setting eyes on their subject? The young man you are about to meet was born in the kingdom of India and studied many years to hone his gift. Four lucky people in this audience will be chosen to have their portraits drawn. I introduce to you Amit, the spirit artist!"

Will doesn't hear most of this. It's just a rattle of words in his head. Maren's gentle nudge tells him he's on. He swallows and walks out. Mercifully he has only a brief moment to see the audience, a solid mass of bodies and heads and expectant heat. He's glad when Maren leads him to the stool and he sits, facing the wall.

"Who will be the first to be drawn?" Mr. Dorian asks.

A veritable roar consumes the carriage.

"You, sir, come forward, please. Stand here. That's it, directly behind him. Now behold. To make sure he cannot see a thing . . ."

On cue Maren holds the scarf in front of the audience. She walks behind Will to tie it around the face of the volunteer.

"Can you see anything, sir?" Mr. Dorian asks.

"*Nyet*. No *thing*!"

"Bind our spirit artist, then," says Mr. Dorian, "and let him begin!"

The scarf is wound around Will's head. He can see through it perfectly. He reaches out blindly with his hands, and Maren gives him his sketchbook and pencil. Then she takes a few paces back and stands in front of him.

He focuses on the ingenious mirrored sequins on Maren's dress. Together they form a kind of mosaic. It's not a perfect image by any means, but it's enough. Will and Maren agreed on a system beforehand. He scratches his ear, she turns to the right; he taps his foot, she turns to the left. He sees the face of the man. A rectangle of solid flesh and bone. A single heavy eyebrow.

Will is nervous and worries they'll see his hand shaking, but he remembers his childhood trick. His eye is the pencil. And so he starts, traveling this little landscape of wrinkles and curves, shading here and there. He works quickly, knowing he cannot let the audience wait too long.

It is not good work, but after one minute Mr. Dorian whisks the portrait away and holds it before the audience.

"Is not the likeness amazing!" he cries.

There is a healthy murmur of approval, then clapping, and then a crush of people, pushing forward to be next. Will does another, more confidently now. In the reflection of Maren's sequins, he glimpses the look of delight when the woman is given her sketch. She shows it to her husband and children. She does not even want to fold it. He wonders if she's ever had her photograph taken.

Two more, and then quite suddenly he is done, taking his bow, buffeted by applause. When he and Maren step back behind the curtain, he feels ignited, unable to stand still.

Maren laughs. "That wasn't so bad, was it?"

"I *liked* it!" It's so noisy all around them, he has no fear of being overheard.

"Told you. You'll join the circus yet!"

"Do you get nervous anymore?" he asks.

"Sometimes."

When Maren is called out to do her act, Will watches intently through a gap in the curtain.

She is calm and poised. In her hand she holds a compact spool, like something you'd see on a fishing rod. As she turns the small handle, wire begins to pay out rigidly in a horizontal line. At its end is a small grappling hook. Round and round she turns the wheel, and the line stretches out. The audience shuffles out of the way as it passes them. Will has never seen such a device, a little magic trick in itself. When the line reaches all the way across the carriage, Maren gives a little twist of her wrist, and the hooked end grips a ledge about three feet up the wall.

Maren then runs to the opposite end of the carriage, paying out more line, and hooks the spool to the wall there. She has created her own tightrope down the middle of the car. She springs onto it, her head nearly grazing the ceiling.

The crowd gives a great cheer. Once on the wire, Maren is like a person transformed. He suddenly doesn't know her at all. He can only stare in amazement as she skips across the wire, does somersaults, closes her eyes and walks backward, lies down on her stomach and pretends to fall asleep.

Despite all the good cheer of the crowd, Will notices how some of the men look at her, a furtive hungry look he doesn't like.

Maren invites people to toss things up at her, and she catches them one after another: a hat, a bottle, a sausage—and proceeds to juggle them all. After throwing the objects back to their rightful owners, she hops down, unhooks her tightrope, and cartwheels down the aisle to the stage.

It's time for the disappearing act. Will watches as chains are placed upon her by an audience member and she is covered by a giant scarf. He stares hard, wanting to understand the trick—and nearly jumps out of his skin when she taps him on the shoulder behind the curtain.

"How do you do that?" he demands.

"I'll never tell," she replies, rosy-cheeked and breathless.

He wishes he could draw her just like that.

Mr. Dorian pulls back the curtain to reveal all of them, and there is a tsunami of applause. Even those lucky men and women who had seats are now on their feet, clapping and shouting "Bravo" and "Brava" and other words Will doesn't understand. A dizzying happiness blossoms inside him.

The audience surges toward them, and Will is worried they'll be crushed. They're all three taken hold of, and hoisted up onto shoulders and carried out of the car into another, where there is a stove, covered with pots.

Bundles are moved, people shift, and Will finds himself eased onto a bench beside Maren. She looks as bewildered as he feels. Scarcely has he been seated, when a bowl of food is put on his lap, and a spoon into his hand. And Will understands they have been invited to dinner.

The food smells delicious, but he's hardly taken a mouthful before people are touching him, and asking him questions in different languages. He knows he mustn't reply in English, so he only smiles and nods, and sometimes repeats the few Hindi words he's memorized.

Across the sea of heaving bodies, he sees someone who looks Indian, trying to reach him. What if the man wants to talk to Will? He'll be found out! Luckily, musical instruments suddenly appear. Strange stringed things, mouth harps, a contraption that looks a bit like an accordion.

The colonists are putting on their own show now, maybe as a way of thanking the performers. Will feels a bit smushed and deafened, but it is all so good-natured that he doesn't mind too much.

A drink is thrust into his hand, and the man looks at him so expectantly that Will doesn't see he has any choice but to slug it back. It sears all the way down his throat. The crowd gives a cheer.

By the time the dancing starts, Will has had two more of the drinks and thinks dancing is probably the best thing in the world. He enters a sweaty web of arms and stamps about the floor, having no idea what he's doing. Nearby he sees Maren being whirled about, a dazzling colorful blur. He wants to grab hold of her, to stop her moving, to feel her skin against his hands.

And suddenly they are pressed together, and the crowd is close around them and clapping hands eagerly.

"They want us to dance," Maren says.

He almost replies in English, tells her he can't dance, but it's too late. She's taken his hands and starts leading him in a mangled version of the waltz. After a few steps he tries to lead, and stamps on her feet, and then she leads again, and before long they are both laughing helplessly.

A woman's cry of dismay suddenly cuts through the music. The instruments stop. There's a flurry of harsh words. The crowd shifts, angling itself in the direction of the noise.

Will looks over to see one of Mr. Peters's burly guards. He towers over a shorter man, whose face is flushed and furrowed with outrage. A woman, maybe his wife, is shouting at the guard, while a small boy watches, clinging to her side, his face pale with fear.

The guard shoves the other man against the wall, reaches inside his jacket, and pulls out a slender bottle. The man tries to grab it back, but the guard strikes him across the face.

For a moment everyone in the car is silent. Then several other colonists shout out and move aggressively toward the guard, but Peters's man primes his rifle, and the passengers halt and step out of his way.

190   KENNETH OPPEL

"Is there a problem?" Mr. Dorian asks the guard as he passes.

"Nothing to do with you," grunts the man, and leaves the carriage.

The woman is crying openly now.

"Their boy is sick," a man says to Dorian. "Mr. Peters sells medicine. The father of boy has not money to pay. Mr. Peters gives medicine but wants money later. The father tries to sell something to makes money, but is no good. Now Peters takes back medicine."

"He has no money at all?" Mr. Dorian asks.

"Only food for trip—but Mr. Peters doesn't want food. He wants deed."

Maren frowns. "Deed?"

"Land deed. What family comes for."

"Ah," says Mr. Dorian. "His government land grant."

Will knows about these. Most of the colonists are on their way to claim their land and start farms and ranches. The deed is their proof of ownership. Without it they would have nothing.

"It seems our Mr. Peters is also a land speculator," Mr. Dorian says.

Will is looking at the little boy, his pinched face. He's never felt such a hot rush of indignation. Without thinking, he marches after Peters's guard.

Maren is close on his heels. "Amit," she whispers, "what are you doing?"

He ignores her, keeps going, all the way to Peters's car. He's aware of Maren at his side, and Mr. Dorian not far behind. She hisses into his ear, "Don't do anything stupid!"

Will has no tricks, no power. But he does have almost three dollars in his pocket.

He bursts into the curtained room to find Mr. Peters eating from a fine plate and drinking a glass of wine. The guards both stand at his sudden entrance.

"Ah, the circus boy," he says. "I'm sorry I missed your show. I've never been one for tawdry entertainments."

From his pocket Will takes the coins and places them before Mr. Peters.

"Medicine," he says.

"Ah, so you *do* speak a little English."

Will says nothing, knowing he's made a mistake—but surely Amit would have picked up a few English words quickly.

"He wants the medicine for that boy," Maren says beside him.

Mr. Peters eyes Will with amusement—and curiosity. "I'm glad to see your ringmaster pays you so handsomely. I've heard some can be terrible slave drivers. I shall happily sell you the medicine." He nods at his guard, who takes the little bottle from the shelf and tosses it to Will.

Will catches and pockets it.

"Not only rich, but a Good Samaritan," says Mr. Peters. "It's heartwarming. We're quite the same. It was lucky I had the right medicine for that boy. If the conductor were to hear there was a sick family aboard, he might turn them off the train, where their situation would be altogether more desperate. It's better this way, handled by compassionate fellows like us."

Will knows this is some kind of threat: Keep quiet about this—about what I do here—or the family will suffer.

Will turns to Maren, pretending he hasn't understood a word, and sees Maren's face pale with rage. This time it's he who puts a hand on her arm, afraid she'll do something rash.

"Don't forget your change," Mr. Peters says.

Will turns back and takes the coins offered him. Mr. Dorian is watching from the curtain silently, and actually tips his hat to Mr. Peters before turning to leave.

Will makes his way through the cars to the boy's family, and holds out the medicine bottle to the mother. Her eyes widen with surprise.

"That man, he will not come to take it back?" the father asks nervously.

"No," says Maren.

The boy looks at the bottle and bursts into tears.

"Why is he crying?" Maren asks.

"The taste," says his mother, "he doesn't like it."

The boy sobs something that sounds like "boat."

"What's he saying?" Maren asks.

"There is a toy, a boat, we leave behind," the mother says. "And he is sad about this still."

Into Maren's ear Will whispers, "Ask her what it looks like."

Maren asks, and Will waits as the mother translates the question for her son. The boy smiles, and his pale face becomes animated. He prattles for a long time. As the mother tells Maren the details, Will pulls out his sketchbook and starts to draw, rapidly but with as much detail as possible.

He tears the page from the book and hands it to the boy.

The boy frowns and points to the smokestack.

The mother says something sharply to the boy, and his eyes fill with tears again.

"What's wrong?" Maren asks.

"He is greedy," the mother replies.

Will looks at the boy and sees him trace an outline of a bigger smokestack on the picture. Will reaches over and with a quick flourish of his pencil enlarges the smokestack and adds a healthy puff of smoke.

The boy beams at Will, and he feels like a hero.

"I hope your boy gets better soon," says Maren.

"Thank you," the father says to them. "Thank you."

"Circus . . ."
　　"*Zirkus* . . ."
　　"*Sirkuksen* . . ."
　　"*Cirkuszi* . . ."
The word that marked Will's entrance marks his exit, with

cheers and clapping, as a surly Drurie leads them through the last of the colonist cars. Hefting his small suitcase, Will feels suddenly exhausted. He's never wanted bed so badly. Drurie brings them to a reinforced door that requires two keys to unlock. When he swings it open, the noise of the tracks pours in. Cold air smacks Will in the face. It's very dark outside now.

Across the couplings a second porter stands behind the lighted window of the other car. He nods at Drurie and opens his door—and Will moves his leaden body after Mr. Dorian and Maren across the shuddering platform to third class.

CHAPTER 10

M U S K E G

"Mind your step, please," says the porter as he ushers them inside. He's a gangly fellow whose narrow wrists shoot past his cuffs. "The mail car's a bit cluttered. We don't get many people coming through here."

Will steps around bulging canvas bags. It's a long double-decker car, windowless, and lit by gaslight. Will is reminded of a beehive. A small army of uniformed men sorts mail at narrow tables, flinging letters and oddly-shaped bundles into open sacks. The entire left side of the carriage is floor-to-ceiling pigeonholes. Workers, each with a bag slung over his left shoulder, stand on tall ladders, sorting mail into the holes. The ladders run on rails and whiz to and fro with astonishing speed.

"This is our postmaster, James Kilgour," the gangly porter says.

A white-whiskered man in an official cap looks up from his clipboard. Will notices he only has a thumb and index finger on his right hand.

"Good evening to you," the postmaster says, and then: "Owney! Where's that package for Edmonton?"

Startled, Will looks down to the floor as a scruffy brown-and-white mutt pushes a parcel toward Mr. Kilgour's feet. Then he sits back and looks immensely pleased with himself.

"Good boy," the postmaster says, tossing the bundle into an open sack and checking off something on his clipboard. He gives the dog a good scratch between his ears. "This is Owney. He's our mail dog."

Owney's brown triangular ears perk up, and his tail thumps appreciatively. From his collar hang so many tags that Will is amazed the dog can raise his head. Will almost asks what they're all for, but stops himself just in time. Mr. Kilgour seems to sense his question.

"People give these to him wherever we stop. He's been all over. Houston. Churchill. Ann Arbor. The mayors, they present him with the tags. He's a good-luck charm, our Owney. Gets the mail through on time, and we've never had a wreck, the fifteen years the mutt's been with us."

"He's a charming little fellow," Maren says, bending to give him a pat.

Will pats him too, mostly to have the chance to bump his hand against Maren's.

"Delightful," says Mr. Dorian, unmoved. "Shall we head on?"

"Give us a moment," says the postmaster. "Mail drop coming, and it gets a bit crowded up ahead." He checks his pocket watch. "Harrison! Reid! Let's open her up!"

Two men rush over and pull a chain to raise a tall metal panel in the carriage's side. Night air gallops in. In the darkness Will can see telegraph posts flashing past.

"Bag on!" shouts the postmaster over the clatter of the track.

Rising like a mast from the center of the car is a sturdy metal pole. Two arms jut from it, one three feet above the other. Harrison and Reid hook a mail bag onto the lower arm, and then swivel both arms so they're sticking straight out through the big window.

"Here we come!" shouts one of the men, poking his head out.

"Get your head back in, you damn fool!" says Kilgour. "How many times have I told you? You want it taken off?" The postmaster rolls his eyes at Will.

There is a blur past the window, and a tremendous clattering noise, and Will sees the bag on the lower arm disappear—and at the same moment the upper arm, empty seconds ago, swings inside with a hefty canvas bag.

"See that!" says Kilgour with a proud shake of his head,

even though he must've seen this a thousand times. "Their arm just swipes our bag of mail, and we swipe theirs! All right, lads. Let's get sorting! We've got an hour before our next drop, and then we're into the muskeg!"

"Bye, Owney," Maren says to the dog as they leave. The mutt wags his tail and then starts snuffling around various bundles on the floor as though he can read their addresses.

The porter leads them through to the next car. Once the door closes behind them, Will notices how much quieter it is than colonist class. There must be more insulation—and better suspension, too, because the ride doesn't feel so rough. The floor is freshly painted white, and there are decorative swirls around the ceiling. Gas lamps are set at intervals along the wall. There's a stove at either end of the car, but no cooking smells or soot.

Right now the carriage is being put to bed. Stewards are handing out pillows and blankets and lowering the sleeping berths. Heavy curtains hang in between for privacy. It is crowded, but much less so than colonist class. People are looking at them, and Will is aware how he, Maren, and Mr. Dorian stand out amongst the weathered cattle hands and farmers in undershirts and denim trousers.

After several more cars the porter leads them past storage compartments and crew quarters, and finally opens the door of a tiny cabin. He stands back to let them inside. There are three bunks against one wall, mostly obscuring the single window.

Against the opposite wall there's a narrow bench. Scarcely room to change your mind—that's what Will's mother used to say of their old apartment.

"There's shelves on the facing wall for your things," the porter says. "I hope this is adequate. It's the only free cabin in third class."

"We're extremely grateful," Mr. Dorian says. "Thank you."

"I had one of the porters prepare your beds, and there's a washroom just at the end of the car. Dining car is a few beyond that. Will you be wanting a meal tonight?"

"We've already eaten, thank you," says Maren.

"Past the dining cars you'll find the saloon, where you'll be performing tomorrow at midday," says the porter. "It's a goodly space."

"Excellent," Mr. Dorian says, closing the door. "Good night."

Will stows his small suitcase on a shelf and perches on the bench. His knees almost touch the lower bunk.

"You were rash in the colonist cars," Mr. Dorian tells him quietly. "You revealed more than you should have."

Will wondered if he'd be reprimanded. "I'm sorry. But it was terrible, what Peters was doing. Why doesn't Sam Steele put a stop to it?"

"The Mounties don't patrol the colonist cars," Mr. Dorian says. "They're left to sort out their own affairs."

"I'll talk to my father about it," says Will. "They're too crammed back there. Cattle are treated better."

"I agree with Will," Maren says. "It's not fair."

"Many things aren't fair," says Mr. Dorian placidly—but for the first time, Will realizes there's anger beneath this unnerving calm of his. "My father's people came from France to claim this land. Then the English came and took it from the French. Later the Americans tried to take it from the English. As a Métis I've seen my people shunted and shamed. I'm not numb to the hardship of these new colonists. But they are, after all, just another group of Europeans come to take land that once belonged only to the Natives."

Will hasn't thought of this, and doesn't know how to reply. It's all more complicated than he can fathom.

"Nonetheless," the ringmaster says, "it was a very kind thing that you did for that boy. And your performance was excellent."

"It was?" Will says, surprised by this praise.

"One of the best debuts I've witnessed."

"I was terrified."

"It didn't show. And those drawings you did were remarkable. Such energy!"

Will didn't even get a chance to see them properly, they were whisked away so fast. He blushes. He can't remember his father ever complimenting him like this.

"You'll give him a swelled head," Maren says.

"I think he's got a very steady head on his shoulders. Now, William, why don't we visit the washrooms and allow Maren to change."

Will wonders how he's supposed to stay clean. He can't wash properly because of the face paint. Brushing his teeth is impossible since his toothbrush and paste are neatly laid out on the gleaming porcelain sink in his first-class stateroom. He supposes he can just use his finger and water. As Will removes his vest, the odd cloth spectacles he bought fall to the floor.

"What're these?" Maren asks, picking them up.

"Oh." He feels foolish. "I got them in the Junction. . . ."

"Muskeg spectacles," says Mr. Dorian.

Will's hardly surprised the ringmaster knows about them—he seems to know about everything bizarre. "Is it true?" he asks. "About the hag?"

"Some people think so. I've never seen her myself. And I only started hearing stories once the train went through." He nods reflectively. "It's like the rails cut a scar across the continent and released all sorts of things. But the explanation may be quite simple. Perhaps some people get hypnotized by the barren landscape and the moonlight. A kind of lunacy. And that's why they throw themselves into the bog."

"All I can see is shadows of things," says Maren, trying on the spectacles.

"That's the point," says Will. "You're not supposed to look in her eyes."

Maren takes them off and slips them back into Will's vest. "Seems far-fetched to me."

"We're passing through the muskeg tonight," Will says

uneasily, remembering the postmaster's comment.

"We'll keep the curtains closed," says Mr. Dorian. "Now, shall we go?"

In the wash car Will and Mr. Dorian wait their turn for the crowded sinks and toilets. A man with a hairy back sluices water under his arms and makes puddles on the floor. He glances suspiciously at Mr. Dorian and Will in the mirror. Will is aware how they stand out—an Indian fortune-teller and a Métis gentleman in a suit.

Afterward, as they walk back to their compartment, Will sees the rear door of the carriage open and Lieutenant Samuel Steele step inside.

Will is overwhelmed by a strange mixture of emotions. Elation, for there's the Mountie in his scarlet uniform, looking as impregnable as a mountain fortress! But disappointment, too. Is his adventure over so soon? It seems too simple, too quick.

All he has to do is call out and tell his story. He'll be escorted back to first class. He'll see his father. Brogan and his men will be apprehended.

He hesitates only a moment before stepping toward the Mountie. Mr. Dorian's hand closes firmly around his upper arm. The sensation is curiously familiar, and he realizes it's how Mackie held him back when he was first brought before Brogan. In confusion Will looks up at Mr. Dorian, fear fluttering through him. The ringmaster stares down at him calmly, and gives an almost imperceptible shake of his head.

Will knows he could shout out for help and the Mountie would come. But he doesn't. He trusts Mr. Dorian. There must be a reason for his wanting silence.

"Ah, Mr. Dorian," says the Mountie, "I saw your performance our first night out. Marvelous."

"Thank you, Lieutenant," says Mr. Dorian. "We're looking forward to performing for you again in a few nights."

"And who is this fellow here?"

"Amit, our spirit artist. He might have drawn you blindfolded, with utter accuracy, but now that he's seen you, he will have to draw someone else."

The Mountie chuckles. "A shame. Take good care. You can find some rough types on board in the lower classes."

"We'll be most cautious."

"We're passing through the muskeg tonight, gentlemen. Best to keep your curtains closed."

"Indeed," says Mr. Dorian.

Will feels a lump in his throat, and can't help looking back as Samuel Steele disappears from sight. With leaden footsteps he follows Mr. Dorian to their compartment. As soon as the ringmaster has locked the door, Will whispers:

"Why didn't you want me to talk to him?"

"What's happened?" asks Maren from the top bunk. She's in her nightdress. Even in his distress Will notices how pretty she looks with her hair down.

"We passed Samuel Steele in the corridor," Mr. Dorian tells her.

"Don't you trust him?" Will wants to know. "You can't think he's in with Brogan!"

"I'd trust Lieutenant Steele with my life. No, he's the most honorable of men. But if you'd gone to him, William, and poured out your story, Brogan would have been apprehended—"

"But that's good!" Will says, confused.

"—and the funeral car would no doubt have been placed under very careful surveillance."

Mr. Dorian says nothing more, just watches Will patiently.

"You want the golden spike too," Will breathes in amazement.

An amused smile twitches Mr. Dorian's lips. "No. What I want is entirely different."

"But you do want something inside the funeral car?"

"Indeed."

"You want to *rob* the Boundless?"

"There's a painting I need."

"A painting!" he exclaims. "You expect me to believe that? Just a painting?"

"As an aspiring artist," Mr. Dorian replies wryly, "I'm surprised you don't have a higher opinion of the arts."

"Is it very valuable?"

"Some think it is. I offered Van Horne a small fortune for it years ago. If he'd sold it to me, I wouldn't need to steal it now."

Will has a sudden recollection of Mr. Dorian on the company train, talking to the rail baron.

"It's the same one?" Will asks. "The blacksmith's shop?"

"Ah. You do remember. Van Horne loved that painting. Why, I'm not sure. I find it rather mediocre myself."

"Then why do you want it?"

"That's my business."

In astonishment Will turns to Maren. When her eyes slide guiltily away, a sinkhole opens inside him. He swallows, his mouth dry.

"You knew about this?"

Slowly she gives a nod.

He looks back to Mr. Dorian. "I thought you were protecting me—"

"We *are* protecting you, Will," Maren says.

"—but you're just using me!" Looking from her to Mr. Dorian, he feels hurt—and for the first time with them, frightened. "My key! That's what you want, isn't it?"

Mr. Dorian sits down on the lower bunk and starts methodically unlacing his shoes. "Not at all. I have my own key."

From a chain inside his jacket, the ringmaster produces a familiar-looking key and holds it out to Will.

"How?" Will asks in amazement.

"It was in your father's pocket during our show. I simply took an impression in a block of clay and had my chief machinist make a copy."

Will plays the scene back in his mind. The audience was stupefied by the train's passage through time zones—or Mr. Dorian's mesmerism, or both. The ringmaster could easily have done many things, invisibly.

"What do you want me for, then?" he demands uneasily.

"All we need is your cooperation—and silence," says Mr. Dorian. "Just two more nights, William. Then you'll be free to return to your father."

"'Free,'" he says numbly, "which means I'm a prisoner now?"

"Perhaps I chose my words poorly," says Mr. Dorian. "I hope you will see your way to helping us."

"Help you?" he says, anger suddenly steaming through him. "Why should I help you? You're just a couple thieves!"

"William, you're tired . . . ," says the ringmaster.

Mr. Dorian is looking at him with his dark eyes, and Will does feel exceedingly tired. Last night he hardly got any sleep at all.

"You've been going hard for a long time," says Mr. Dorian. "Anyone would feel very, very tired."

Will wrenches his gaze away from the ringmaster.

"Don't hypnotize me!" he says.

"I'm saying you need rest, William," Mr. Dorian says. "Rest is what you need more than anything else right now. If you'd just listen to me, listen to sense—"

Will raises his voice to drown out the ringmaster's. "Brogan's trying to kill me! The longer I wait, the more chance he has of finding me!"

"Yes, and we've disguised you so Brogan *won't* find you. We took you in without asking you a single question and harbored you."

"We'll protect you, Will," says Maren.

He can't meet her eye. He's been stupid. He thought she truly liked him, but she was just pretending so they could string him along like a puppy.

"You can't protect me against a knife, or a pistol!" he scoffs.

"You'll certainly make it much harder if you draw attention to yourself," Mr. Dorian says softly.

"And what about my father!" he carries on. "Who's to say Brogan won't try to kill him!"

"Keep your voice down, Will!" Maren says sharply.

"I've got to warn him now!"

She looks ill at ease but says nothing.

Mr. Dorian says, "Your father is safe."

"You can't know that! You probably don't even care!"

"Two nights, William. That's all I ask."

Mr. Dorian stands and walks to the door, blocking the exit. There is nothing menacing about his posture, but Will knows if he were to try to reach the door, Mr. Dorian would stop him. Will could never overpower him, and the thought fills him with fear.

So he nods and says no more.

But he already knows what he will do, later tonight.

* * *

Brogan shivers as he enters colonist class, glad of the heat but not the ripe stench. He makes his way to Peters's car and finds the Englishman stretched out on a cushioned bench, reading the newspaper.

"How's business?" says Brogan, eyeing the shelves, trying to judge how much trade Peters has done.

"Bit slow today," says Mr. Peters.

"I told you, you gouge too deep, you'll cut off your own leg."

"You'll want your share, I daresay," says Peters, stirring himself reluctantly and reaching under the bench for a strongbox.

"Keep it for now," Brogan says. "As a down payment. You get the stuff I asked for earlier?"

"Ah. Indeed I did." From a shelf he takes down a small wooden box, and then pries off the lid. Nestled in sand is a slim wooden vial.

Brogan draws it out carefully, reads the label, then opens the vial and sniffs.

Peters smirks. "An acceptable vintage?"

"Suits me just fine."

Brogan takes a pouch from his pocket, fills it with sand, and slips the vial inside.

"You're very casual, sir," says Peters a little nervously.

"When you've worked with this stuff as much as I have, you know what's allowed and what's not. And I think there was something else you said you could sell me."

"Of course," says Peters. From the counter he takes a shallow case, and opens it.

"That's the stuff," says Brogan, reaching for the pistol.

Peters pulls it back. "Expensive things you're purchasing."

"You'll get your payment. Don't you worry."

"Before you blow yourself up, is preferable to me."

One of Peters's guards clears his throat and taps his rifle butt against the floor.

Brogan sniffs and pulls a small wad of bills from his pocket. He peels a few off and hands them to Peters. "I'm feeling generous."

"Big plans, no doubt," says Peters.

"Yep. You ain't seen that boy I told you about by any chance?"

At this, Peters's eyes became more sly. "The redheaded boy?"

Brogan looks at him, hard. "That's the one."

"I believe you said you'd pay for that information."

Gritting his teeth, Brogan peels off a couple more bills and hands them over.

"You might want to take a look at the Indian boy traveling with Mr. Dorian."

"Why would I want to do that?" Brogan's voice is hostile.

"He's not who he says he is."

"My men saw that kid when he was walking up the train."

Peters shrugs. "The porter, Drurie, said he doesn't speak English, but one of my men overheard him talking. And he had three dollars on him. Seems an awful lot for a circus brat."

"I hope this ain't some goose chase, Peters."

"You won't know unless you chase the goose."

In his guts Brogan knows Peters might be right. "They still here?"

"Moved on to third class for the night."

"I'm much obliged to you."

"My pleasure. Do you plan on buying some bullets for that pistol?"

In the middle bunk Will waits, seething with anger and fear.

Below him Mr. Dorian snores softly; above him Maren is silent. The room is nearly pitch-dark, except for the faintest moon glow coming from around the curtains. He's lost track of how long he's been waiting, but surely they must be asleep by now.

What a fool he's been, to be taken in by these two. All those stories about circus folk being scoundrels—all true! Despite Mr. Dorian's fancy manners and clever tricks, he's just a common thief. And Maren, too. Didn't she steal his sasquatch tooth? He wants to transform her into a villain, but he keeps seeing the lively-eyed girl he met three years ago in the mountains. Furious, he crumples the image up like a ruined drawing. He's got to get out of here.

All he has to do is swing himself quietly off the bunk and

make it to the door, and then he'll be free to run. He's worried about passing between cars. If the brakemen are still watching, he might be spotted. And what about passing between classes without his ticket? Surely the porters will believe his story. If he makes a ruckus, they'll at least drag him before Samuel Steele—unless they're working for Brogan. But not everyone can be working for him.

He takes a slow breath and tenses his muscles.

"Will," whispers Maren from the bunk above.

He says nothing, just closes his eyes. He hears her shifting and knows she's leaning over the side, peering at him. She prods him in the shoulder.

"I know you're awake."

He doesn't reply.

"Don't go," she says.

He lies still.

She pokes him in the eye.

"Ow!" he gasps.

"Sorry—did I get your eye?"

"Yes!"

He can see the shape of Maren's head, her hair spilling darkly down. Below them Mr. Dorian stirs, but then resumes snoring softly.

"I'm sorry," she whispers. "I just meant to poke your head. I know you're planning on leaving."

"What're you talking about?"

"If you go, Mr. Dorian won't be able to rob the funeral car."

"You get a cut, I suppose?"

"Not really."

Will frowns. "Not *really*? What does that mean?"

"I don't care about the painting. He just needs me to turn off the electricity."

"Why can't he do it himself?"

"The keyhole's underneath the funeral car—and the train will be moving."

"Moving?"

Her voice is unconcerned. "I can do it. I've been practicing."

He remembers her in the gymnasium, shimmying down the tightrope on her back. The image makes him queasy now.

"Is he forcing you to do this?"

"Not exactly."

"How, then?"

She sighs. "If I do it, he says he'll release me from my contract—my brothers, too. And he'll pay me five thousand dollars."

Will inhales sharply. That's a lot of money.

"We'll be able to start up our own show, my whole family. My father's leg won't heal properly, ever. No one'll ever hire him again. I need that money if we want to be together in one place. This is my chance to get free."

"Still. Thieving, it ain't right. There's gotta be another way."

Without noticing, he has fallen back into his old way of

talking, words smacking together like shunted boxcars.

"And what would you do for me, Will Everett? Are you going to rescue me?"

Will blushes, glad it's dark. "I wouldn't know how. It just don't . . . doesn't . . . seem right, your risking your life."

"I'm not worried."

"No chains can bind you, no lock hold you."

"That's right. Please, Will. Stay."

He doesn't want to be swayed by her. He still doesn't trust her. He thought she liked him, but how can he know properly now? Yes, they're helping him, but they're also using him. And what kind of man would ask a girl to do something so dangerous? And all for a painting?

"You'll stay with us?" Maren asks him.

"Yes," he says.

"You're lying."

She's right, but he still doesn't trust her. For all he knows, she's invented her father's injury and her plans to start her own show. Maybe the painting is a lie too, and they're really both after the gold spike.

"I'm going to sleep," he says.

"I'll stay up all night, watching you."

"Suit yourself," he says, and turns to face the wall. He has no intention of falling asleep. He'll wait her out. But he can no longer fight his exhaustion, and before long he's fast asleep.

* * *

Guided by lantern light, Brogan, Mackie, and Chisholm make their sure-footed way, single file, atop the Boundless.

On either side of the track stretches the Shield, a crust of ancient rock broken only by huge swaths of bottomless muskeg. Wizened trees crouch, rocking like old crones trying to stay warm against the cutting wind. The water glints restlessly, as though it wants to rise and spread. Brogan has seen this landscape in daylight and moonlight, in lightning and in blinding sun—and nothing improves it. It's the most godforsaken waste he can imagine.

"We shouldn't be out here," he hears Chisholm say behind him. "The hag."

Brogan glances back with a sneer. "What about the hag?"

Chisholm's cheeks are sunken in shadow. "Just that they say she's more active in moonlight."

"There ain't no hag," Brogan says. "And if there is, I'll give her a thumping she won't forget. If you'd recognized that boy when you seen him, we wouldn't need to be out here at all."

"Had that giant with him anyway," says Chisholm.

"Not anymore," says Brogan, turning.

If that half-breed magician thinks he can spirit away the boy, he's sadly mistaken. A bit of face paint might fool the likes of Chisholm, but Brogan will know if he sees him. He should've suspected something when Dorian called him by his real name back in the circus cars. Who'd told him that? If it was the boy, that meant he was still alive and on the train.

And if he's on the train, he'll be in third class. There's not too many places they could put three circus performers for the night. They'll be sleeping by now, and the butt of Brogan's pistol will keep the ringmaster and the girl that way.

And for the boy, nice and quiet—the knife.

From the locomotive comes the long hard blast of the whistle. There is no more urgent sound to a brakeman. Sudden stop.

"Get back to your cars!" Brogan shouts to Chisholm and Mackie.

Down the length of the Boundless, lantern lights flicker as men rush to the rooftops, hustling for the brake wheels. Another long desperate whistle blast fills the night—and then another. It's an emergency, maybe something up ahead blocking the tracks. . . .

As he bolts back to his own station, Brogan already feels the train slowing. He glances down and sees the water nearly at the tracks, and lapping higher still. He knows what's happened.

Muskeg.

Will dreams there is a woman standing at the foot of his bed, screaming. She looks directly at him and, with a quick jerk of her hand, drags the covers off his body.

When he wakes, the screaming has become the frantic blast of a steam whistle and the shriek of brakes. His body presses hard against the bunk's safety rail as the train comes to a nervous standstill. A tremor runs through her steel skin, like a horse eager to bolt. Beyond the walls of their tiny compartment, Will hears the rumblings of surprised passengers. A baby's thin-edged cry wells up from a distant berth.

When he tries to sit up, he realizes he's been handcuffed to the bunk.

"Hey!" he says, yanking against the manacles.

"She's locked you up," Mr. Dorian says quietly from the darkness. "No doubt for your own protection." He's sitting on the bench, and appears to be already dressed.

"My own protection?" Will exclaims.

"You were thinking of running," the ringmaster says. "You might've been caught."

"You can't keep me locked up!"

"William, your voice, please."

"I could holler for help!"

Mr. Dorian is suddenly beside the bunk, his face fierce in the shadows. "You could, but you won't. Because if you do, a porter will eventually come. Questions will be asked. While they're trying to figure out what to do with you, news will spread quickly through the brakemen. Before you even reach second class, Brogan will visit you, and his knife will find the soft place between your ribs."

Will says nothing for a moment, breathing hard. "Why've we stopped?"

"I was just going to find out. There might've been an accident."

He thinks instantly of his father. "What kind of accident?"

"Stay here."

Will jangles the handcuffs defiantly. "I can't go anywhere else, can I?"

Mr. Dorian slips out the door and closes it behind him.

"Maren!" Will says, thumping the bottom of her bunk.

She mumbles something that sounds like "No," and turns over, deep asleep. He kicks at the underside of her bunk and only succeeds in hurting his toes.

Outside the door he hears some footsteps and then someone, maybe a porter, saying, "Part of the track's been flooded. They're working to lay new rails . . . nothing to worry about. Shouldn't be too long . . . used to this kind of thing . . ."

Will twists himself around in the bunk and parts the curtains. The muskeg is barren, yet strangely beautiful, in the moon's silver light. There is scrub and black spruce and darkly lustrous pools of water. Because the train tracks curve gently to the left, he can see the entire length of the Boundless and, far, far in the distance, the silhouette of the locomotive. It's like a small mountain on the flat horizon. Pinpricks of light twinkle from the cab. It looks undamaged. His father is most likely fine.

In that moment he feels an almost smothering sense of longing. It is a big distance, but he could run it. He wouldn't have to bother with porters and passports. He could just run along open ground, right to the locomotive. He could jump aboard and be with his father. And he would've rescued himself—without anyone's help.

With a gasp he spots a woman standing at the side of the track, looking in at him. Their eyes meet. A chill sweeps over Will's body, and he realizes she's the woman from his dream.

He lets the curtains fall back, presses his hand against them, as if he can erase what he's just seen.

What have I done, what have I done?

He blinks, trying to flush the image from his mind. But he can't.

A wind blows outside the carriage, carrying with it the faint whinny of horses and the rusty moan of cattle. Will doesn't want to turn his head, because he is afraid—no, he is *certain*—that there is someone beside him on the bunk. In vain he tries to trace the wavery lines of the curtains, but his eyes won't cooperate. They want to slide away. He feels his head turning, as though some brutish schoolmaster has a hand on his skull.

She is crouched beside him, her limbs unnaturally folded, looking at him in terrible ecstasy.

He wants to scream, but his terror is bottled inside him, like in a nightmare, and the only sound he hears from himself is a dull grunt.

The hag reaches out and touches his handcuffs. They spring open.

You wanted an adventure, she says without speaking.

His heart races. Yes.

Come have an adventure, then. You can run to the locomotive. You can be with your father.

His legs swing themselves over the bunk, and he slides down to the floor, trembling like a marionette. In his long johns and vest, he jerks over to the door, opens it, and steps into the corridor. He stares straight ahead. He doesn't need to turn his head to know she's right there beside him, tied to him like a shadow. He can feel her clawlike grip on his forearm.

In another moment he has reached the door to the car. There's no porter here, and he steps outside onto the platform. Four steps take him down to the side. Thick murky water laps against the rail bed like an oily tide.

Just look, she says inside his head. *The locomotive's so close.*

He starts toward it. If he can only keep his eyes fixed on the smokestack, and not look at the woman beside him, he will get there.

But his route is taking him away from the track, and he splashes into the wet muck. It flows over his feet. He doesn't notice until it's up to his ankles.

Keep going, the voice in his ear tells him helpfully. *The shortest distance between two points is a straight line.*

The bottom is mossy, sucking at his feet as he lifts them with each slow step.

He keeps going, up to his knees now. The cold clench of

water moves up his thighs. Then the bottom drops away and he flounders up to his neck.

"Help!" he cries from his wordless mouth.

He lifts his chin high, trying to tread water without swallowing any. He flails out for something firm, but every bit of earth dissolves instantly the moment he touches it. He kicks out, trying to find purchase. The water sucks at him hungrily, and he knows it isn't normal water. It wants to pull him under. It *wants* to fill his lungs.

Not five feet away there is a blighted tree, and he thrashes toward it, spluttering, getting nowhere. The muskeg hag is crouched there amongst the gnarled roots.

He knows he will never reach that tree.

Are you enjoying your adventure? she asks soundlessly.

She is close enough so that she could reach out a hand and pull him up. Her face is expressionless. She sits watching as he sinks deeper.

Gently, she says. *Go ahead. Breathe.*

He can barely lift his arms through the dense muck.

She smiles, her eyes dead. *It's all right. Just take a deep breath.*

He goes under.

Breathe.

He fights against the urge to fill his lungs. Something pokes him hard in the side of the head, and then again, and he feels roused from a sleep. Terror pours through him. Sluggishly he lifts a hand to protect his head, but is poked again in the shoulder. He closes his hand around the thing, and feels it give a tug. Instinctively he grasps it with both hands. Dragged upward, his head breaks free. He gulps air.

He sees Maren at the other end of her long tightrope wire, his pair of muskeg spectacles over her eyes. She pulls and reels him in with all she's worth.

He kicks toward her.

"Don't look back!" she shouts.

Look back.

He starts to turn.

Look at me, William.

"Look at *me*, Will!" Maren calls, and he keeps his eyes on her, as intent as if he were drawing her. Before long her hands are gripping him and tugging, and he lurches out of the muskeg.

She is panting and crying a little too. She turns her back to the muskeg hag and hurries Will toward the train. His legs have both gone to sleep, and he can barely feel them.

"Let's get you inside," she says. "Your makeup's half washed off."

"Thank you," he wheezes.

He's startled by how far they are from the train. He stamps his feet against the earth, trying to batter feeling into them. And then he sees three figures walking toward them.

"Hey!" Brogan shouts out. "What are you doing out here!"

"Who are they?" Mackie says.

"I can't see 'em," Chisholm replies, squinting his buggy eyes at the two figures staggering out of the muskeg.

Brogan lifts his lantern, trying to catch them with his light. One of them is a girl, and the other one's leaning on her—a boy, he thinks, but can't be sure because his head is down. Who'd be stupid enough to wander out here . . . unless they were making a run for it? Brogan finds the knife in his pocket and grips it tight.

Suddenly the two figures start hobbling for the train, fast as they can.

"Get 'em!" Brogan barks, and they give chase. It's dark, his lantern light jangling around all over the mushy earth. The moon disappears behind cloud, and Brogan trips on something and goes down. The lantern is dashed from his hands and extinguished. Blind for a moment, he pushes himself up, and thinks he sees a woman's face, cheek pressed to the mud, smiling at him. Can't be right, just a shadow, and now the moon's back out and he's on his feet again and the boy is right in front of him. It's him—William Everett.

There he is. Couldn't have asked for more.

Brogan tackles him, and they both go down into two feet of muck and water.

You can drown him nice and quietly, the voice says inside his head.

"Brogan!" the boy is shouting. "Brogan! Stop!"

He's thrashing hard, the boy, dragging both of them deeper

into the bog. Brogan tries to stand, and feels his feet sink. He steadies himself, punches the boy in the face, gets his hands round his throat and pushes. The boy's head goes under, comes back up gasping, and Brogan pushes it down again, this time for good.

There you go, she says inside his head. *Hold him down. . . .*

"Brogan!" someone is shouting beside him. It's Mackie. "Brogan! Let him up! That's Chisholm!"

"Just run!" Maren hisses.

Will takes a last backward glance at Brogan, struggling with one of his own men in the bog. What happened? A third man—maybe Mackie?—is hollering from the shallows, trying to pull them both back to solid ground.

Then Will looks straight ahead and forces his numb legs to carry him as swiftly as possible toward the Boundless.

THE WORLD OF WONDERS

Mr. Dorian is waiting for them at the door to their carriage and hurriedly ushers them inside.

"Thank goodness," he says with obvious relief. "I was just about to go looking."

Will is sodden and shivering and covered in bog mud. There are a few other people in the corridor, and he hangs his head so they won't see his washed-away face.

"Just a little stroll in the muskeg," Mr. Dorian says to the curious.

Inside their compartment the ringmaster locks the door. "What happened?"

"I can't believe I opened the curtains," Will mutters.

"I woke up," says Maren, "and you were gone, and I saw the handcuffs on the floor. When I looked out the window, you were there—and there was just something about the way you were walking, like sleepwalking. It wasn't normal. So I put on those glasses of yours and hurried out."

"Well done, Maren," the ringmaster says.

"You saw her, didn't you?" Will asks her.

"It's all shadow through the spectacles. But there was definitely someone with you. She moved around a lot. Sometimes it was like her feet weren't even touching the ground."

"She came right inside," Will says. He points to the handcuffs on the floor. "She took those off. What is she?"

Mr. Dorian takes a breath. "That, I don't know. What she does is quite beyond my understanding or abilities. The world is full of wonders. Especially along this road."

"Brogan and some of his men were out there too," Maren tells the ringmaster.

Mr. Dorian turns intently to Will. "Did they recognize you?"

"I don't know. He was shouting at us. We just started running."

"I thought we were finished," Maren says, "because you were really slow at first. But then suddenly Brogan tackled one of his own men. It looked like he was trying to drown him!"

"He must've seen the hag," Will says. "She puts ideas into your head."

"Maybe he thought it was you," says Maren.

Will shivers at the thought.

"You'll want to get out of those wet clothes," Mr. Dorian tells him.

"I'm sorry," he mumbles, for the underclothes have a rich stink to them. He still feels dislocated from his body, like all the sensation hasn't quite returned to his limbs. He starts peeling off the soaking garments, then glances awkwardly over at Maren.

"I won't look," she says, turning. "Here, I'll set out your dry clothes on the bunk."

"I'll take these to the washroom to clean them," says Mr. Dorian, pushing the filthy clothes into a burlap sack and leaving the room.

Gratefully Will dries himself with a small towel and pulls on clean trousers and a shirt.

Maren is going through her bag. "Madame Lamoine gave me some extra paint for touch-ups." She produces several small jars and a brush.

Will sits on the bench, and Maren kneels before him.

"Can you fix it?" Will asks.

"It won't be nearly as good as what Madame Lamoine did, but I'll try."

Staring at him intently, she brushes paint over his cheekbones. She bites her lower lip as she works. Will knows she's just concentrating, but he still feels embarrassed to be the subject of such attention from her. He gazes at the floor, though keeps sneaking small peeks at her face. Her eyes unexpectedly meet his.

"You handcuffed me to the bunk," he says.

"I just saved your life!"

"You turned me into a prisoner!" He's still angry with her but can't quite muster the same outrage he felt earlier.

"I knew you'd run, so I manacled you."

Mr. Dorian returns and locks the cabin door behind him. He's carrying two steaming mugs.

"Hot chocolate," he says, handing them to Maren and Will. "Your clothes are hanging up to dry in the washroom."

"Thank you," Will says. "Is the train all right?"

"Quite all right. I made inquiries. A sinkhole opened up beneath the tracks, but they're working hard to fill it up with sand and gravel."

"Will we be able to get through?"

"The Boundless carries extra steel for just such eventualities."

"No one was hurt up front?" he asks, thinking of his father.

Mr. Dorian shakes his head. Will takes a sip of his hot chocolate. It's just the right sweetness and very creamy. He still isn't sure how to speak to Mr. Dorian. Is he a friend, or a prison warden?

"Are you going to handcuff me again?"

"That depends. Can we trust you?"

"Trust *me*? I'm not the thief."

"I have my reasons for being one," says the ringmaster.

"What's so special about this painting?"

"Quite simply, I can't live without it."

Will gives a sniff of laughter, but then sees the serious expression on Mr. Dorian's face.

The ringmaster looks from Will to Maren. "You have a right to know. You especially, Maren, since you're helping me. I am the inheritor of a family curse—medical in nature, not magical. My great-grandfather, a man of immense strength and vigor, died at the age of thirty-nine. My grandfather died at the same age. As did my own father. All three were felled by a sudden and massive seizure of the heart. I am two weeks away from my thirty-ninth birthday."

Looking at Mr. Dorian, Will finds it almost impossible to believe that he could suffer from any illness.

"Have you seen a doctor?" he asks.

"Many. And all say the same thing. I have some tragic flaw in my heart. There is nothing to be done about it. It is a clock that will eventually trip over itself and stop."

Will isn't sure what any of this has to do with stealing a painting.

"Given my parentage, carving out a life for myself was no easy thing," Mr. Dorian says. "But I did it. I built my circus into one of the finest in the world. But there is still too much I want to do. Too much left to achieve. I will not be snuffed out in my prime."

"But you can't know it'll happen to you, too," Maren says.

Mr. Dorian gives a dry chuckle. "The history is not promising. But I mean to thwart it."

"How?" Will asks, glancing at Maren. She looks just as confused as he feels.

"You've heard the legend of the fountain of youth, yes?"

Will nods. "But—"

"Listen a moment. The Arawak people of the West Indies told the first Spanish settlers about it. There are many accounts of a natural spring in Florida that bestowed permanent youth. A Spaniard called Juan Ponce de León found it. But he left no written record. I spent years searching for that fountain."

"But I thought you didn't believe in magic," Will says.

"I don't. Why is it any more magical than the sasquatch or the muskeg hag? You've beheld both with your own eyes. There's no magic about these things. We may not understand them yet, but they're part of our world, and anything that exists in the world is real."

"Did you find it?" Maren asks.

"The site only. The pool had long ago dried up. But I did learn that an enterprising fellow had devised a way of secretly transporting the water. He soaked up the last of it with fabric, and divided that fabric into a number of canvases. And it turned out that if you painted someone's portrait upon the canvas, that person remained young, and only his picture aged."

Will says, "This . . . it can't be true."

"Time is a mysterious thing. You've seen how it can falter when we cross a time zone. This water simply helps time forget itself. Beyond that, I have no understanding of the water's properties.

Apparently one of the canvases made its way to England, where it's been keeping a very unpleasant fellow young for many years; another went to Persia, another still to a Russian prince. One found its way to our shores and fell into the hands of a painter, one Cornelius Krieghoff. He painted a blacksmith shop on it. Clearly he had no idea. Nor did Van Horne."

There have been moments—and Will remembers each one—when he has sensed his life shift. He felt it that day in the mountains when he met Maren for the first time. And he feels it again now. The entire world seems much larger and stranger than he could ever have imagined. It now contains not only sasquatch but a muskeg hag—and canvases that can trick time itself. He certainly doesn't understand it, and he's not even sure he believes it.

"I need that painting," says Mr. Dorian, "and I happen to know it's inside Van Horne's funeral car. It's just hanging unseen, like a relic in an Egyptian pharaoh's tomb. I want my portrait painted on the back. From that moment on my body will not age. My heart's clock will not snap its spring. And that, William Everett, is my story. What do you say? Am I a villain?"

Will thinks carefully. It's still stealing, but it's hard to care very much, when it's something that otherwise is just going to hang in the darkness forever. Why leave it there when it could save a man's life? And yet . . .

"Getting Maren to crawl underneath . . . ," he says hesitantly. "You shouldn't. It's not right to ask her to do something so dangerous."

Mr. Dorian smiles. "Your chivalry is a credit to you, William. But I think Maren has made her own decision."

"Yes," she says, surprising Will with the annoyance in her voice. "And please don't bring it up again."

He frowns. "All right. . . ."

"It's bad luck having someone around who doesn't think you can do something," she says. "Hands."

He stretches out his hands so she can reapply more skin paint. "I think you can do it," he says as she roughly brushes makeup on. "But that just turns the power off. Do you even know where the door is?"

"Of course," says Dorian. "It's in the right side, ten feet back from the front of the car."

Will tries to conjure it before his mind's eye. He saw it only briefly that day in the Junction—he was in such a hurry to find Maren. He remembers his eyes getting lost in the complicated contours of the decorations. All those sculpted metal wreaths and garlands and ivy and blossoms and fruit. He supposes the door must be hidden there.

"And if you get the painting, who'll do your portrait?"

"Madame Lamoine," says Mr. Dorian. "She's got quite a fine hand."

"Ah," says Will, disappointed somehow.

The car gives a little forward jerk, and then another longer pull.

"There we go," says the ringmaster. "We're on our way again."

"What about Brogan and his men?" Will says. "They must've been looking for me. Why else were they out there?"

"I hope they all drowned," Maren mutters.

"I doubt that," says Mr. Dorian. "But I'm hopeful they might not have seen you properly. In any event, there are too many people up and about tonight for them to try anything. Our door is locked, and I have no need of more sleep. I hope you're not thinking of running again, William."

Will lets out a deep breath. Twice they've saved his life—and that counts for a lot. Even if he wanted to run, he doesn't have an ounce of energy left.

"I'm not going anywhere," he says, and is rewarded with a smile from Maren.

"Good." From his breast pocket Mr. Dorian takes one of the Native tools Will saw mounted on his stateroom wall.

"What is that?" Will asks uneasily.

"A Cree hide-scraper. Tricks can be useful, but I've often found this can be equally persuasive." He rests the wickedly sharp metal blade on his lap and turns to face the door.

"Are you standing guard because of Brogan? Or because of me?" Will asks.

Mr. Dorian glances back with a smile. "You should try to get a little more sleep before daybreak, both of you. We have a performance at noon."

CHAPTER 12

IN THE SALOON

Will sleeps late, and when he wakes, Maren is already dressed, sitting cross-legged on the floor and looking out the window.

"Where's Mr. Dorian?" he asks.

"He's gone to get us some breakfast. He doesn't want us walking around."

Outside the window, trees flash past, their leaves bright with the morning sun. The Boundless has left the muskeg behind. Will sees farmland, enclosed with rough fences, mist still pooled in the low fields. There's a house and barn in the distance, a horse in a pasture.

From his bunk he pulls his trousers and shirt from a peg. He dresses under the covers.

"Do you think it's true?" he asks.

"The canvas? I don't know. He knows so much about so many things. Nothing tricks him—he *knows* all the tricks." She shakes her head. "If he thinks the fountain of youth is real, it must be."

"How well do you know him?"

"Not well. I don't think anyone does. He's charming when he wants, fiercer than he needs to be sometimes."

"Is he a good man?" Will says hopefully.

"Well, he runs a good circus. No one's better at finding talent and putting together new attractions. He's got the best show in the Dominion, and he wants to be the best in the world. Some people think he's a slave driver, because he gets people to sign contracts for a long time."

"Like yours."

She nods. "He pays pretty well, and treats the marvels pretty well, but he keeps most of the money they bring in. I heard he had a pretty hard life, growing up."

"Because he's Métis," Will says.

"He hardly talks about it. But I think something bad might have happened to his mother. That's about all I know. He's a mystery—like everyone, I guess."

"It's just . . ." Will shakes his head, searches for the right words. "Why should *he* get his portrait on that canvas? Why not the sick boy in colonist class? Why not you? Why does he deserve it? They say the world's full of saints, and I'm pretty sure he's not one of them."

He looks at the door to their compartment. No one's guarding it right now.

"Still deciding whether to help him?" Maren asks.

Will sighs. "I'm not sure about him. But I want to help *you*."

"You'll stay?"

"I'll stay."

Will feels his face heat up in the glow of her smile.

She takes her remarkable spool of tightrope from the shelf and brushes some dried muskeg muck off it.

"Why'd you bring it with you last night?" he asks.

"It's kind of a habit. You'll think it's silly, but just having it with me makes me feel better. Like I can get out of any scrape."

"That doesn't sound silly," he says. "It makes complete sense to me."

"I have a dream sometimes that I'm crossing a big space on my wire. . . ."

"Niagara Falls?" Will asks.

"Maybe. And I'm halfway across, and there's water beneath me, mist churning. I'm so far from land, I can't even see either shore."

"Is it scary?"

"Not at first. It always starts off peaceful. But then I don't know which way I'm supposed to go."

"If it were my dream, I'd probably fall," Will says.

"Oh, I have those, too. Anyway, my spool comes with me everywhere. Just like your pencil, I suppose."

Will laughs in surprise. "Yeah. I guess my thoughts . . . well, they float free when my hand and eyes are busy. It helps me think things through. Also, I love it."

"I can tell."

"It's fun when you get to certain parts."

"Like what?"

"Oh, I don't know. There's parts you just know are going to be fun. Like a curtain, with all the folds. And shadows, I love those too."

"It seems like it'd be hard."

He laughs. "Not as hard as wire walking!"

"When I'm up there, I feel like I can do anything."

"Well," Will says. "I'm not that good a drawer yet. But I want to be." He thinks of the conversation he had with his father on the first night. "My father wants me to join the company as a clerk."

"Is that what you want?"

"Well, I was thinking, if I worked for the railway, I could maybe make things better for the colonists. Get rid of people like Peters."

"That would be good," Maren agrees.

"And I might be able to help design things," Will tells her. "Bridges and ships maybe."

"I'm sure you'd be good at it."

"It'd be a good job," Will says.

"Yeah. You don't really want to do it, do you?"

"No. There's an art school in San Francisco I want to go to."

"So why don't you?"

"My father doesn't want to pay."

She sniffs. "You could work. Pay your own way. I was working from the age of five."

He feels childish. Even when he was poor, Will never had to work. Those years when it was just him and his mother, he took care of himself, and ran errands and chopped wood and pumped water and helped wash and clean. But he never worked. Plenty of kids did. In factories, or workshops. He was spared that, anyway. It sounded hard to make money on your own.

"Maybe I'm not suited for a hard life," he says. "That's what my father thinks."

"Do you believe that?"

He shrugs. "If Mr. Dorian hadn't taken me in, Brogan would've killed me. I got hagged—I didn't even remember to put those muskeg spectacles on. I would've drowned if it weren't for you. . . ."

"You're looking at it the wrong way around," she says. "You got free of Brogan! You ran the deck of the Boundless—*at night*! That's something!"

He nods, and smiles a little. "I like your way of looking at things better."

"So you should go to this art school of yours."

* * *

When Will opens the door to the saloon car, noise pours over him like a cascade of poker chips. A song peals from the upright piano in the corner, nearly obliterated by the laughter and stamping of the patrons.

A high wooden bar runs almost the entire length of the carriage. Men perch atop stools, their boots on the brass foot rail, drinking and jetting their tobacco juice into spittoons. Behind the bar the wall is a long stretch of mirror, reflecting the room back at itself, so it seems even bigger and more crowded. A pair of stuffed pheasants stands startled atop the counter. The antlered head of an elk watches solemnly over the gambling tables.

Gusting through the maelstrom of smells (stale beer, cigar smoke, sweaty leather) is the scent of women's perfume—something Will hasn't smelled since his first night aboard the train. But this fragrance is totally unlike the pale scents he's used to sniffing in drawing rooms, and on his mother. This smell is big and loud, to match the colorful pleated dresses he sees on the women serving tables, or dancing with the men. The dancing seems all the more raucous because of the general rocking and rolling of the train. Everyone lurches and reels.

The saloon is a double-decker car, and on the second level, men stand against the railing with their drinks, watching the dancers and the card tables. Doors lead into small rooms, and Will spots a man being led into one by a woman with bare shoulders. He catches Maren looking at him and blushes.

Their porter ushers them over to the middle of the saloon. Against a wall they've made a small platform out of whiskey crates and hung a curtain across it so there's a little backstage area for the performers.

"I hope this is all right," the porter says.

"I'm sure we'll have their undivided attention," Mr. Dorian replies drily.

"Oh, they've come to see you," the porter says. "That's why it's so crowded."

At one of the card tables a man stands up with a whoop of glee and a fistful of cash. Immediately one of the other men launches himself at the winner, and they tumble about on the floor, beating each other. Behind the bar the barkeep takes a sledgehammer from its brackets on the wall and slams it loudly onto the counter. Quickly the fight breaks up and several men limp away, bloodied.

"Well, I'm looking forward to this," Maren says as the porter swiftly departs.

"Shall we prepare?" Mr. Dorian says, ushering Will and Maren behind the curtain.

Hidden from the saloon, Will removes his coat and thinks: *After this, just two more performances, and then I'm back in first class.* But another part of him surges with nerves and excitement for the show.

They arrange their props carefully. Removing his jacket,

Mr. Dorian suddenly winces, his face pale, but then he takes a breath and stands taller.

"Are you all right?" Will asks.

Without a word the ringmaster steps through the gap in the curtain.

Will and Maren put their faces to the opening. He's aware of the faint metallic mustiness of her jeweled costume, but also the gentler fragrance of soap and skin and hair that seems such an innocent smell in the saloon's oppressive beeriness.

Mr. Dorian stands on the makeshift stage, saying nothing. Somehow his mere presence quiets the crowd. The noise ebbs like a gale that has blown itself out. Silently, methodically, Mr. Dorian rolls back his sleeves to the elbows.

Will has no idea what the ringmaster will do. He doesn't discuss it ahead of time. So Will is just as curious as everyone else. Mr. Dorian lifts his arms into the air, fingers spread. Then he closes his hands, and when he opens them again, he's holding a card in each one, between thumb and first finger. Will can see they're both the two of hearts.

A few grunts and whispers rumble across the saloon.

"My granny does it better," someone sneers.

Behind the curtain Will whispers to Maren, "They don't seem too impressed."

"Just wait."

"What's he going to do?"

"You'll see."

Mr. Dorian holds the cards aloft, turning them from side to side, showing the crowd they are just single cards he holds, no more.

With a flick of his wrists, a three of hearts is added to each hand. There are a few grunts of appreciation, and a smattering of tepid applause. Mr. Dorian stamps his foot against the crate floor, as though reprimanding them for their disbelief, and a third card appears in each of his hands. Very slowly he waves his arms in the air like entranced snakes, closer together, farther apart. And more cards keep appearing in his hands: a five of hearts, a six, a seven . . . and he is moving faster, stamping time with his heels like a flamenco dancer, the cards forming fans.

The room is totally silent now except for the furious beat of Mr. Dorian's heels. Even the poker games have come to a standstill, all the cardsharps staring in frank admiration.

A jack of hearts, a queen, a king. Mr. Dorian's arms flash in the air in ever more intricate patterns—and then with a flourish an ace of hearts appears in each hand, completing the full suit.

The room bursts into applause, but Mr. Dorian isn't done yet. He throws his two sets of cards into the air, and they fan out in slow intersecting arcs, shuffling themselves in midair. The ringmaster stands observant, hands uplifted as if conducting them, urging them on as they spiral about one another.

"Enough!" he shouts to them, and they cascade back into his hands. He combines them into a single pile and starts to put them back into his trouser pocket. Then he changes his mind and hurls the cards into the audience—but they become two dozen white pigeons that soar up to the ceiling and disappear through the high windows.

The applause is redoubled, with floor stamping and whistling.

"Gentlemen and Ladies, I am Mr. Dorian, and this is Zirkus Dante."

He has them now, completely, as he effortlessly takes them through several more feats and wonders. He hypnotizes a few members of the audience; he turns a man's hair into a bat, and returns it to his head; he walks up six invisible steps.

Through the fug of cigarette and cigar smoke, Will sees a man shoulder his way to the bar. He throws a bill onto the counter and points at a bottle on the shelf. Will's entire body tenses. Drink in hand, Brogan turns and watches Mr. Dorian.

"He didn't drown," Maren whispers, before Will can say a word.

And then to a great surge of applause, Mr. Dorian steps back behind the curtain.

"Brogan's in the crowd," Will tells him.

"Should we keep Will back?" Maren asks the ringmaster.

"He may leave before you go on," he tells Will. "If not, we'll keep you back."

Mr. Dorian steps out to introduce Maren and help her rig her tightrope between the mezzanine railings. Wolf whistles rise up from the crowd.

Will stares at Brogan, who's got his back to the bar. Beer in hand, he is watching Maren as she hops onto the tightrope. He looks pretty comfortable. Will doesn't see him leaving anytime soon. When Maren finishes her first act and comes backstage, Brogan is still there, a fresh drink in hand.

"We'll go straight to the finale," Mr. Dorian tells them. He steps out before the audience.

"Ladies and Gentlemen. To conclude our performance, I welcome the Miraculous Maren once more."

Maren is about to make her entrance, when from the audience someone cries, "Little Sultan!"

The breath catches in Will's throat.

"Where's the Little Sultan!" calls someone else.

"The brown boy who draws!"

"We want to see the Little Sultan!"

"Someone must have spread the word about you," breathes Maren.

"I want me portrait done!" a woman with a terrifyingly loud voice shouts.

Mr. Dorian steps back behind the curtain and looks at Will. "There's nothing to be done. Will you go out?"

Will's throat is dry. He nods. He walks out to a cheer that does not seem altogether well-meaning. He avoids looking at Brogan but is aware of him staring his way, a hot spot in Will's peripheral vision. After bowing, he turns his back on the audience. As Mr. Dorian makes his introductions, Maren appears with the scarf. The first volunteer is selected.

Seated on the stool, eyes covered, Will begins to draw the image reflected in Maren's sequins. His mind feels scattered and his hand shakes. The drawing is a clumsy one, but Mr. Dorian whisks it away after the customary minute and holds it up for the audience and the subject. With relief Will hears the man say:

"Ain't half-bad! That brown boy's got a gift!"

Another cheer rises from the audience, this one sounding more genuine.

"He's making asses of you all!" says a voice from the crowd.

Will does not need to see the speaker to know it's Brogan.

"Is there a problem, good sir?" Mr. Dorian asks.

"None of this 'sir' nonsense, Mr. Dorian." His voice is getting closer. "You and me, we're old friends, ain't we, Mr. Dorian?"

Reflected in Maren's sequins, Will blurrily sees Brogan moving through the crowd toward the stage. He sits rigidly, trying to control his breathing. He wants to bolt.

He killed the guard—he could kill me.

"I got myself a feeling this boy of yours is a fraud, Mr. Dorian."

"I assure you, sir, Amit is nothing of the sort."

"I'd like a portrait done, then!"

"Very well, sir. I always enjoy making a believer from a non-believer. If you would stand here . . ."

"No, no," Brogan says, and Will sees him pulling a black scarf from his neck. "Use this."

There is a taut silence in the room, like a storm about to break. Why doesn't the bartender do anything? And why doesn't Samuel Steele come on his rounds?

"If you have any doubts," Mr. Dorian says, "you are free to tie our scarf around your own face."

"No, there's some trick to it—that don't fool me. You use mine."

Will swallows.

"Very well," Mr. Dorian says. "It has no effect on Amit's abilities."

"Well, allow me, then," says Brogan snidely, thumping onto the stage.

Will's head snaps back as the trick scarf is dragged from his head. He hasn't felt such mortal danger since he was chased through the forest. He forces himself to meet Brogan's gaze, praying that the man will not see the secret behind his eyes. His heart thrashes against his ribs.

Will looks at Mr. Dorian, who says something to him in Hindi for good measure. Will repeats one of the three phrases he's learned, and Mr. Dorian nods.

The brakeman's scarf reeks of tobacco and hair grease. Brogan ties it tightly. With difficulty Will swallows, but knows he must remain calm.

"That's it," he hears Brogan say. "Let's see him draw!"

"A portrait of you, sir?" Mr. Dorian asks.

"Nah. He's had a good look at me. Let's see him do this

lady here. Come on over, darling, and have your portrait done. Stand right here in the magic circle."

A huge whoop rises from the bloodthirsty crowd, and laughter, too. They're with Brogan now, wanting a good show.

A great wall of blackness separates Will from the world. Within him, panic cavorts up its spiral staircase.

"And get that girl away from him," Will hears Brogan say behind him. "She's probably telling him things."

"Of course," says Maren, and Will hears her come closer and press the pencil and sketchbook into his blind hands. Very quickly, with the point of the pencil, she traces something across his palm. Was it the letter *B*? *B* for Brogan?

Is it a trick, then? There's no woman standing behind him, just Brogan himself? Will takes a breath. Even if he's right, does he know Brogan's face well enough? He tries to recall its details, but they're all out of focus. Putting his pencil to the paper, he instantly feels calmer. His shoulders unclench. Blind, his hand travels more quickly than usual, the tip of the pencil never leaving the paper, following the conjured contours of lips, then nose, then eyes. With a flourish he rips the page from his book and holds it aloft. He feels Dorian take it from his fingers and hold it before the saloon.

"Ladies and Gentlemen, behold his psychic powers!"

Applause and mocking laughter roils from the crowd, as well as some jeering. Is it directed at him, or Brogan?

"The boy got you there!" he hears someone cry out. "He did you good!"

Will feels the scarf being gently unwound from his head, and is surprised to see Brogan before him, staring at him intently. In Brogan's hand is the portrait. Will can't help but take a quick peek at his own work—not half-bad. The brakeman forces a smile and pats Will on the head, his thumb rubbing hard across Will's brow.

"That's a good trick, lad," he whispers. His breath smells like pickled eggs.

Will raises his eyebrows, feigning ignorance, but he worries his fear transmits itself through his pores.

"Is this man proving troublesome, Mr. Dorian?"

Will's gaze snaps instantly to the imposing form of Samuel Steele, his scarlet uniform ablaze amidst the crowd. The Mountie's eyes are fixed on Brogan. The brakeman stiffens at the sight of Steele, and then his eyes slink over to Mr. Dorian, awaiting the ringmaster's reply.

It's all Will can do to keep silent.

"No, Lieutenant Steele," Mr. Dorian says cheerfully. "A circus always welcomes audience participation."

"Very well, then," the Mountie booms out to the crowd. "Comport yourselves in an orderly manner. Any damage to person or property will be dealt with very severely. Also any low moral behavior." His eyes stray to the gallery, where the painted women smile down at him angelically.

Brogan retreats to the bar and sits watching the rest of the show with his back to the counter and an unnervingly serene look on his face. Samuel Steele remains in the saloon.

Will is glad to escape behind the curtain. For the finale Maren appears once more onstage, to whistles and kissing sounds, to perform the disappearing act. Mr. Dorian makes sure to choose a female volunteer to come and tighten the chains. But the cheeky miss can't resist chatting up the audience and shaking her lacy pleated skirt. She strokes Maren's bare shoulders and says, "Ooh-la-la, isn't she a fresh young thing, gents?"

Will wishes Maren would disappear all the faster.

Mr. Dorian covers her with the scarf. "Ladies and Gentlemen, it's been a pleasure performing for you here today. I hope that you will cherish fond memories of the Zirkus Dante, and when we next appear in your town, come and visit us properly, and you will see that the wonders you have sampled here today are but a flicker of the full flame."

And when he whisks the scarf off Maren, she is gone.

"Will you ever tell me how it's done?" Will asks when she appears behind him.

"You'd be disappointed," she says. "Isn't it better just to wonder about some things?"

"I don't know," says Will.

They put their coats on, pack up quickly, and leave the saloon, escorted by the gangly porter.

Samuel Steele nods at Will as he passes.

* * *

Will is glad when the heavy door to third class is bolted shut behind them, though he knows it won't stop Brogan. He still feels the pressure of the brakeman's calloused thumb across his temple. Did Brogan rub some of his face paint off? Will hasn't had a chance to check himself in a mirror.

A short bustling porter escorts them through a carriage lined with crew berths and maintenance compartments. Then, to Will's surprise, he opens the door to a blinding abundance of sunshine and sky. Men and women stand against the railings of a roofless flatbed carriage, taking in the view of the rolling prairies. Breathing deeply, Will smiles. After being inside for so long, it's wonderful to feel a breeze against his face.

"Observation car?" Maren asks the porter.

"No, miss. This is the shooting gallery."

Looking closer, Will now sees rifles in the hands of the passengers. At the far end of the car there is a large cabinet of more firearms. A man pays some money to a steward and selects one.

"What do they shoot?" asks Maren.

"Oh, sometimes they just like shooting off their guns," says the porter. "Soothing to some folks, I suppose. We pass wildlife from time to time, and it's good sport to see if they hit anything."

Will looks to the far horizon. There is something hypnotic about it: nothing but grassland, showing the first signs of green after the long winter—and the tracks of the Boundless cutting through it like a scar. The blue sky sits atop it all like a dome.

"Do you hear something?" he asks Maren.

It's difficult to tell above the din of the train, but he senses a deep earthly vibration, as much through the soles of his feet as in the air. And then they come. On the left side of the train, a dark wave crests a hill and swells toward them. Massive bundles of hair and brawny shoulders and horned heads. Their hoofs thunder on the ground.

"Looky here!" bellows one of the passengers, raising his rifle and taking aim. "We are goin' buffalo huntin'!"

The prairie has become a dark roiling sea. For a moment Will wonders if the sheer force of them will capsize the Boundless, for they're coming head-on. But at the last moment the animals veer off, charging alongside the train.

All the passengers push for position against the left railing now, firing shot after shot into the sea of buffalo. To Will it seems like the most senseless and unsportsmanlike thing he can imagine.

"I think I downed one!" a man shouts.

"Me too! Look at that!" another bellows.

Will sees one of the mighty beasts crumple at the front legs, plowing dust and earth before it. Other buffalo careen into it from behind.

Will glances at Mr. Dorian and sees, beyond the familiar calm of his expression, a pale fury.

"This is how you exterminate a people," the ringmaster says bitterly. "You kill all their food."

"Indians!" one of the passengers shouts.

Hard on the heels of the massive herd come dozens of Natives on horseback, some with rifles, others bows. They divide the herd expertly, shunting it in new directions. Will spots a young brave brandishing his rifle angrily at the train.

"We'd be wise to go inside now!" the steward shouts from the front of the carriage.

"Not when the hunting's this good," says a fellow, taking another shot.

"Damn redskins!" shouts another passenger with a flushed face and small close-set eyes. "They're steering them away from us!"

In horror Will watches as the fellow takes aim at the closest Native and fires off a couple of shots.

Mr. Dorian steps forward and grabs the barrel of the rifle. "What are you doing, sir?" he shouts, his eyes blazing.

"Just a warning shot is all," says the man belligerently. "What's it to you?"

"They rely entirely on these hunts for food and hides."

"Well, I'm not taking their buffalo, am I? I'm helping them!"

"Not by shooting at their hunters."

"What's one less Indian?" snorts the man just before an arrow buries itself in his heart. He staggers back, dead before he hits the ground.

"Or one less white man," murmurs Mr. Dorian.

Panic breaks out across the car. Some men run for the

exit, but most reload and start shooting at the Natives.

"Stop this!" shouts Mr. Dorian at the passengers. The ring-master's face has lost all composure; the color is high in his cheeks as he snatches one man's rifle and cracks it across his knee. "Stop this, you fools!"

"Everyone inside!" shouts the steward again, in vain.

"Mr. Dorian, sir!" the porter calls out. "Come inside now!"

With a cacophony of gunfire the Natives converge on the train. Arrows slit the air. Will crouches low and grabs Maren's hand. "Come on," he says, pulling her through the panicking crowd toward the next car.

Will smells singed fabric and notices a tendril of smoke curling from his small suitcase, just inches from his chest. He looks up in alarm. Through the churning bodies he catches a glimpse of a man at the railing, a cap shadowing his face—his rifle trained on Will. Will tenses at the sound of a dozen simul-taneous shots, and suddenly Mr. Dorian is in front of him, his thick coat swirling before Will like a cape. A rifle bullet falls from the folds of the coat and dances across the floor.

"Run now!" Mr. Dorian shouts.

Will bolts after the ringmaster, trying to stay low. As Will nears the door, he sees a Native rider pull fearlessly alongside the carriage on an amazing black horse. Its speed is incredible, outpacing the Boundless, passing unscathed through the barrage of rifle fire. The hunter pulls back his bowstring and shoots one of the passengers, then pulls another arrow from his quiver and notches it. An instinct makes Will grab Maren and push her down. There is no sound as the arrow embeds itself in the wooden post behind where Maren stood seconds before. She looks at Will, eyes wide in astonishment.

Suddenly a voice—and Will never thought a voice could be so loud—carries above the shouts and rifle reports and train clatter.

"Put down your weapons at once!"

Will turns back to see the scarlet figure of Sam Steele striding across the platform, anvil-size pistol raised high. He fires off a warning shot.

"Weapons down, do you hear, or I will open fire upon you and mow you down!" He turns to the Native hunters. "And that goes for you, too! This ends now!"

The gunfire ceases at once, and then Will, panting, is being pushed inside the next car by their porter. A group of sweaty men talk jubilantly about their skirmish. Uniformed stewards are pushing through the crowd to assist the Mountie.

"You'll need to hand over the rifles now, gentlemen," one steward says, taking the guns from the reluctant hands of the passengers. "These are the property of the Boundless and for use only on the shooting car."

"We showed those redskins!" one of the passengers whoops. "We showed 'em!"

The porter leads Will and Maren and Mr. Dorian through the car. Will's knees are wobbling, and Maren, too, looks badly shaken. She puts her lips to his ear and whispers, "Thank you."

As the porter shows them inside their compartment, Will is hardly paying attention. Mr. Dorian locks the door and then parts the curtains, peering out onto the prairie. There's no sign of buffalo or the Natives.

"Lieutenant Steele seems to have put a quick stop to the madness," he remarks, his face still drawn. He looks at Will. "That wasn't a Native that shot at you. You know that, don't you?"

Will nods. "I think it was Chisholm."

"I caught a glimpse of him. It was a perfect chance to kill you in the confusion. No one would've known."

Will looks at the bullet hole in his suitcase and feels ill.

"Thank you," he says. "You saved me from that second shot."

"A good coat serves many purposes," the ringmaster replies.

"They know who I am," Will says, fighting panic. "They're going to come for me again!"

"Quite possibly, yes," Mr. Dorian responds.

Will blinks. He was hoping for a shake of the head, some kind of reassurance.

"But they won't attempt anything during the day," Maren tells him.

"They just did!" Will exclaims.

"We'll change compartments before nightfall," Mr. Dorian says. "Until then I think it might be wise to spend as much time in public areas, the busier the better. Let's begin with a visit to the dining car. Both of you must be famished."

Eating is the last thing Will feels like doing. Someone has just tried to kill him. But after Maren changes out of her tightrope costume, the three of them venture out to the dining car.

Second class, though still a far cry from the luxury of first, is a lot more comfortable than third. The corridors have wood paneling and fabric wallpaper. Thick carpet cushions Will's footsteps and insulates the carriage from the noise of the tracks. The windows are larger and the gaslights more numerous.

In the dining room Will feels people's eyes on him, and recognizes a pair of men from the shooting car. Everywhere Will glances, he thinks he sees Brogan or Chisholm or Mackie.

When the meal arrives, it looks delicious, but Will is afraid to eat it. How does he know one of Brogan's men hasn't crept into the kitchen and drizzled poison all over it? Enviously he watches as Maren tucks into her chicken pie. She catches him looking, and notices his uneaten food. She seems to understand what's worrying him, because she raises an eyebrow, forks some of his food into her mouth.

"Pretty good," she says, and then swallows.

Will eats. Everyone is talking about the gunfight with the Natives, and Will hears all sorts of gossip flitting between tables. Ten passengers killed. Fifteen Natives. Three passengers. Two Natives. A brave jumped aboard and scalped a steward. Sam Steele leaped onto a Native horse, chased off the hunters, and then reboarded the Boundless with a tomahawk.

Will feels better after his food. Having all these people

around almost tricks him into believing he's safe—he could stand up and walk off into his normal life.

Toward the end of the meal, Sam Steele strides into the dining car and speaks to one of the senior stewards before moving forward up the train.

"Ladies and Gentlemen," the steward says, "Lieutenant Steele has asked me to pass on the news that there was a brief skirmish with some Indians. Two of our passengers were tragically killed."

Gasps of horror engulf the dining car. Men thump the table and vow bloody revenge. Mr. Dorian eats, staring rigidly ahead. The two men from the shooting car look over darkly, and Will thinks he hears them muttering the word "half-breed."

He stares longingly in the direction where Sam Steele disappeared. Forward. He catches Maren looking at him anxiously. Is she worried he'll make a run for it? He wants to, but he won't. They've saved his life three times now. He's made his promise to Maren, and he means to keep it.

"Nearly had him," says Chisholm, nervously forking some meat from a tin. "All lined up, and then Dorian waves his coat in front of him. How does a coat stop a bullet?"

"You should've let me take the shot," says Mackie. "I wouldn't have missed the first time."

"Ease up, Mackie," Brogan says, flicking some food from between his teeth. "Sounds like it was a tough shot." He's angry about Chisholm's cock-up too, but he wants to jolly him along, especially after nearly drowning him in the muskeg. He needs all hands on deck for what's coming.

The three of them have fallen back to Peck and Strachan's brakemen's cabin, not far behind colonist class.

"We won't get another chance like that," Mackie says sullenly.

"Maybe we don't need one," Brogan says.

"What d'you mean? You said we needed to take that boy."

"Oh, we're gonna take him, all right."

"So what's the plan?" asks Chisholm, his eyes bulgier than usual.

"When I was in the saloon car, that Mountie was right there. I thought I was sunk. Why didn't the boy go to him? The boy wants something, that's why—or Mr. Dorian does, more like. He's got his hands on a key to the funeral car. I reckon they've got their own plans."

"I don't like this waiting," Mackie says.

"That Dorian can disappear things," says Chisholm. "How we know he won't disappear what we're after—and himself?"

Brogan thinks about this, and shakes his head. "That's magic," he says. "And I don't believe in magic."

After the porters have made their last rounds, putting the train to bed, Will, Maren, and Mr. Dorian slip silently out of their compartment. Luggage in hand, they move five doors back and enter a smaller, empty room. After bolting the door behind them, Will starts quietly helping the others pull down the sleeping berths.

"When are you doing it?" he asks as he spreads a sheet and blanket over the middle bunk. "The robbery."

Mr. Dorian takes out his watch and consults its two faces. During the afternoon he several times asked the stewards about the train's precise location and speed. "We need to be inside the funeral car no later than four o'clock this morning."

"You can just stay here, Will," Maren tells him. "Lock the door behind us. No one knows where you are. We'll be back before breakfast."

Will shakes his head. "I'm not staying here alone."

"It's best if you don't get mixed up in this, Will," she says.

He laughs. "Could I be any *more* mixed up? I'm coming with you. I'll feel a lot safer."

Mr. Dorian regards him. "I warn you, Will. You might regret your decision. I have a feeling we may run into resistance."

Still, it's not a hard decision to make. He's truly horrified by the idea of being left alone in the compartment. Even more, he wants to be there to help Maren if she needs it.

"I'm coming," he says again.

"Very well. I suggest you both get some sleep."

"You're not sleeping?" Maren asks the ringmaster.

"Not yet."

Later, under the covers, Will is still wide-awake. The

gaslight has been turned low. Maren shifts above him, already asleep. Opposite him, Mr. Dorian stretches out in his berth, fully clothed, writing. He looks over and sees Will watching.

"Will you be young forever?" Will asks. "After your portrait?"

"I think not. The portrait ages, and presumably when it reaches a goodly age, it will die, as it were."

"What happens to you then?"

Mr. Dorian looks up from his writing. "Perhaps all my years will catch up with me, or maybe I'll just start aging again normally. That would be an unexpected bonus. I merely want my allotted years, William. Is it greedy to want that?"

Will doesn't know the answer. "Maren says you have big plans for the Zirkus."

Mr. Dorian smiles—and it's a different kind of smile from the impassive ones Will has seen so far. This is the kind you get when you're thinking of your favorite thing. "Yes," he says. "I'd like to open circuses overseas, and add more animals to my menageries—make Noah's ark look paltry!"

He chuckles, and Will laughs too.

"You must be the only person with a sasquatch."

"I believe I am, for the moment. But there are always more animals, and more marvels to collect. Imagine if I could trap a Wendigo!"

"Have you seen one?" Will asks, caught up in the ringmaster's enthusiasm.

"Not yet, but I plan to. And there's a man in the Far East

who can fly. Imagine that, William. Flight! I hope to enlist his services before Mr. Barnum does. Everything on this earth I want to gather, and every feat that's possible. A new world to let us escape our own."

There's a wistfulness, Will thinks, in his last words. The ringmaster folds his piece of paper away inside his pocket, and then writes a brief note on a second piece.

"Just a little message telling my Zirkus friends how we're faring," he tells Will.

"How's it going to reach them?" Will asks quietly.

"A favorable tailwind," Mr. Dorian replies.

As Will watches, Mr. Dorian folds the paper in half lengthwise, then makes a series of other folds, ever more complicated and ingenious. When he's finished, he has something that resembles a goose. He pulls a little tab at the tail, and its wings flex and quiver expectantly.

"It really flies?" Will asks, incredulous.

"It really does."

Mr. Dorian goes to the window and slides it open. Night air tinged with coal smoke gusts in. The ringmaster puts his face out, turns it from side to side, then makes a slight adjustment to the paper wings.

And then he launches his bird into the air.

Will wishes desperately he could somehow follow its journey. If he could, he would see the paper bird swoop up, wobbling slightly. The train shuttles past so quickly, it's hard to tell if the paper bird is moving at all, but occasionally the wings give a flutter or flare and the bird rises and banks. The cars flash past beneath it.

The paper bird soars toward a brakeman standing atop a freight car, smoking. He squints, then reaches out to grab it, but the bird veers around his outstretched hand.

Farther down another brakeman sees it and, thinking it's a bat, punches it with his hand, sending it tumbling through the air, away from the tracks. The bird rights itself and flaps, but the train is far away now, and the mindless paper craft just keeps sailing straight ahead, into the night.

But perhaps it is cleverer than it appears, for straight ahead comes the last half of the Boundless, still rounding a big curve. The paper bird banks slightly, to come in line with the train. Whatever paper mechanism animates it now seems to falter. The wings stop fluttering, and slowly the paper bird begins to sink, toward the roof of the freight cars.

Lower and lower it glides until it flies right into some kind of web jutting from the window of a car that says: ZIRKUS DANTE.

It's not a web but a Native dream catcher, and the paper bird is tangled snugly in its threads. The dream catcher is pulled swiftly inside.

The paper bird is unfolded, the note read.

CHAPTER 13

THE FUNERAL CAR

Will feels a hand shaking him awake.

"It's time," says Maren.

The gaslight is turned low. She's already dressed, as is Mr. Dorian, who's slinging a coil of light rope over his shoulder. Hurriedly Will pulls on his trousers beneath the covers.

"Sure?" Maren asks him when they're ready to leave.

He nods. Mr. Dorian takes up an unlit lantern and unlocks their door, and they slip out into the corridor. Will feels like a ghost as they make their way through the sleeper cars. On both sides thick curtains are drawn across berths, muffling the sounds of snoring, murmuring passengers. Will's eyes sweep from side to side, terrified that an arm will shoot out at them.

Every cough and snuffle makes him start. Mr. Dorian has a sixth sense for avoiding the few porters and sleepless passengers who come their way—ushering Will and Maren into washrooms or empty berths until it's safe to emerge.

The dining car is deserted, all the tables already laid with linens and cutlery. As the three of them pass the kitchens, Will glances through the round window in the door and sees long gleaming counters and blazing ovens, and pots as tall as smokestacks, spewing steam. Already the cooks are chopping vegetables and kneading bread for the breakfast onslaught.

Every time they're ready to cross to another car, Mr. Dorian has them stand back while he peeks through the window to see if a brakeman is poised on the roof, watching. Then he quietly opens the door and the three of them dart across the couplings.

In the laundry car the air is heady with starch and bleach. Line after line of tablecloths and sheets and uniforms silently sway to the motion of the train. The fabric glows in the pale gaslight. Watching the shadows, Will hurries through.

At the door to the next car, Mr. Dorian pulls back suddenly from the window.

"There's a man on the roof," he whispers. "Brogan definitely wants to know what we're up to."

They wait several minutes for the brakeman to move along, then several more.

"He's not budging," says Mr. Dorian. "We need to distract him."

"I've got an idea," Will says.

He retraces his steps into the laundry room. He takes a starched white shirt from the line and slides open one of the windows. After feeding out the shirt, he closes the window tightly so half of it flails about in the wind, like a man wildly signaling for help.

"Nicely done," says Mr. Dorian. "Let's see if he bites."

They return to the carriage door and wait. Will kneels and peeks out the window. The tip of the brakeman's cigarette flares orange. Then there's a sudden movement of the head, and a lantern flares. The brakeman jumps over to the roof of their car and treads in the direction of the laundry room.

"Now," Will says.

He pulls open the door and leads the way across the coupling to the next carriage. Inside, Maren smiles at him. "That was a good idea. You're quite an accomplice."

"I'm not an accomplice," he says, shocked at the idea.

"Anyone who helps is an accomplice," Mr. Dorian points out.

Will frowns, then chuckles softly. "I suppose so, then."

He knew Van Horne pretty well; maybe the old fellow wouldn't mind if his painting were stolen. After all, the rail baron always had a flair for the extraordinary. He was so full of life himself, no doubt he'd have been miffed to know he could have had more. But he'd also like all the intrigue his painting was causing.

When they near the end of second class, Mr. Dorian stops

them and says, "We need to go to the roof now. There will be porters on guard at the border, and we mustn't be seen."

Will knew this moment was coming, but he is not looking forward to it.

"Are you ready for another walk atop the Boundless, William?" Mr. Dorian asks. "The train's a bit slower now. We're slowly rising toward the mountains. The route's dead straight."

Will nods. "I've done it before; I figure I can do it again."

"That's the spirit. We need to move as swiftly as we can. There may be other men on the roof."

At the next coupling, they cross, and Mr. Dorian climbs the ladder. He pokes his head above the roof, takes a good look each way, and then gestures for Will and Maren to follow.

Despite his coat, Will shivers as the wind meets him atop the Boundless. He steadies himself. The passenger cars are different from the boxcars. They have no running boards, and their roofs slope down even more than the freight cars'.

There's a fingernail clipping of moon, and Will can see only a few feet ahead of him. Mr. Dorian does not light the lantern. Good for staying hidden, terrible for jumping cars. Mr. Dorian walks with ease, and Maren strolls along like she has no cares in the world. To a tightrope walker this is nothing.

At the end of the first car, Will watches as Mr. Dorian and Maren make their jumps, getting swallowed up in darkness. Only the lanterns along the train's sides tell Will that the Boundless is still moving in a straight line. He quickly rubs the sasquatch tooth in his pocket. He can barely see the other car as he takes a run and launches himself into the night. For a second, midjump, he feels a hot pulse of vertigo, but then he's coming down and Maren is waiting to offer a steadying hand.

"You did it," she whispers.

Car by car his confidence grows, his body reacquainting itself with the train's restless pitch and sway.

Up ahead Will catches a flicker of lantern light, maybe three cars distant. He moves to touch Maren on the shoulder, but she's already turning, and he sees Mr. Dorian, jabbing his finger to go backward. Will crouches and hurries back to the end of the car.

"Down!" he hears Mr. Dorian whisper.

Will climbs back to the platform, stands to one side of the car door so no one can spy him through the window. Maren and Mr. Dorian quickly descend and join him.

"He may not have seen us," says Mr. Dorian. "We'll go past underneath him."

He checks the window, opens the door, and ushers them inside. It's strange for Will to be back in first class again. It feels like a different world—or maybe it's the same world and it's him that's different. He's dressed as an Indian spirit artist, part of a band of thieves come to rob the funeral car of a rail baron.

He looks around, trying to figure out where they are, and then catches a whiff of roasted almonds and popcorn. "The cinema's just up ahead," he says.

Stealthily they pad along the plush carpeted hallway. Edison bulbs glow from behind decorative pink shades. The trio reaches the end of the car. Maren checks the rooftop and nods at the others, and they silently open the door and cross to a double-decker car.

Inside, the sound of water greets Will. He climbs six steps to the black-and-white-tiled deck of the swimming pool. The silver fountain in its center sends spray into the fish-flecked water. The only light comes from the pool itself and casts undulating pale blue reflections on the ceiling.

Will follows the others along the deck, past the cloth changing tents. From the far end of the car, above the noise of tinkling water, comes the precise metallic sound of a doorknob turning.

He grabs Maren's hand and pulls her inside the nearest tent. There's a zipper to close the flaps, but Will doesn't want to make any noise. Through the narrow crack, he sees Mr. Dorian disappearing into the tent in front of theirs.

Climbing the steps to the deck, a brakeman comes into view, wearing a peaked cap. Even though Will can't see his face clearly, he thinks it belongs to Mackie. In his hands is a long metal pole with a pronged end. He stands for a moment, listening.

Walking slowly along the deck, Mackie casually swings his metal pole into the first changing tent. With a smacking sound the heavy fabric puckers deeply. He moves on to the second

　　　　　　　　　　　KENNETH OPPEL

changing tent, strikes it hard at chest level, keeps going. Will watches in horror as Mackie nears Mr. Dorian's tent. Will grips Maren's hand tightly. The brakeman hits the tent hard. The fabric dents, and an almost comical squeak comes from inside.

"That really hurt!"

"Come out here!" barks Mackie, taking a step back and adjusting his grip on the pole. Will expects a bloodied Mr. Dorian to stagger out, but no one emerges.

"Out!" Mackie snaps. He strikes the tent again at knee level.

Another high-pitched yelp comes from inside, and then, "Come and get me!"

Mackie scowls. With the end of his pole he parts the flaps, and then strides in, ready to wallop. The moment he's inside, Mr. Dorian, to Will's huge amazement, steps out of another tent altogether. With one swift movement Mr. Dorian zips Mackie into the tent and delivers a high kick. The tent topples over, thrashing. Mackie curses from inside.

"Give me a hand!" the ringmaster calls out.

Will runs over with Maren, and they take hold of the tent and bundle it into the pool. Exotic fish dart away like colored bolts of lightning. The fabric is soaked within seconds and proceeds to sink.

"He'll drown!" Will says, but already he can see Mackie's hand thrust from the churning tent and start to unzip the flaps.

Outside the swimming pool car Mr. Dorian leads them once more onto the roof of the Boundless. On the double-decker cars Will feels the sway of the train more strongly. Twice the distance to fall.

Slowly his eyes readjust to the night as he pushes himself to keep up with Maren and Mr. Dorian. He knows the three of them need to put distance between themselves and Mackie.

Heart hammering, he makes his first jump and lands in a crouch, slightly off center. By the third jump he starts to feel more confident again. He tries to keep track of where they are in first class, and guesses the dining cars. Up ahead he spots the pale glow of the Terrace car, gaslight still burning faintly inside. Several minutes later they leap onto it—the place where he stood just days ago as the train left Halifax station. It seems like a memory from someone else's life. Through the domed glass he sees a solitary gentleman dozing in an armchair, his hand still closed around his glass of brandy.

Another jump, and another. Beneath him: the parlor cars, the billiards room, the library. And there, ahead of him in the long distance, is the locomotive. Rising above the coal-packed tender, it's a small engine city, a symphony of pistons, its vast smokestack reaching into the sky.

Too hastily Will makes the next jump. His feet have just left the roof when the wind shifts and a cloud of soot and heat washes over him, singeing his eyes. He blinks furiously and sees the next car curve away from him.

A grunt escapes his throat as he stretches out his arms. He

hits the corner of the roof with only one foot, and crashes onto his shoulder, scrabbling to grab something.

Maren hears his cry, turns, and throws herself toward him. Sliding along the sloped roof, she seizes his wrist. She is small, but he feels her amazing, compact strength as she pulls. With her help he gets both feet against the roof and pushes himself to the center of the car.

"Careful," she says, leaning her forehead against his.

Breathing fast, he nods and follows her. Before long he realizes he's walking over the top of the bedroom he spent all of one night in. And after that the cars become single-deck again, and the three of them have to proceed more quietly than ever, for these are maintenance and crew cars, where the porters and stewards will soon be waking and preparing for another day aboard the Boundless.

Will can see the ornamental metal plumes of the funeral car now, and after another two cars, they've arrived. He climbs down after Mr. Dorian and Maren to the small juddering platform. At his back is the doorless end of a maintenance car—and before them, the darkly gleaming steel of the funeral car.

"Stay back," Mr. Dorian warns them.

There is a great deal of noise from the tracks, but Will is aware of an extra vibration: electricity coursing through the metal exterior.

The ringmaster pulls out his timepiece and examines its hands. "We have thirty-five minutes."

"Until what?" Will asks, but Mr. Dorian ignores him and lights his lantern.

Maren crouches and removes her coat, taking out her amazing spool of wire. It was one thing to talk about it, even to imagine it, but now that Will is peering beneath the funeral carriage, seeing the speed of the ties as they clatter past, feeling the sway and shudder of the train—he feels terror for her.

"You don't have to do this," he says.

"Shush." She pulls on rubber-soled slippers. "You never say that to someone before a performance."

"This isn't a performance," he says.

"She trained for this," Mr. Dorian reminds him.

"Are you even sure there's room?"

"It can be done," Mr. Dorian tells him. "I made careful measurements."

Again Will stares at the tiny hurtling space and imagines her falling.

"Why can't you wait until we're at a stop?" he demands.

"It has to be now," Mr. Dorian says sharply.

"Why?"

"That's enough, William!"

"But this isn't safe!" Will exclaims, suddenly trembling with fury. "If it's so important to you, why don't *you* do it?"

"Be quiet!"

It's Maren who speaks, and Will turns in surprise to her angry face.

"Go if you want!" she says. "But stop interfering!"

His face burns as if he's just been slapped. He was trying to protect her, and she treats him like a squalling baby.

"Go ahead, then!" he snaps, to cover up his hurt. He feels close to tears. He wants to climb the ladder and head back to first class. Leave them to their death-defying feats and insane robbery! But he stays put.

As Maren slides toward the edge of the platform, he takes the key from his pocket and hands it to her. "Here. Use the original. It might work better."

"Thank you, Will."

Mr. Dorian arranges the shutters of his lantern to send a strong skinny beam into the whirling world beneath the carriage. Oiled steel and truss wires and spinning metal rods—and the clattering din of the ties hurtling past.

Maren turns the handle of the spool. The rigid wire extends, longer and longer.

"Remember you can't touch any part of the undercarriage," Mr. Dorian warns her.

She nods and pays out the miraculous wire, guiding it beneath the bottom of the carriage until it hooks across a horizontal rod on the far coupling. She secures her end to the underside of the platform. She has her tightrope.

In a single fluid motion she swings herself onto the wire, arms held out, balancing on her back. Her feet, in their rubber-soled slippers, push her deeper under the train. Her legs can only bend slightly, so they don't hit the steel undercarriage.

The ringmaster lies flat so he can angle the light for Maren. Will presses his cheek against the cold metal to see better. He dares not say a word. The train jolts, and Maren sways violently, hands dancing through the air. He wants to plead with her to come back.

"The lock is coming up now," calls out Mr. Dorian calmly, for Maren can't see what is behind her. "Another few pushes. . . . There."

Maren balances beneath a black box. She takes the key from her sleeve. Swaying side to side in sync with the train, she inserts the key into the lock and turns. The faint buzzing in Will's ears ceases.

"You've done it, my girl," breathes Mr. Dorian. "You clever girl, you've done it. Come back now, and carefully!"

The return trip is no less anxious for Will, watching as Maren slides back—though this time she can reach up with her hands and use the undercarriage to balance and propel herself.

She slides out onto the platform and springs to her feet with a huge smile. Will can't help wrapping his arms around her and squeezing her tight with relief.

"I'm sorry I snapped at you," she says into his ear.

"I'm just glad you're safe."

"Let's hurry," Mr. Dorian says.

They climb the ladder to the roof and walk forward. Mr. Dorian fastens his measure of rope to a metal rung and rappels swiftly over the side. Will watches as the ringmaster traces the dense metal foliage with his hands, and finally inserts the key. A section of the car pops out and slides back flush. The ringmaster swings himself inside.

"You go," Maren tells Will. "I'll hold the line still for you."

"Thanks," Will says gratefully.

If someone told him, days ago, he'd be lowering himself over the side of a hurtling train car, he would've laughed, and wished he had the courage. But he has it now, even though his hands are sweaty with fear. He stares back up at Maren, and the mere sight of her gives him confidence.

Mr. Dorian is waiting for him inside the hatchway and seizes his arm to pull him in. Within seconds Maren stands beside them. Mr. Dorian lights his lantern again.

The interior is heavy with a cloying musk: candle wax, dust, furniture polish, and a faintly sweet odor that Will fears is the slowly decomposing remains of Cornelius Van Horne. The carriage reminds Will of pictures he's seen of a pharaoh's tomb, all manner of things piled and jumbled about. A chair and footstool that must have been favorites. A tall urn with peacock feathers. A chess set with the pieces set out, as if about to be played. A battered pair of snowshoes. The taxidermy of a beloved dog. Hanging from the wall is a large framed photograph. Will walks closer, and gasps.

It's a photograph he's never before seen—but *he* is its subject. It's from Craigellachie. There he is, front and center, the hammer frozen just as it connects with the head of the last spike.

"That's incredible," Maren says. "How come no one knows this?"

"Donald Smith liked the other photo better," says the ringmaster. "Even though he just bent the spike and it needed straightening."

"But this one's the truth," Maren says, smiling at Will.

He thinks there's admiration in her eyes, and he drinks it in. He's never really made much of the story—has never seen it as an achievement of his own. He just happened to be sitting there on the platform at Farewell, and Mr. Van Horne took a liking to him.

"The last spike of the railway," she says. "You're sort of famous."

"No," he says. "I did nothing to build it."

Will sees Mr. Dorian's eyes sweeping the walls.

"Where's the painting?" Will asks.

"Not here. He loved it a great deal. It will be farther in."

The ringmaster moves to an inner wall that, Will realizes, must divide the carriage in half. In its center is a metal door that looks like the entrance to a bank vault.

"We'll never get through," Will murmurs. "We've no key to that. Can you pick it?"

Maren lets out a deep breath and shakes her head.

"No need," Mr. Dorian says, surprising them both. "The lock is on a timer."

Faintly Will hears a tick emanating from within the door, where two clocks sit side by side.

"You'll see," says Mr. Dorian, "that the first clock has our current time, and the second the time and date when we arrive in Lionsgate City. The lock is timed to open only then."

"So what're we to do?" Will asks, exasperated. If Mr. Dorian has known this all along, why on earth has he led them on this fool's journey?

Mr. Dorian consults his watch. "As I've shown you, time is an unreliable thing. In five minutes we'll be passing between time zones."

Will remembers how the hands faltered on his watch. "But I was never sure if that was just . . ."

"A trick?" Mr. Dorian asks with a smile. "The universe plays the best tricks of all."

"You knew all along about this lock?" Maren asks, amazed.

"Of course," replies Mr. Dorian. "I know the man who designed the lock. Me."

"So when we pass through the time zone . . ." Maren begins.

"The hands will falter. The clock will stop, and for a few moments the lock will think we've reached our destination— or at least have no notion of time at all. In either case it will open."

The sound of slow applause makes Will whirl. Brogan stands behind them, clapping. Flanking him are Chisholm, a knife gripped in his jittery hand, and Mackie, his damp clothes plastered to his powerful body. Brass knuckles rim his right fist. Brogan holds a pistol.

"Good thing we let you lead the way," Brogan says. "The key was just the beginning, wasn't it? I didn't realize there'd be more trickery inside. You're the real key, ain't you, Mr. Dorian?"

Will can only stare, taking in the bulk of Brogan and his men.

"That's a nice disguise, boy," the brakeman says. "I knew when I saw you in the saloon—I knew you were up to something. I wondered to myself, why ain't he talking to that Mountie? And then I knew you wanted something from that funeral car, as much as me."

Mr. Dorian says, "That was a fine piece of deduction, Mr. Brogan."

"So go ahead, work your magic. . . ."

"I don't believe in magic, sir."

"Do what you need to do and open that door!"

Mr. Dorian consults his watch, and Will glimpses the double clock faces: one terrestrial time, the other cosmic.

"What is it you're hoping to find inside, Mr. Brogan?" the ringmaster asks calmly, still inspecting his watch.

"Never you mind. You just get us in."

"I see no reason why we can't all walk away happily with our prizes."

Brogan laughs sarcastically. "How d'you know we're not after the same thing?"

"I gather you're after gold."

"You've no interest in that, I suppose?"

"Not at the moment."

"Lucky you. How's this work, then?" Brogan demands.

"We just have to wait a moment."

Brogan glances nervously at Mackie. "Watch him, boys. He's cunning."

And then Brogan puts his pistol against Mr. Dorian's temple. "Don't try your tricks on me, my man."

"I wouldn't dream of it."

Will looks at Maren, thinks of the gun going off, and how easily the bullets would pass through her—through all of them—their flesh so soft and helpless.

Mr. Dorian holds his timepiece up for all to see. "Here it comes, gentlemen. . . ." It's a strangely dramatic gesture, but everyone looks up. Will's eyes rivet themselves to the second hand of the clock.

"Any moment now . . . ," says Mr. Dorian. "Any moment . . . you'll feel it when it's upon you—"

"Stop talking!" shouts Brogan. Will sees the strain on the brakeman's face—the lines stretching down his cheeks like dried riverbeds. "I know what you're trying to do!"

"There's nothing at all I need do," says Mr. Dorian soothingly. "It's completely beyond my control."

"Stop talking," says Brogan again, but his voice sounds muted now.

"Nothing at all to be done . . ."

The strangest feeling wells up within Will, as though his senses want to float free of his body.

"Any moment now," he hears Mr. Dorian murmur quietly, a small voice a long distance away.

Will sees the watch's second hand pause and tremble. He's aware of the thunder of the tracks beneath his feet, unnaturally loud. But rising above that is the slow tick of the vault door. He drags his gaze over to it, feels as though he's moving through water. The first clock embedded in the metal door falters and stalls. From within the door comes a surprisingly dainty click, like fingers being snapped.

The moment is just a moment, but it contains multitudes. The carriage seems to expand around Will. He's aware of Maren beside him, and the hulking presence of Brogan and his two men. Curiously, only Mr. Dorian seems absent—but then he is right beside Will, his hand reaching out to take the wheel on the door.

It spins with such beautiful slowness, the lantern light flashing off the spokes. The door drifts outward. Will's nostrils fill with a deep, metallic odor, and then the clock hands begin moving again.

With a sharp intake of breath, Will comes back to himself. Brogan snatches Mr. Dorian's lantern and waves his pistol at them.

"Inside!"

As Will steps through, he hears a metallic thunk from the door. He sees that Mr. Dorian has noticed too—there's a look of surprise in his eyes—but there is no time to ask him what this sound means.

Light darts about from the impatient lantern. Compared to the antechamber this room seems empty. In its center is an enormous sarcophagus. Will spent the last three years in a port city that whispers ghost stories. Ghost lighthouses and ships, drowned mines, hauntings and forerunners. But never has he had a stronger feeling that he is in the presence of the supernatural. It's a tingling in his toes, a weakening of his joints, and a faint but insistent whine in his ears that quickens his pulse.

The lantern light sweeps over hanging photographs of Van Horne's family—and then Cornelius Krieghoff's *The Blacksmith's Shop*. Will glances at Mr. Dorian and sees his eyes fixed to the canvas like a desert wanderer spying an oasis.

"Fancy that, do you?" says Brogan. "Well, you'll have lots of time to admire it. Boys, let's get what we came for."

"It's the spike, isn't it?" Will says.

Brogan sniffs. "The spike?"

"You tried to steal it in the mountains."

"Oh, I'll have the spike, but that's just the beginning." Brogan's eyes narrow. "Your father never told you, did he?"

The train judders, and Will takes a step to keep his balance. "Told me what?"

"In the mountains, we weren't just building the railroad. We was digging for gold, your father and me. The railway was bust, boy. Van Horne was a desperate man. No one would bail him out. Us men hadn't been paid in two months. You remember going hungry, don't you? What did your ma feed you those months?"

Will does remember those times, when they ate the same flavorless soups and stews because his father sent no wages home. Without their mother's factory work they would've been turned out on the street.

"Van Horne was a desperate man. No one'd give another penny for his blessed railway. But he heard from some Indians that there was gold in the mountains. He set a team of us workin' to blast tunnels to see. And we found gold, by God we did. Enough to save his railway. But he kept it secret—didn't want people to know he was saved by sheer luck. And whether that gold really belonged to the company, well, that was a thorny question. One thing's certain. Didn't see Van Horne with soot and nitro on his hands. That fat cat's soaked in the sweat and blood of others, and I hope he's drowning in it now. We mined it, and Van Horne took it. But there's plenty left over. This car ain't just carrying a dead man."

Brogan swings his lantern so it illuminates three large crates against the rear wall. One of them is open, revealing the sly luster of gold bars.

"That's what your father was gonna use to launch the steamship line across the Pacific," says Brogan. "But I'll have it instead."

"You can't!" Will says, his outrage sudden and fierce. "You can't steal from him!"

"I dug up that gold!" Brogan roars. "Same as him. Why shouldn't I have my share of it? I didn't get no promotion. I didn't get handed the railway like your pa!"

"He saved Van Horne's life!" Will retorts. "And he worked for what he got. He's no thief like you!"

Will feels the nauseating fork of pain in his stomach before he even knows he's been punched. He's on his knees, gasping, streaming tears. Brogan spits beside him.

"Thief? You ask your pa if he slipped some of that mountain gold into his pocket—if you ever see him again." He turns to his men. "Fetch it up! Haul them crates to the doorway."

Mackie hasn't taken two steps before he stops short. From within the sarcophagus comes the sound of someone dragging a breath into his lungs.

Will jerks as the lid slides violently back. Maren's fingers grip his arm and bite deeply. His whole body feels struck by lightning.

From the darkness of the coffin, Van Horne rises. His mighty beard and sideburns obscure his shrunken face. A jacket hangs loosely about his collapsed chest. His once powerful hands are webbed with flaccid skin. As though he's in the grip of a seizure, his torso quivers, then gives a great twitch, and Van Horne springs upright like some diabolical jack-in-the-box.

There's a crackling sound, a sudden acrid odor—and a

terrible high-pitched gagging emanates from Mackie. His back arches and lifts him onto his tiptoes, chin angled high, as though being yanked by some invisible chain. His damp clothes steam; his arms tremble stiffly at his sides. The tendons in his neck stand out like knotted twine. To Will the sight is almost as terrible as the corpse towering before him.

Chisholm grabs Mackie to drag him back, but the moment he touches his stricken friend, they seem welded together, and he too makes horrible choking sounds.

Will looks back at Van Horne's corpse—half convinced it's working this devilish effect on Brogan's men. But he sees now that it's merely a mechanical wonder, like the ones he saw in the Zirkus car.

"It's just a puppet!" Brogan bellows at his men.

"They're being electrocuted," Mr. Dorian tells him calmly. "It's a trap."

Brogan levels the gun at Mr. Dorian. "I thought you turned it off!"

"This runs off a separate battery."

There's another *snap*, and Brogan's two men collapse to the floor.

Without turning his back on Mr. Dorian, the brakeman warily kicks at his fallen companions. They groan and tremble, their wide eyes unblinking.

"They'll recover," says the ringmaster. "You needn't worry."

As Will watches, Van Horne's swaying corpse silently

stretches out its skeletal hand and closes it around Brogan's forearm.

Brogan whirls with a cry, and tries to pull free. But with a metallic ratcheting sound, one finger after another locks around the brakeman's flesh. The puppet's arm is stiff and freakishly strong, holding Brogan at a distance from the sarcophagus.

Brogan whirls on Mr. Dorian in fury. "You knew about this!"

"Of course. I helped design this room for Mr. Van Horne."

"Get me free, or I shoot!"

"I'm afraid I won't be doing that," says Mr. Dorian.

Brogan squeezes the trigger. The hammer clicks. He squeezes again and again—six empty chambers.

"Difficult to fire a gun without these," says the ringmaster, holding out the bullets as if returning them to Brogan. Brogan lunges for them, but is brought short by Van Horne's grip.

"You'll be released when we reach Lionsgate City." He turns to Maren. "The painting, please. Don't touch the floor. Beyond where we stand, every inch is booby-trapped."

Like a cat Maren springs across the carriage and lands on a small bureau near the wall. She lifts the painting off its hook and flings it toward Mr. Dorian, who catches it. Then she leaps nimbly back beside Will.

Mr. Dorian is already savagely knocking the Krieghoff painting from its frame. Taking the hide-scraper from his coat pocket, he slits the canvas right off the stretcher. He hurriedly folds it and crams it inside his jacket. His hands are shaking.

"We're leaving!" he shouts, ushering Will and Maren out ahead of him.

"Don't be a fool!" Brogan shouts. "We can split the gold! You'll be rich!"

In the antechamber Will watches as Mr. Dorian swings the door shut—but with a bang, it won't close. Mr. Dorian pulls harder. Something is jamming the door.

"The bolt," Will says, now understanding the sound he heard earlier. "It shot back out."

Mr. Dorian looks. Sure enough, a large metal bolt now protrudes. "Once we were through the time zone . . . ," he murmurs, "it must have tried to lock itself again."

"What a shame!" crows Brogan from the other side of the door. "Can't lock us in now, can you?"

For the first time since Will met Mr. Dorian, he looks flustered.

"Quickly," the ringmaster says. "We need to get back."

Snow-laden trees flash past the open doorway. Maren climbs up the rope to the top of the funeral car. Will's next. Going down was one thing, but lifting himself hand over hand is altogether more difficult. She helps pull him over the top.

Will looks about, astounded. From the east the first light gilds the wrinkled slopes of the mountains that rise up all around the Boundless. The sky throws an icy cloak around Will, and he shivers.

KENNETH OPPEL

Below him, Mr. Dorian starts to pull himself onto the roof, and falters, his face pinched. Will and Maren kneel, grab hold of an arm each, and haul him over the edge. He nods gratefully, pulling the rope up after him.

Will is shocked by how ill Mr. Dorian looks in the sun's glare.

"Are you all right?" Maren asks.

"Just winded," he says, standing.

"It's done," says Will softly. "It's over."

"Not quite yet," says Mr. Dorian.

Will turns. Silhouetted by the rising sun, six brakemen loom large as they make their way across the roof of the Boundless toward them.

CHAPTER 14

ATOP THE BOUNDLESS

"Get up!" Brogan roars. He kicks out at Mackie with his boot, catching him under the chin.

Mackie splutters and then rolls over and retches on Brogan's boot.

"What . . . ," he moans.

"You got jolted. Move back before it does it again, and pull Chisholm with you."

Chisholm's weasely face begins to twitch, and he opens his eyes and sits groggily.

"Jaysus," says Mackie, looking at the towering corpse of Cornelius Van Horne, its chest raggedly rising and falling.

"Puppet is all," says Brogan, "but it's got a grip on me. You'll need to bust its arm."

"I don't like puppets," says Mackie.

"You wanna spend the rest of your life in prison? Get over here!"

Wincing with revulsion, Mackie steps closer to the corpse. He grabs the skeletal wrist and tries to snap it.

"Strong," he mutters, pounding his fist against the forearm.

The corpse puppet shoots out its other hand and latches on to Mackie's bicep.

"It's got me!" he wails. "It's got me bad!"

"Idiot," growls Brogan. "Chisholm, haul your lazy carcass over here and free us up!"

Chisholm draws closer, eyes buggy with fear. "You sure this ain't the man himself?"

"He's underneath somewhere. This here's mechanical," says Brogan. "Peel its sleeve back!"

Chisholm gingerly undoes the cufflink on the corpse's sleeve and rolls it back. The color of the flesh is surprisingly lifelike, not hard like a mannequin's.

"Look there," says Brogan, "there's a little hatch or something."

Chisholm digs in with his pen knife and pries open a panel. A series of taut wires runs like vein and sinew through the arm.

"Cut it—that'll do the trick," says Brogan. "You got wire cutters."

"Here," says Mackie, pulling a pair from his back pocket and handing them to Chisholm, who drops them to the floor.

"Still a bit shaky," Chisholm says.

"Hand 'em over!" barks Brogan.

Brogan gets the teeth around the main wire and squeezes hard. Finally there is a sharp crack, and the corpse's fingers go limp. Brogan pulls his arm clear.

After freeing Mackie, Brogan looks furiously across the chamber at the crates of gold—unreachable. One step deeper into the room, and the floor would deliver another lightning bolt of electricity.

"We'll come back for the gold," he says. "Right now let's make sure the other lads have taken care of Dorian."

The six brakemen pause, one car away from Will and the others, blocking their way to first class.

"Where's Brogan!" the tallest of them shouts.

Will realizes this isn't what they were expecting. Probably they thought they'd arrive to find the gold ready for the taking.

"He's locked up in the funeral car with Mackie and Chisholm!" Mr. Dorian shouts back. "It's over, gentlemen. You've failed. And if you value your freedom, you'll have the sense to turn back and resume your posts. We've not had a good look at your faces yet."

Will waits tensely. Maybe they'll think Mr. Dorian has a pistol. In their fists Will sees a flash of a knife, a long wrench, the glint of brass knuckles. They don't seem keen to back down.

"We can go forward to the locomotive," Will whispers to Mr. Dorian. "There's the firemen, engineers. My father . . ."

Mr. Dorian says nothing, his pale face still fixed on the brakemen. He looks like a strange raven more than ever, his black jacket blowing in the wind like spread wings.

"What do we do?" Maren asks her ringmaster.

He looks about, bewildered, and mutters to himself, "They should be here. . . ."

"Who?" Will asks.

"Get rid of 'em!" a voice behind Will shouts, and he turns to see Brogan, clambering like a monkey up the side of the funeral car, followed by Mackie and then Chisholm.

Will swallows. They're surrounded, front and back. With a shout the six brakemen rush forward.

"We'll get past them," Will says to Maren. "They can come at us only one or two at a time. Get back to first class and sound the alarm."

"I'll take care of Brogan," says Mr. Dorian, and from his jacket he pulls out his hide-scraper and strides threateningly toward the other three, making vicious swipes through the air.

"Here they come," says Maren as the first brakeman leaps the gap to the funeral car.

All Will's body wants to do is retreat, but he forces it forward to meet the torrent of men. He has nothing to fight with, but suddenly remembers Mr. Dorian saying, "A good coat serves many purposes." Two brakemen rush toward him, their arms spread like predatory birds come to feast.

"Take hold of him!" one shouts to the other.

Will shrugs his coat off and slings it at the two brakemen. The wind plasters it against their faces. Their hands fly up to drag it off. Lurching, they throw each other off balance. One stumbles right off the roof. With a cry he hits the gravel and rolls out of sight into the scrub. The second brakeman claws the coat off but trips. He grabs hold of the roof's edge, legs swinging in empty air. Will can't bring himself to kick the man off.

And then Will is seeing only little bits of things, because everything is happening too fast. Behind him Mr. Dorian is squaring off with Mackie, Brogan, and Chisholm. His terrifying hide-scraper slashes the icy air. Even more terrifying is the expression on Mr. Dorian's face—teeth bared, his eyes blaze with menace.

To Will's right a brakeman grabs hold of Maren, but with an easy twist she's free. He grips her again by both arms. With a shrug she is loose, and this time there are handcuffs dangling from one of his wrists. Cursing, the brakeman comes at her once more, and a second man crowds in on her from the other side and grabs her tightly. They've got her now, but Maren steps nimbly out from the tussle, and when the two brakemen lunge for her, they find they have been manacled together. They yank each other off balance and tumble to the roof in a heap.

There are only two men in front of Will now, with a gap between them. If he can just cross five or six maintenance cars, he'll be above the crew cars. Get inside one of those, and he can spread the alarm. He runs for it.

He dodges a brakeman and is about to jump to the next car, when his legs are seized from behind. He crashes to the roof, all the breath knocked from him. Gasping, he turns over and kicks out at the fellow trying to shove him off. Will has never struck someone before, but it's instinctive. He surges forward and drives his fist into the man's face. The brakeman staggers back with a surprised grunt. Then his brawny arm pulls back and punches Will so hard, he blacks out for a moment. When he comes to, his head is dangling over the edge of the car. The tracks blur past. The brakeman leans down to heave him off altogether. Desperately Will looks for something to grab hold of, but there's nothing.

A long wooden pole catches the brakeman in the stomach and tosses him off the train—like a chopstick flicking a bit of beef. Will looks up and sees the Zhang twins striding past atop the train on their stilts. Li nods down at Will.

"Hello, little bug!" he shouts.

As Will scrambles back from the edge, he squints and sees another stilt walker emerging from the sun's glare. It's Roald, a brace of throwing knives strapped across his chest. At his side lopes Mr. Beauprey. He no longer has to stoop as he moves across the train, but stands to his full eight-foot height. He jumps cars and is in the fray.

Will is about to keep running to first class, but he sees Maren throwing herself back from a brakeman swinging a lug wrench. He isn't sure if she trips or the wrench strikes her in the shoulder, but she falls. Her head hits the roof hard. She doesn't move. He shouts her name and runs into the thick of the fight.

Mr. Beauprey is already trying to wrestle the wrench from the brakeman's hands, as a second fellow pummels the giant from behind. Maren's body starts to slide off the roof. Will throws himself toward her, skids, and grabs her arm.

Instantly her hands are tight around him and she's dragging him to the edge.

"Maren!" he shouts.

"Oh!" she cries, blinking. "I thought you were one of them!"

"You're okay?"

"I was just faking. I was going to flip him off the roof!"

"We've got help!"

"I know!"

"Tunnel!" someone bellows, and Will whips round to see a mound of stone rushing toward them like a troll's head, mouth agape. Already the locomotive has steamed inside. The Zhang twins drop to the roof, their long wooden limbs askew.

"Roald!" screams Maren, and Will catches a glimpse of her startled brother as the mountain roars over him. There's a dull thud and a clattering sound, and then it's all darkness and noise and smoke for a few long seconds before—

Light crashes over them again, and Will is coughing and blinking.

"Roald!" Maren cries out again, and her brother springs up from his crouch, holding his one remaining stilt.

"I'm fine!" he shouts, and launches the stilt along the rooftop. "Heads up!"

Mr. Dorian steps deftly out of the way, and the stilt hits Mackie and knocks him off his feet. Brogan lunges at the ringmaster, and then recoils, blood welling from a cut across his cheek.

The two brakemen who've been manacled together charge the Zhang twins and hurl themselves against their stilts, snapping one in half. The Siamese twins crash to the roof. Like a crippled spider, they try to rise. Suddenly they're up on just two stilts, pirouetting like a ballerina. One of the manacled brakemen screams as Roald's knife buries itself in his shoulder.

Will turns to see Roald with another knife at the ready, but before he can hurl it, a great gust of smoke and steam from the locomotive rolls over, making the world disappear. Wrapped in pungent fog, Will feels dizzy, there is no up or down, and he drops to his knees and clutches at the roof.

When the smoke clears, Will catches sight of Mr. Beauprey giving a howling brakeman's arm a twist. The giant then picks the man up, roars, "I will throw you from the train!" and does just that.

Will looks forward. They're steaming straight for the stone flank of another mountain.

"It's the Connaught!" one of the brakemen shouts.

Will has heard of it—a tunnel that makes three complete spirals through the heart of the mountain—and here it comes, the gaping black hole lunging toward them.

The darkness is total. Three blasts of the locomotive's whistle nearly blow his head off. He's aware of the ceiling overhead, roaring past.

A faint glow from the train's side lanterns illuminates the shape of the tunnel. The roof is higher than he thinks, for the locomotive needs to pass through with its tall smokestack. As it begins its long, looping descent through the mountain, the train slows considerably—though not as much as it should, with so many brakemen missing from their posts.

"I'm here," he hears Maren say beside him, and she takes his hand.

Icy droplets patter down on him from the ceiling. Without his coat he's starting to feel the deep cold. The roof is getting slippery.

Locomotive smoke funnels densely through the tunnel, and ash stings his eyes. He can't see more than two feet in front of him. He wants to roll himself up like an armadillo and disappear. Shivering, he tenses, afraid of who might touch him. The smoke clears.

"Look out!" cries Maren, gripping his shoulders and twisting him out of the way. A large shadow blurs past. In the fading light he sees a tortured green and brown icicle of stone.

"Stalactite," he breathes, and ducks as another one rushes past.

Around him, in the steam and darkness, he hears shouts and has no idea what's going on. He tries to figure out how many brakemen are left. Five? Six? The two manacled together, but one of them has a knife in his shoulder. The one with the big wrench. Then there's Brogan and Mackie and Chisholm. . . .

Another long gust of blinding smoke, and then a shadow looms over them. Mr. Beauprey bends down, smiling.

"I tossed another man from the train," he says happily.

He sits down suddenly, and Will sees the dark spreading stain on his chest.

"You're hurt," Will says in horror.

"One of them had a knife," he says matter-of-factly, and then his head lolls as if he's falling asleep. Will and Maren try to cushion his fall as he crumples against the roof. As the train continues its sharp turn, his body rolls. Will grabs at it, but it's too heavy and Will has to let go or else be dragged off with it. With a sob he watches Mr. Beauprey's body slide off into the tunnel and disappear.

Another bank of smoke washes over them, and when it clears, this time Will sees Chisholm stooped before him with a knife.

"There you are," he says, coming at Will.

He scrambles back with Maren. The knife quavers in Chisholm's hand. The brakeman is not altogether steady on his feet as the train turns and turns. Behind him, a pale aura begins to spread. They must be nearing the tunnel's end.

Will sees the wickedly curved form of a stalactite spiking down from the side of the tunnel.

"Look out!" he can't help shouting.

Chisholm's smirk of disbelief is frozen on his face as the stalactite smacks him off the roof and against the tunnel's wall.

The Boundless bursts from the tunnel, and Will is momentarily blinded by sunlight and mountain snow. Squinting, he rises to a wary crouch, looking quickly about. He sees the two manacled brakemen in retreat, limping back across the neighboring car—and a third jumps the gap, hurrying after them. There is no sign of either Brogan or Mackie. Have they already fled, or were they thrown off in the tunnel? Will lets out a big breath, and his shoulders drop a bit. The Zhang twins hold the remnants of their broken stilts. Mr. Dorian looks about, his eyes wild, the hide-scraper still clenched in his fist. Roald retrieves one of his knives from the roof and hurries over to his sister.

"Mr. Beauprey . . . ," Maren begins to say, then bursts into tears.

"I know," says her brother, hugging her. She presses herself against his chest, and Will feels a sharp pang of longing.

"What happened?" Mr. Dorian asks, his face ashen.

"He was stabbed," Will tells him numbly. "We couldn't hold on to him. He slid off in the tunnel."

Heavily, Mr. Dorian sits down.

"Did you get what you came for?" Roald asks him.

For a moment it seems the ringmaster hasn't heard the question, but then he nods. "Yes. Yes, I did."

"I hope it was worth it!" Maren says hoarsely. "You spent someone's life to get it!"

"Shhh," Roald tells her gently, but Will notices that the Zhang twins are watching their ringmaster a bit warily. Mr. Dorian says nothing, and Will wonders what he's feeling, if anything at all.

It starts to snow, huge beautiful flakes flashing past, hitting Will's clothing and melting instantly.

"I need to get back to first class," he says. "We're done." The idea seems impossible. The last four days have expanded into an entire lifetime. He has survived—but he doesn't feel exultation right now, only hollowed-out with exhaustion and sadness. He takes a breath. He will enter the first-class cars. He will tell Lieutenant Samuel Steele what happened in the Junction, and everything afterward. At the next stop he will see his father in the locomotive. And then . . .

"We're not done," says Mr. Dorian, looking at Will. "Not quite yet. I need your skills, William."

Frowning, he asks, "What for?"

"I need my portrait done."

"But what about Madame Lamoine?"

"It has to be you, William. And it has to be now."

With effort the ringmaster stands.

Will swallows. "Your heart?"

"Yes."

"I'm not sure I can," Will says desperately. He doesn't just mean he's worried about his skill as a painter. He's not sure he wants to help Mr. Dorian any longer.

"You listen to me," says Mr. Dorian, wincing with the effort. "I have spent precious years of my life, and a considerable fortune, working toward this moment! I have the canvas now, and *you* will paint my portrait!"

"Why should I?" Will shouts back, his own fury suddenly flowing out of him. "Why should you get to live? When Mr. Beauprey died! When you risked all our lives? Maren might've died too! Do you even care?"

"Of course I do," he says wearily. If he looked ill before, now he looks deathly.

"What's this all about?" Roald asks in obvious confusion.

"He's dying," Maren says to Will.

Will looks at Mr. Dorian, and his anger cools to pity.

"Yes," he says. "I'll paint your portrait."

CHAPTER
15

THE PORTRAIT OF DORIAN

Maren picks the lock of the maintenance car, and they all hurry inside, Mr. Dorian leaning heavily on Roald. Pungent with grease and paint fumes, the space is tight. Crowded shelves line both sides. Maren lights a lantern. Will is already rummaging around, knocking things to the floor in his exhausted haste. He grabs brushes, several cans of paint, a jug of what looks like turpentine. His studio.

Roald settles Mr. Dorian gently on the floor, his back to some shelves, then goes to Meng and Li Zhang.

"Keep watch from the rear of the car," he tells the twins. "No surprise guests." He gives Will a confused look. "I still think he needs a doctor."

"No doctor," says Mr. Dorian through gritted teeth. "What I need is right here." He drags the canvas from his pocket and hands it to Will.

"I'll keep an eye out for Brogan and Mackie," Roald says, and heads to the front of the car.

"We need to mount it on something," Will says, kneeling and unfolding the canvas, painted side down.

"No time," says Mr. Dorian with a cough.

"I won't be able to work it otherwise." He looks around and finds a piece of plywood. He drops it to the floor and rummages in a few bins for some nails and a hammer.

"Hold it tight for me," he tells Maren, and proceeds to bang nails around the perimeter. He's almost afraid to touch the canvas. But it doesn't burn with cold or heat. His parents were never much for Bible learning, but he can't help wondering if there is something wicked about this fabric. He finishes hammering. The canvas is still slack in places, but it'll have to do.

Mr. Dorian sits upright, as dignified as possible. "My left side is my best," he says, managing a pained grin.

Will looks at the scraggly brushes and paints. There is black and white, green and red—all the colors of the Boundless's exterior. He can make more from the primaries.

"How good does this have to be?" he asks, starting to worry now. Another man's life is in his hands, and how does he know he's skilled enough to make this work? He's a good copier, but he's never done a proper oil portrait.

"This is the chance you've been waiting for, William," Mr. Dorian says. "The birth of the artist."

Maren places the lantern beside him, and he shivers in the faint warmth of the flame. The shadows chisel Mr. Dorian's features so his head looks almost skull-like.

Will knows there's no time to prime the canvas. He searches his jacket for his pencil stub—it's a small miracle it's still there. This pencil's a survivor. If he can pull off this painting, he will keep the pencil forever as good luck. Hunching over the canvas, he starts an outline of Mr. Dorian, sketching in the features, capturing the angle of the head and shoulders.

The truth is, he can't paint. Not well anyway. His drawings are sound, but his paintings are dead—this is how he thinks of them. Once he starts putting the paint on, the picture loses all its vitality. He slowly buries it, killing it with every brushstroke. He forces his eyes back to his subject, working hurriedly.

Maren pries off the lids of the paint cans. "How do you like them arranged?" she asks.

"Just here to my right," he tells her. "I can use the lids to mix the colors. Can you find me some rags for the brushes?"

The touch of his pencil to the canvas has sent no spectral sparks through his hands. He wonders if this is all nonsense and Mr. Dorian has risked their lives for nothing. Mr. Beauprey is dead. Some of the brakemen are almost certainly dead. Will thinks of the man he sent over the edge. Is he dead too?

"Will?" Maren says quietly.

He realizes he's just staring at the canvas.

"Start," Mr. Dorian wheezes.

He's terrified to start. The drawing's a fair likeness. He fusses with it a bit more but knows he's stalling.

After dolloping some red onto a lid, he adds white, mixing until he has a passable pink. The light is so poor, it's hard to tell how fleshlike the color is. On another lid he mixes red and green to make brown, and then adds a bit to his pink to tone it down. He thins the paint with turpentine. This way his lines can be finer and more careful.

With the smallest brush, using his drawing as a guide, he begins painting in Mr. Dorian's flesh. Maybe he should have made the color whiter, for Mr. Dorian's skin is terribly pale now. The brush bristles are hard—they haven't been cleaned properly. His strokes are impossible to control. Panic mounts within him. How will he ever manage the mouth and eyes?

He keeps staring up at Mr. Dorian, trying to force his eyes to follow and feel, but his eyes don't want to see right now. His head is filled with worry, crying out like a raven's ceaseless cawing.

"William, please hurry," says Mr. Dorian, and he flinches again.

Will knows he needs to get the paint down faster, but he's worried about getting lost as he obliterates his drawing bit by bit.

With a rag he cleans his brush and switches to dark brown to make a start on Mr. Dorian's hair. Then he changes brushes and works on the shadows around the ringmaster's nose and eye sockets. With careful strokes he chisels deep hollows in the cheeks.

"Will," Maren says, "are you all right?"

He stares at his work, and it's happening again, just like it always does.

"The painting's dying," he murmurs.

"*He's* dying!" Maren reminds him.

"Stop being so careful, William!" Mr. Dorian says, wincing. "Look at me, and paint *me*."

Will looks hard at the ringmaster. The shadows deepen and his pale face seems to hang, suspended in space. There is nothing but the blazing head in the darkness. And suddenly Will beholds Mr. Dorian for what he is, beyond his flesh and bones. It's like his whole life is pouring out of him, and Will sees all the desperation and fear and longing and a terrifying will to live—like a fire that will burn everything in its path.

Feverishly Will slops paint on a lid, mixing. He makes the colors he needs and does not thin them this time. He works wet on wet, putting more paint on the canvas, trying to keep it thick. The canvas seems hungry for more.

The ringmaster is wheezing now.

"Hurry!" says Maren.

Something inside Will gets unlocked with these bigger, faster strokes. It's as if he can feel Mr. Dorian's face with the brush. He is mixing hastily, not bothering to clean between colors, just putting the paint down on the canvas.

"I'm done!" says Will.

Brogan stares down at the coupling behind the funeral car.

"You can't do it," says Mackie. "Not when we're in motion."

"It can be done," says Brogan. And he shows Mackie the vial of nitro he's been carrying in his sand-filled pouch.

Mackie's all he's got left. Chisholm disappeared in the tunnel, but Mackie had the sense to get himself hidden when the cavalry showed up with their stilts and throwing knives. They both retreated over the front of the funeral car.

"We've gone too far to stop now," he tells Mackie, sensing his doubts. "You're with me or you're against me. Decide now, but know it's a bloody road we're about to take."

"I'm with you," Mackie says angrily. "I'm getting rich or going to hell."

Brogan spent years blasting. Drilling the coyote holes in the rock face, packing in the powder or the nitro, and running out the fuse. He's seen men blasted to pieces more times than he can count. But he never got so much as a scratch. He's like a cat. Nine lives.

"We blow this coupling and leave the rest of the Boundless behind," he tells Mackie. "We've got the funeral car, and then we take the locomotive."

"How? There's the firemen and engineers!"

"We tell them to hop it. They'll hop it." He shows his gun.

Mackie reminds him, "There's no bullets."

"They don't know that. Would you risk it? And if they don't hop it, they get the knife."

Mackie says nothing.

"Then we drive the locomotive into the foothills, near Farewell. We blow the funeral car to bits, get the gold out. We're away down the river and across the border before the Mounties even saddle their horses."

He knows exactly what he's doing. He's bloodied but not beaten.

"And look at it this way." He forces a grin at Mackie. "We got fewer people to share with."

Will gazes down at the portrait. It's good. What he's painted is *good*. Despite his clumsy mixing, the colors seem startlingly vibrant. It is not careful and realistic. No one would praise its photographic accuracy. But it captures the man himself, his soul somehow.

"Show me," whispers Mr. Dorian.

Will turns the painting round. It is a violent collision of colors and textures. Mr. Dorian's face is still as he beholds his portrait. He smiles and nods.

"Yes," he says. "That's it." He exhales deeply.

"Are you feeling better?" Maren asks.

"I am," he says. He begins to stand, and without warning his entire body jerks and he cries out, clutching his left hand as though it has just been seared.

"Mr. Dorian!" shouts Maren.

But he can't hear her, because he is moaning, the most urgent and heartrending lament Will has ever heard. Mr. Dorian slumps over. Will helps Maren ease him to the floor.

"What's wrong!" Roald cries, hurrying over.

"It's not working," Maren says, looking at Will in desperation. "Why isn't it working?"

"I'm going for the doctor!" Roald says.

"No . . . no . . ." moans Mr. Dorian, but Roald is already barreling down the carriage. "There's nothing to be done."

"Is there something wrong with the portrait?" Will asks, stricken.

"Not the portrait," Mr. Dorian says, wincing. "The canvas."

"What?" Maren asks.

Mr. Dorian shakes his head, his eyes rolling back. His lips are bluish. He mutters something Will can't understand, then grimaces and sighs: "The trickster, tricked. . . ."

Several times his body twitches, and then is still.

"Is he dead?" Maren asks.

Will touches Mr. Dorian's cold wrist, tries to find a pulse, can't.

"His heart gave out," Will says.

"I don't understand," she whispers.

"The canvas," Will says, understanding Mr. Dorian's last words. "There was nothing special about it. He was wrong. He got tricked."

The sound of a huge explosion reaches him at the same moment the carriage shudders—so violently that Will thinks the car has been knocked from the tracks. It tilts as the left wheels leave the steel. Then it crashes back level.

Will climbs the ladder and crests the roof. He sees the funeral car up ahead and can tell, just by the gap, that the Boundless has been severed. The locomotive is slowly pulling its tender and the funeral car away from the rest of the cars. The back of Van Horne's carriage is disfigured from the blast, paint scoured off, the decorative plumes mangled. On the roof Brogan and Mackie are moving forward in the direction of the locomotive.

"How did they do it?" Maren gasps, hauling herself onto the roof beside Will.

"Nitroglycerine," he says.

He is trying to judge the widening gap between the maintenance car they're on and the funeral car. If Brogan has explosives, who knows what he means to do. His father is on that locomotive.

Urgent whistle blasts pierce the mountain air, the alarm to bring the train to a halt. Will can only hope that there are enough good brakemen left on the severed part of the train to slow it down—for it's headless now, and there are surely steep turns and trestles up ahead.

Brogan and Mackie have jumped across to the bunk car where the firemen and engineers sleep when off shift. And beyond that rises the back of the massive tender, heavy with coal and water. To cross over top would be impossible. But along the right side runs a narrow catwalk to allow the crew to pass between the locomotive and their bunk car.

Will starts to run forward, hunched over.

"Will!" Maren shouts behind him. "What are you doing?"

"I need to get across!" Will hollers back at her. "My father!"

He reaches the front of the maintenance car. The gap to the funeral carriage is more than fifteen feet now, and growing. He knows he can never make that jump.

"Can you get me across?" he asks Maren, who has run after him.

She looks ahead. Will sees a long stretch of straight track. Without a word she takes her spool of wire and starts to swiftly unwind it across the gap. She hooks the grappling hook around a ladder rung at the back of the disfigured funeral car, and latches her end to the rooftop. The Boundless is connected once more, briefly, by tightrope.

"We're at fifteen feet now," she tells him. "There's thirty feet in the spool. We don't have much time. You're going to have to walk with me. You'll need to trust me, Will. Can you do that?"

"Yes. You can do this, right?"

"I've carried an anvil. I can manage you. Go. I need to be behind you."

His will falters a moment.

"Go!" she says. "Just walk and don't stop. Don't look down. I'll do the rest."

He takes his first step, and then another, and he's about to teeter off when he feels Maren's hands, one on his waist, another on his opposite shoulder, guiding him. Instantly, amazingly, he's steadied. He forces himself to keep going, looking only at his destination—the shuddering back of the funeral car. It takes concentration, but more than that, surrender.

"Don't fight me," she whispers.

He wasn't aware he was. He tries to breathe.

"You're doing well," she whispers into his ear.

Their destination looks just as far away as it did when they began, but he knows the gap between the cars must be growing, their tightrope line paying out, foot by foot.

"Will, I need you to go a little faster," she says in his ear. "Just a little. Good. . . ."

In his peripheral vision something tumbles past on his right and is gone. Moments later another shape flashes by, and this time he realizes it's a person. He catches a glimpse of the overalls that the firemen wear.

"He's forcing them off the train!" Will gasps.

"Don't worry about that now!"

A third person rolls past. Will doesn't know if they're dead or alive. Were any of them his father? He doesn't think so, but— He feels Maren roughly push him.

"Will!" she says. "Pay attention!"

Up ahead he sees the track begin to curve. "We're going to bank to the right," he gasps in alarm.

"I've got you. Keep walking. Just look at the end of the wire."

The train starts to lean, and Will feels his body teeter. Maren's hands are firm, pressing, nudging. He looks down—he can't help himself. He's going to fall! He's going to be crushed between the cars!

"You're okay, Will," she says. "We're straight again. You're walking straight. And we're almost there."

He lifts his gaze to take in the back of the funeral car. They're getting closer, but it still seems that for every two steps he takes, the train moves ahead one.

A shock travels through the wire. Suddenly it softens underfoot.

He's aware of Maren, looking back over her shoulder, but he dares not do the same.

"Run!" she's shouting. "Just *run!*"

And he doesn't need to look back, because he can see it in his mind's eye. The wire has gone as far as it can, and has snapped, and is sailing through the air behind them, falling swiftly.

He runs, Maren's hands guiding him, her body so close that he feels like they're one person—one person with four legs in perfect synchrony. The wire is as soft as snow beneath his feet, and they're running uphill now as the wire sags to the tracks.

"Go! Go!" Maren shouts, and he puts on a burst of speed, accelerated by her body behind him.

He reaches out for the mangled ladder at the back of the funeral car and seizes a rung. He swings to one side to make room for Maren. Glancing back, he sees the tightrope wire dragging behind them on the tracks, sending up sparks. The rest of the Boundless seems impossibly far away.

"Not quite Niagara Falls," he pants, "but close."

"No one's ever done *that* before," she says with some satis-faction.

Mountains, their peaks bathed in the rising sun, tower around them, old as the planet. With Maren he runs across the roof of the funeral car and jumps to the bunk car.

"We should check inside," he says. His father might have been off shift, but he doubts it. He would've wanted to be at the controls through the mountains. And if Will's right, Brogan and Mackie cleared out the bunk car and forced the men off the train.

He hastily climbs down and sees the knob smashed apart, and the door ajar. He enters. Empty bunks, breakfast dishes shattered and food scattered on the floor.

"They definitely forced them off," Will says.

"How many should be here?" Maren asks.

"I don't know. They do shifts, that's all I know. Maybe two extra firemen and an engineer."

She nods grimly. The three people they saw tumble past the train.

Will recognizes his father's jacket hanging on a peg, and the sight of it makes his throat ache. They parted on such cold terms.

"Big fellows, these firemen, aren't they?" Maren asks. "Brogan doesn't even have a gun."

"He has a gun, but no bullets. But they don't know that. And he's good with a knife."

"Do they have weapons up there?" Maren asks.

Will shakes his head. "Don't know."

Back outside, the tender rises before them like a cliff. Along the catwalk at its side there's no sign of Brogan and Mackie. They've already reached the locomotive.

Single file, he and Maren edge along the narrow walkway. It starts to snow again. As they near the locomotive, the flakes are wheeling down in thick sheets, matting the metal surfaces.

Will hangs back and leans out to peer into the locomotive's lower level. Normally a fireman would be stationed here, ready to shovel coal from the chute into the firebox—but the compartment is empty now.

He swings himself inside the open doorway, Maren close behind, and looks around. A shovel lies askew on the floor, a spill of coal beside it. He listens but can hear nothing above the titanic chugging of the pistons. Fire blazes from the open furnace. Steam hisses through the many escape valves around the boiler.

Here at the very front of the Boundless, there's an incredible sense of propulsion. The landscape flies past on all sides, and for the first time Will can look straight ahead, to the tracks that are being devoured by the locomotive as it hurtles into the mountains.

Outside the compartment, metal stairs continue up to the second fireman platform, and then upward again to the engineer's cab. Quietly Will heads up, snow driving at him, hard. He keeps his body close to the side, and when he's halfway up, he peeks into the second-level compartment. It too is empty. But overhead he hears footsteps from the engineer's cab—and shouting, though he can't make out the words.

"They've got all of them up there," he whispers to Maren.

"Someone's coming down," she hisses, and they both dart up inside the fireman's compartment and press themselves to the wall. Through a small window Will catches a glimpse of two firemen, their hands raised wretchedly above their heads, descending the outside stairs. They don't carry on to the lower level but head out along a narrow footboard that slants down against the boiler to the very front of the locomotive. Snow flies hard.

Following the two firemen comes Will's father, his hands also raised. Behind him is Brogan, his pistol held out. He marches them into the driving snow.

Will peeks his head out the open doorway to watch them make for the pilot—a small platform atop the cowcatcher at the locomotive's very front.

Will pulls back inside, looks frantically around the compartment for some kind of weapon. He seizes a shovel.

"Is this a plan?" Maren asks worriedly.

Before his courage fails, he steps out onto the footboard and stealthily follows Brogan, hoping the brakeman won't turn around. Scalding heat pours from the boiler's massive flank, and the noise of pistons and venting valves is almost blinding. Whirling snow turns the world black and white. Will tightens his grip on the shovel. Another twenty feet and he'll be close enough. . . .

"Hop it!" Brogan bellows at his prisoners when they've reached the pilot. "You're low enough you'll likely survive with a few busted ribs."

"There's no bullets in the gun!" Will shouts.

"William?" his father calls out, and there's a question in his voice.

For the first time in a long time, Will remembers his painted face and dyed hair. "Pa, it's me!"

Brogan looks back at Will, but the gun's still aimed at his father.

"You sure about that, boy?" he says. "You want me to test my aim on your father, do you?"

"Mr. Dorian took all the bullets out!" Will hollers.

Brogan smirks. "A man always has extra ammo."

"He's lying!" Will shouts, but is thinking: *What if he's telling the truth?*

KENNETH OPPEL

"Will! Get back!" his father yells.

Brogan charges up the footboard toward Will, who swings his shovel at the brakeman. He hits Brogan hard in the shoulder and knocks the gun from his hand. It clatters down the metal catwalk. But before Will can swing the shovel again, Brogan wrenches it from his grasp and slams it into his chest. The cracking pain swells to fill Will's entire body.

"Brogan!" he hears his father bellow.

Will feels the prick of a knife point against his throat, and Brogan wheels him around in a headlock. His father, pistol in his hand, stops short.

"Let him go!" James Everett yells.

"Shoot," Brogan pants. "It ain't got no bullets."

Will's father takes aim at Brogan's head and squeezes the trigger. Nothing.

"Now," says Brogan, "I've killed already. I got no compunction about doing it again. You want your boy alive, you and your men hop it, and I'll let him hop it after you."

Will feels the blade press harder against his skin. He stays very still.

"Go on!" Brogan bellows. "Or I slit his throat! All of you! Go!"

There is a lull in the driving snow, and the sky opens enough to let the sun through. Will sees the mountains rising up to the right. The air trembles. A rumbling builds above the roar of the steam engine. On the distant slopes the snow puckers and begins to slide.

"Avalanche," he gurgles against the choking hold around his throat. "Avalanche!"

His father turns his gaze to the mountain. "Brogan, let me back to the cab!"

Will can't see Brogan's face, but he feels the twitching tension in his body. "Stay right there, Everett! Mackie's in the cab. He's doing fine."

"You need to stop the train!" Will's father waves his arm at Mackie up in the cab. "Stop!"

To Will it doesn't feel like they're slowing much. The locomotive rounds a bend, and up ahead, five hundred yards, snow spills across the tracks and then down into a deep river gorge, spray rising as from a waterfall.

Now Will hears the shriek of the brakes, and the train slows faster—but not fast enough. They're in the snow now, deeper and deeper, the cowcatcher sending torrents of ice back at them. Dead ahead Will can see a looming wall of snow.

And then he's in the air, half stunned by the concussion that stopped the train in its tracks and yanked him off his feet. He has spun free of Brogan, everything white. He curls to protect himself, for he doesn't know how or where he'll land, but he hopes it's soft.

No one sees this.

At the back of the Zirkus Dante cars, Goliath paces his cage. The Boundless has finally been brought to a standstill in the driving snow. The sasquatch's nostrils flare, again and again as he breathes in a scent that is acutely familiar. It provokes in him a frenzy of restlessness. He wails up at the narrow vents. He thumps his fists against the reinforced walls.

He crouches, crushing handfuls of straw in his fists. Then he stands tall, ears straining at the faraway cry. Goliath bellows again, and when he hears a return call, it's closer.

He whirls about in his cage, thrashing against the bars, throwing himself so hard against the wall that the wood creaks.

Something thuds atop the roof of his car, and he stops and looks overhead. A second thump, then a third. Dark shapes move past outside the vents. Powerful hands thrust inside and begin to rip the wall apart. Goliath sets up a wail of jubilation as, plank by jagged plank, his view opens up: sky, mountains, and the high forests whose smell he recognized as home.

Snow is packed up Will's nostrils. He thrashes about, not knowing how long he was unconscious, or which way is up. He fights his way toward the light. His head breaks the surface. Gasping, he realizes that the snow isn't moving. The avalanche is over, but just. A low layer of mist still hangs over the ground. The stillness is remarkable—it feels like a force, squeezing against him. Gone is the clackety motion of the train that had come to feel natural to him over the past days. Wind shushes against his eardrums, and he hears a trill of birdsong and the distant rumble of water.

He looks about for his father, for Maren, Brogan—they too must have been thrown off the locomotive when it collided with the wall of snow.

"Help! William!"

"Pa!" Will paddles his way atop the snow, in the direction of the call—in the direction of the gorge. He remembers the snow spilling over the edge like a waterfall.

Carefully he slides down the slope, and spots his father clinging to a shrub at the edge of the precipice.

"I'm coming!" Will says. "Hold tight!"

He swims as close as he dares. "Grab hold of me!"

"You'll need to hold something first," his father says, "or you'll get dragged over!"

Will looks around. There's a tree behind him, but it's too far for him to reach.

"We'll just have to manage it," he says.

From the slopes comes a sound that Will first heard three years ago in these same mountains. An animal call unlike any other. It begins as a low, mournful hoot, and builds in intensity and pitch to a terrifying shriek. The voice is joined by another, and another, until it's a ghostly chorus, wafting through the snow-curtained pines.

"Will! Wait!" Maren swims toward him, caked in snow.

She grabs hold of the tree and stretches out to Will. They lock hands. Now Will can reach his father.

"Good," his father grunts as he takes hold. Will pulls. Maren holds him tightly. James Everett scrambles and kicks, trying to get himself up over the edge. With a lurch he makes it, and they all scramble into the safety of the tree's branches.

"You're all right?" Will asks his father. There's some blood matted around his ears, but he seems otherwise unharmed.

"I'm fine. You, too?"

"Yes."

James Everett wipes snow off his shoulders and chest. Some papers rustle in the large pocket of his overalls, and he pulls them out and carefully brushes off the melting snow. Will catches a glimpse of the hand-sewn sketchbook he gave his father three years ago.

"Don't want it getting wet," his father says.

Will can't help smiling. Another chorus of animal sounds wafts over them. Near the buried rail bed Will sees the solitary figure of Brogan, slogging through the snow, in the direction of the locomotive.

In the mist, silhouettes appear. At first Will thinks they're people come from the Boundless to help. But he soon realizes they are too tall to be human, their shoulders too broad. They stand eerily still. Then the closest suddenly moves, hurling himself forward to land on all fours, then pushing off with its legs. It lands ten feet in front of Brogan and stands tall.

Will squints. "Is that—"

"Goliath," breathes Maren. "He must've escaped!"

Brogan takes a few steps back, knife in hand. Goliath steps

forward. Then Brogan turns clumsily and starts thrashing through the snow. Goliath overtakes him easily, pushes him deep into the snow. Will can see Brogan struggling, his hands and feet kicking up, but the sasquatch leans down, and there's a scream and then silence.

Will feels his insides flash hot and then cold. He thinks he might be sick. Goliath looks up from Brogan's body at them.

"Don't move," Will's father says.

The other sasquatch are silent. Will can hear Goliath punch air through his nostrils. He's sure the sasquatch is looking right at him.

A gunshot cracks the air, and then another. A man in a scarlet uniform, on snowshoes, comes into sight from the direction of the train. The sasquatch disperse as quickly as dry leaves in a sudden breeze—all except Goliath. He reaches down to Brogan's body and, with a swift movement, rips his head off and spikes it on the branch of a tree. He gives a final bellow before disappearing into the forest.

And then Lieutenant Samuel Steele and two firemen are calling out to Will and his father and Maren, and unfurling ropes to help them out of the deep snow.

CHAPTER
16

CLEARING THE
TRACKS

"You can't arrest her!" Will protests as Lieutenant Sam Steele manacles Maren.

"By her own admission she helped rob the Boundless," says the Mountie.

"But Mr. Dorian was forcing her!" Will insists.

"He wasn't forcing me," Maren says quietly.

"He *was*—in a way!" Will counters, irritated that she's not helping him with his lie.

They are all in the locomotive's bunk car, shivering themselves warm around the stove. Will's father shovels in more coal and sets a kettle atop to boil. Their boots make puddles on the floor. Maren sits looking at her manacles with amused curiosity. The two firemen have laid Mackie's body out and covered it with a blanket. His neck must have been broken inside the cab, by the same impact that sent everyone else flying clear. Amazingly, the locomotive wasn't derailed when it plowed into the wall of snow. The tender, the bunk car, and the funeral car all stand on the track, unharmed.

"In addition," the Mountie says, "she endangered the lives of others aboard by not telling us sooner about Brogan's plot."

"But I didn't tell either!" Will exclaims.

"I'm aware of that," says the Mountie. "Three times I saw you in the carriages, and you said nothing to me."

Recklessly Will says, "Well, you should arrest me, too!"

"Will!" Maren and his father say at the same time.

"I am considering it, young sir," says Steele.

This makes Will pause a second, but he pushes on. "She saved my life in the muskeg. Without her I couldn't have warned my father—or stopped him going over the edge just now!"

"Remarkable heroism, no question," says Samuel Steele. "And it will certainly weigh in her favor when she's brought before the magistrate in Lionsgate City."

"Is this truly necessary, Lieutenant?" Will's father asks.

"I'm afraid so, Mr. Everett. The law must be upheld. When we get things a bit more settled, I'll transfer her to the jail in second class."

"May I have a blanket?" Maren asks, shivering.

Will takes a large blanket off one of the bunks and drapes it over her shoulders.

"Thanks," she says.

"I'm sorry," Will says awkwardly. "I didn't see it ending like this."

"Neither did I." She smiles. "Well, at least you've got a good story to tell. And I think this one definitely happened *to* you."

He nods. "I guess so." He wishes he hadn't used the word "ending." Is that what this is?

The kettle starts shrieking atop the stove.

"Can I offer you a mug of tea, Miss Amberson?" Will's father asks, moving to the boiling kettle. "It'll help warm you up."

When Will looks over at Maren, she has pulled the blanket right over her head and wrapped it around her like a tepee. She must be really cold.

"Maren?" says Will's father, offering her the cup of tea.

She makes no reply, nor does she move. Will holds his breath, watching.

The Mountie steps over. "What're you playing at, girl?"

He takes the blanket and yanks it off, revealing a pair of manacles on the empty bunk.

"This is unacceptable," mutters Lieutenant Steele.

While the Mountie and James Everett hurriedly check the inside of the bunk car, Will charges to the doorway and climbs onto the roof to get a better view. There's no sign of her in the snow-strewn landscape. He wants to cheer, and call her back all at the same time.

"I gather that's called the disappearing act," says James Everett, climbing onto the roof with Sam Steele. Will thinks there is a trace of a smile on his father's lips.

"She's foolhardy if she thinks she can run for it," Steele remarks, "with the sasquatch on the move."

Will looks about, feeling suddenly desolate. She wouldn't really strike out alone into the wilderness, would she? No one could survive out here. She must have a plan. The emptiness inside him contracts into a hard ache. Is this it? Is this how she always imagined it? That after the robbery she would say good-bye and never see him again?

"There's no time to worry about her now," says the Mountie. "I need a rescue party for the men who were forced off the locomotive. They're likely injured. And I need deputies to apprehend those last three brakemen." He looks at Will. "Two of them manacled together, or with wrist bruises, yes? Shouldn't be too hard to find."

Will follows his father's gaze to the funeral car, the door in its side still open.

"Let's get that door closed," his father says. "And then we need to start digging ourselves out."

"I'll assemble a team for you," says Steele.

Will points. "I think it's already assembled."

Slogging their way along the tracks is a steady stream of

crew and passengers: men in fine overcoats, colonists in their bulky woolen layers—and amongst them two stilt walkers, and an assortment of oddly dressed people who could only belong to the circus.

"All we need are shovels!" one of them calls up.

Will digs in and tosses more snow to the side. All along the buried track, people are working to clear the rails with shovels, buckets, soup ladles—anything they could lay hands on. Their muffled voices and laughter carry through the clear mountain air. Kitchen staff bring sandwiches and hot drinks, and the mood is almost festive. He has a memory of winter mornings in Halifax, when all the neighbors would be out shoveling after the night's snowfall. He looks over at his father, working alongside him.

"Can you put the train back together?"

"We'll need to repair the couplings they blasted apart, but we've got a welder aboard. Shouldn't be a problem. I want to get clear of here by nightfall."

Will glances up at the fireman atop the locomotive, a rifle in his hands, scanning the slopes for sasquatch. So far there's been no sign of them. Will hopes Maren is safe, wherever she is. Most likely she struck out with her brothers. He hopes at least Christian is with her. Will likes the idea of her having an animal handler along, especially one used to dealing with sasquatch. And what about the reward Mr. Dorian promised her, the five thousand dollars to start her own show? It seems too unfair if she doesn't even get that. The ache in his throat gives another contraction.

"Do you think Sam Steele will try to catch her?" he asks his father.

"Not right now certainly—and maybe not ever. I'll have another word with him, see if he'll drop the charges. I've no wish to pursue them. She seems like quite a remarkable young woman."

From the corner of his eye, Will sees his father watching him, and keeps digging. His cheeks feel hot. He's not worried about Maren getting caught—not if she doesn't want to be. No locks can hold her, no chains bind her. She'll always have her freedom. But maybe if the charges were dropped, she'd come back . . .

His father claps him on the shoulder. "You did well. I don't know many lads—or men—who could've done the things you did."

Will grins. "Thank you."

"But I wish you'd come forward sooner, for your own safety."

"I promised them. That I'd wait till he got the painting. I thought I owed it to her. And Mr. Dorian," he adds carefully. "He saved my life too."

His father pauses from his shoveling. "It seems incredible to me he really thought the painting would keep him young. He was too clever a man for that, I thought."

"It doesn't seem so much stranger than other things," Will says.

He thinks of the ringmaster's body, laid out cold in the first-class infirmary. He worked so hard, and for so long, and bloodied his hands to change his fate. But in the end he wasn't able to cheat time.

"I can't help wondering," Will says, "if all the strain actually brought on his heart attack."

His father shakes his head sadly. "He shouldn't have put so many people in harm's way. It was more than selfish. It was monstrous."

Will supposes he should feel angrier at the ringmaster, but when he remembers the fear pouring from Mr. Dorian's face, and his terrible moans—he feels only sadness.

"What will happen to his portrait?" he asks suddenly.

"Well, I imagine it'll have to be removed from the canvas, without damaging the Krieghoff."

"It was good," Will says wistfully.

His father looks at him. "Or maybe we can just leave it. Have it reframed. A secret on the back of the Krieghoff."

"I like that idea."

"You know," his father says, leaning on his shovel, "we're not so far from where you drove the last spike."

Will looks into the mountains. He had the feeling they were close to Craigellachie, but it's hard for him to super-impose this view with the one he saw three years ago, when he was a boy coming to see a father he barely knew.

"Brogan said you and he mined for gold."

His father turns to him. "This is true."

"To save the company from going bankrupt."

"True again. If we hadn't struck a seam, the railway never would've been finished. Thousands of us would've lost months in wages."

Will has to force himself to ask, "Did you take any for yourself? The gold?"

"Is that what Brogan said?"

Will nods.

His father takes a deep breath, and Will catches himself holding his. "There wasn't a day I wasn't tempted. Some of the others pocketed what they could. I didn't report them. We'd gone unpaid for a long time, and it was hard to think of it as stealing. Who owned it? Maybe the Dominion. Maybe the Natives. Maybe no one at all. But we were employed by the company, and I followed orders. I never took any, William. I hope you believe me."

Without hesitation he says, "I do."

Despite the cold, the sun feels warm on his face, and he thinks of spring. The smell is coming back to things. Grass and mud. They dig for a little while in silence, and then his father says:

"This art school in San Francisco. If your heart's set on it, you should go. I'll pay your way."

Will looks at him in astonishment. "You will?"

"I will. Now you keep clearing these tracks, and I'm going to see how the welders are coming along."

Will leans on his shovel, dumbfounded. This thing he wanted, that seemed impossibly far away, is now right before him, and it hardly seems real. So why isn't he happier? His father has agreed to let him go to art school. But somehow the thought has no luster right now.

He scratches his neck, and his fingertips come away with a bit of face paint. He tried to wash it all off earlier in the bunk car, but it was stubborn stuff. When he looked at himself in the mirror after scrubbing hard, he felt disappointed, like some part of him had gone swirling down the drain with the dirty water. He was just William Everett again.

Something brushes his head, and he turns to see a small bird bouncing off his shoulder as it flutters to the ground. Bending, he realizes it isn't a real bird at all but an ingenious paper creation, like the one Mr. Dorian made the night before. Heart beating faster, Will picks it up. Standing, he looks all around, but he can't see who threw it.

Carefully he unfolds it and starts reading the handwritten note. Even though he's never seen her handwriting, Will knows almost instantly that it's Maren's.

He gave me the circus! He left the will in my pocket.

He has to read the lines a second time, he's so astounded. Mr. Dorian *gave* her the circus? Was this his way of repaying her for all the danger he put her in? Will remembers how, before they set out for the funeral car, the ringmaster wrote two notes and put one inside his jacket. This must be what he secretly slipped into Maren's pocket. Eagerly Will keeps reading:

We'll be in San Francisco in two weeks. Ready to join the circus properly? Write your answer and send the bird to the west.

Don't be late this time.

Will feels a little short of breath. It's almost too much to think about. This is more than just a door opening in his life— it's the door being blasted right off its hinges, and a circus troupe bounding in, picking him up, and carrying him off on its shoulders.

He looks along the tracks that, once cleared, will take the Boundless to Lionsgate City, to his future. And what exactly will his future be? His mind is noisy, and he forces himself to take a deep breath.

His hand shakes as he fumbles inside his pocket for his stub of a pencil. At the bottom of the page he writes his answer, twice to make sure it's good and dark. He's worried about putting the bird back together, but the paper seems to know which way it wants to be folded.

Lifting the bird high, he faces west, and launches it. Up it swoops, and he can't quite tell, but he thinks its wings are fluttering. It skims above the trees, in the direction of the setting sun, carrying his answer of yes.